*a Trumpet*

Simon & Schuster

*in the Wadi*

# Sami Michael
## Translation by Yael Lotan

New York • London • Toronto • Sydney • Singapore

SIMON & SCHUSTER
Rockefeller Center
1230 Avenue of the Americas
New York, NY 10020

Originally published in Israel in 1987 by Am Oved Publishers, Ltd., Tel Aviv

Simon & Schuster and colophon are
registered trademarks of Simon & Schuster, Inc.
For information regarding special discounts for bulk purchases,
please contact Simon & Schuster Special Sales at 1-800-456-6798
or business@simonandschuster.com

Manufactured in the United States of America

10  9  8  7  6  5  4  3  2  1

Library of Congress Cataloging-in-Publication Data

Michael, Sami
[Hatsotsrah ba-vadi. English]
A trumpet in the wadi / Sami Michael ; translation by Yael Lotan.
p.      cm.
I. Lotan, Yael, 1935– . II. Title.
PJ5054.M44H3813 2003
892.4'36—dc21             2003042716
ISBN 978-0-7432-6148-7

*To Rachel*

*A Trumpet in the Wadi*

# Chapter One

Grandpa Elias, smiling his Egyptian smile, remarked that small troubles are heaven's gift to the unfortunate. Mother sank into a chair and pointed with a stubborn chin at the door. "Allah's a humorist like you if he gives such presents," she said, looking as though she expected the door to break open and rough feet to barge in, violating the brightness of the living room floor. This mother, who married, bore me and Mary, and was widowed, was still virginally house-proud. Perhaps because she married late, or because Father hurriedly begot us and left this world without delay. From the little I heard about him, I knew that he did not have the sense of humor of his father, Grandpa Elias. Maybe I'm like him. We've been living in the wadi for many years, but I have no Arab friends, male or female. I'm trying to be more Israeli than the Jews themselves. Like a fisherman whose nets keep coming up empty, I've wandered from one fishing ground to the next, and now Yehuda Amichai is nearer to my heart than any Arab poet. Mary makes no effort. She's the most Israeli offshoot of this family. Two years younger than I, she's bold and reckless. She gambles on her own life with a fetching smile. I don't preach at her. That's the main difference between us, that I fantasize and she tries, I dream and she tastes. The rough noisy footsteps on the stairs going up to the roof infuriate our neighbor Jamilla, growing old with her cat on the floor below, and trouble Mother's rest. Whereas I hear these footsteps twice as noisy but only in my dreams. The muscular hairy legs trouble my sleep in steamy nightmares. I wake up ashamed of my dreams, loathing the muscles in the dream, its shrieks and smells. Mary listens attentively and senses the real existence of the boys. Perhaps there are not so many of them. Maybe not more than five or six peasant boys from the West Bank. But the stairs are rickety, and to hear Jamilla yelling downstairs you'd think the house is about to fall down. They run up there as if they're chasing each other, stomping heavily with their boots, and our flat rattles like a closed trap. The flooding feeling that seizes Mother does not affect me, as I retreat at once into my body, into the throbbing pain in my right shoulder whose tentacles distort my back. It is the pain that shakes my chair, not the pounding of the rough feet on the stairs. By contrast, Mary yields to the vibration of the flat, like a child yielding to the rising and plunging of a roller coaster. Now she looked into a small round mirror, plucked her eyebrows and said in a singsong, "Maybe we should open the door to them sometime and offer them something to eat or drink." In Hebrew she added, "Why not?"

Mother choked, though she knew Mary was joking. "I'm going up in flames and you're pouring oil on the fire," she scolded Mary, seeing Grandpa grinning and knowing he was not in sympathy with her.

"Work is work, never mind what other people tell you," he said. "When I was young I also felt like singing and running at the end of the day."

"What, like these savages?"

"No. We worked from dawn to dusk. And I had to do the cooking too. When your husband was a boy he also ran and yelled a bit."

"And then he went silent and stayed silent until he was gone."

Grandpa hummed under his breath, bent over the narghileh and stirred the embers with his dark fingers, but did not utter a word in his son's defense. The bubbling of the water in the narghileh hinted that it was not right to speak like this of a dead husband. I've always wondered about the nature of the relationship between my mother and her father-in-law. The age gap does not always deter. Amichai was writing poems before I was born, but if we had lived together, if we had known the cold of winter and the loneliness of spring, if he were the breadwinner and I the nest maker, if I were enveloped in restrained manly warmth and wordless regard, as Grandpa Elias envelops Mother, maybe . . . I wouldn't have been shocked to discover that there was something between them. Today he's an old man whose exact age nobody knows, but he is still sturdy and supple and smiling. He must have been an impressive young man. What kept them apart during the long years after his son's death? Or did anything keep them apart? Before I knew Bahij, and when Bahij came and brightened my soul with the radiance of another world, and also in the leaden days after Bahij, I was constrained by shyness. I was too shy to ask, thinking that only dirty people inquire about certain things. I knew it was hypocritical, but then hypocrisy is the timid person's shield. Nevertheless, my curiosity was considerable. My sister, who detested sanctity, shouted at me, "And you blame me for being what I am!" I thought she was shouting because the idea had crossed my mind and not hers. But then she grinned and said, "Mother and Grandpa? You ever heard of a bird and a stone making love? Only I don't know which of them is the bird and which the stone."

Grandpa wound the red tube around the narghileh, sat back on his sleeping bench in the living room and said, "The boys upstairs have calmed down. We can watch television."

Mother got up to make his coffee. In the middle of the living room she froze and tucked her head between her shoulders, as though afraid that the ceiling was about to collapse. On the roof someone gave a ferocious kick to an empty bucket. Three bottles were smashed one after the other, and a tremendous voice roared, "Damn God who forced me to see your face, you animal!"

Mary tapped her teeth excitedly, as though she was sitting in the front row at the stadium.

"Listen, listen," Mother said to Grandpa reproachfully.

"They'll get tired."

The ceiling shook. Clumsy feet ran around and kicked. A terrified voice shrieked, "Put me down, put me down."

"Throw him into the street," urged another voice.

"The night before last," Mother related softly, her face pale as though it had just happened, "I opened the window and their stinking urine almost spattered in my face. Is that right, urinating over the banister?" she asked Grandpa like a pious schoolgirl.

Grandpa refused to play the teacher and laughed. "Who opens a window in the autumn chill?"

Mother looked at her hands which had almost been defiled and said, "I can do without such heavenly gifts."

Grandpa is not a believer. His God, if he has one, must be a bachelor, free from life's burdens, who relishes good jokes. "You're wise," he said to Mother, "not to chase after His gifts." He turned and addressed Mary's profile, "Sometimes He ties to His gift an invisible string and pulls it, laughing His head off at the fools who chase after them."

"Are you talking about me?" Mary smiled.

"Me?"

Mother didn't give up. "They're disturbing my sleep. They go up and down in the middle of the night. They yell when they're playing cards. Not to mention the drugs and the dirty women they take upstairs."

"Best not to mention it," said Grandpa.

"Go ahead and laugh, if you like, but that Abu-Nakhla is doing it deliberately. He lets the room to these types in order to make us sick of our life here."

I loved these arguments. They were anchored in the ground of time, like an alliance that can withstand the storms. I often wondered if this was not the essence of a deep love that grows between two people who have stopped chasing after gifts tied with invisible strings.

"And what about these girls?" Mother asked.

"What about the girls?" he asked. For the first time a trace of worry appeared in his voice. He even moved on his seat, as if about to rise.

"You forgot how they attacked the door when they were drunk. Who'll protect us?"

Grandpa pretended to feel hurt, stood up and declared, "I'm here."

Mary was unimpressed by his long shadow which reached the lintel of the kitchen door. "They'll blow on you and you'll fly away, Grandpa."

He turned to her as though to clarify the issue. "You think so?"

"You're older than you think," she replied affectionately.

All three of them ignored me. Perhaps they knew that it was in my heart that the real, hard, depraved fear was lurking. These boys who supposedly work in restaurants and building sites are in fact the demons who operate in Abu-Nakhla's dark dens. Night after night they conquer the darkness which comes down on me. In their sweat-encrusted clothes, their stiff rumpled hair, their faces sprouting black beards like a scorched forest, their yellowed teeth, the smiles melting on their moist lips, all these blended them into a single creature. Their hands trail on the house walls, slither through the cracks, gripping the gutters and the window bars. I would drown in this growling creature, my strength ebbing before the struggle. I gave in before the encounter.

"Your shoulder again?" Mother asked.

I was ashamed of the pains. "No, no," I replied.

"She's gone pale," Mary stated.

"Where's the arak? You and your doctors. Woman," Grandpa ordered Mother, "smear and rub in the arak."

Out of consideration for the budget he'd open a new bottle for himself alone, wait for a suitable excuse, such as guests or ailments, then drink up the remainder. I loathe the smell of arak, which has accompanied me since childhood. My mind associates the smell and the pain. Mother's fingers slid under my blouse, skillfully undid my bra and began massaging energetically, as though following the tentacles of pain piercing my back and chest. Grandpa stamped lightly with his foot, his voice interweaving with Mother's fingers, "More, more, more, woman. More, more, more." I shut my eyes and rocked on my chair with Mother's massaging movements, and the pain seemed to submit to the touch, or the arak fumes, or Grandpa's monotonous voice. "More, more, more," he repeated in a soporific intonation like an African witch doctor. When I opened my eyes I saw his face close to those of Mother and Mary. I noticed the tension behind his smiling countenance. In my childhood he used to stand beside my bed when I was ill, his lips mumbling incantations, probably from his early years, as he was not a believer. I liked the rustle of these incantations, but he never gave in to my pleas to repeat them aloud.

Now too his lips were moving, and unwittingly he pushed himself between Mother and Mary until he'd moved them away from me. His brown palms embraced my face and I closed my eyes. When I opened them again I saw his face sweaty and weary.

I seized his wrists and kissed his hands. "Enough, Grandpa."

He leaned over me as if to kiss my hair, as if I was still a child. But he straightened up, took the opened bottle from the table and went to the bench. When there was a knock on the door he quickly took a good swallow and hid the bottle under the bench.

Jamilla, the downstairs neighbor, came in. "Sick again?" she scolded me, as people scold children who give their parents a lot of trouble. She was a kind, lonely old woman, addicted to coffee. Her sensuality repelled Grandpa, but he forgave her because she dearly loved Mary and me. She would come in at all hours. If she happened to come in when we were eating she did not retreat, but sat down on Grandpa's bench and refused to taste a thing. We got used to eating in her presence and chatting with her during the meal.

Now she came up to me with her forefinger extended and touched my forehead before I could dodge. I've noticed that Jews don't touch each other so much. Once I said to Grandpa that it is better than our oriental habit of handling each other. He disagreed.

"They're like the Europeans. Love from a distance and kill from a distance."

"You're still young," Jamilla said to me, as though diagnosing a medical complication. "You should get married. Who made you angry?" she demanded.

Grandpa's face went blank. The word "still" grated on him.

"We were talking about Abu-Nakhla and his tenants," Mother explained.

Jamilla put on the table a plate with freshly baked cookies she'd made for us, and was clearly waiting for coffee. "Devil's spawn!" she said. "I have to keep rescuing the cat from them. Last week they tied a beer can to his tail. Poor thing went crazy. Day before yesterday he came home half dead. Threw up all over the place. They fed him fish with hashish."

Grandpa surreptitiously drew the bottle from under the bench. He disliked Jamilla's chattering. Mother's face brightened. Here was an ally. "Abu-Nakhla brings these animals here on purpose. He wants to evict us from this flat and get the lease money."

"He won't get me out."

"No," Mother agreed with her. "Your nephew Halim's a lawyer. But we're like orphans. He was a miserable little thief who got fat with the State. Ever since he turned informer he's been getting away with everything. Why shouldn't he be after a widow's flat? You know how much he can get for these walls?"

"He's a millionaire," said Mary. "This is small change to him."

"A robber remains a robber," Mother insisted. "He'll rob for the pleasure of it. How long are they going to protect him? His boys are already selling drugs to Jewish girls on the Carmel. Now he's touching their own flesh and blood. They won't put up with it—oh no, they won't!"

"No they won't," Jamilla repeated, and beamed when I turned on the gas in the kitchen. "Sugar in moderation, daughter," she called out to me, leaning forward.

Grandpa's fingers ploughed through his crisp silvery hair. "God preserve us from women's wars. Have you threatened him already, woman?" he questioned Mother.

"I'm not stupid. I've been measuring my wings since I was a girl, and they still haven't grown. I know I'll break my neck with some-body like Abu-Nakhla."

Through the kitchen door I saw the smile that Grandpa gave her. It was the smile that always puzzled me, the smile of a real man to a real woman.

Clever Mary, the expert in the male department! Maybe she knows all about the dramatic events, but after the letdown of the Bahij affair, I withdrew behind the oriental veils. I was back amid the subtle hints, the soft notes, the brief glance like the twinkling of one tiny star among the multitude of stars.

"Are you sure," he asked, "that you didn't, perhaps by accident, blow on his face?"

It annoyed her that he was questioning her and mistrusting her words. "I said I didn't utter a word."

"Then I don't know," he said. He was silent while I served the cof-fee. Mary finished plucking her eyebrows and gathered her tweez-ers and things.

"He'll be here this evening," he said.

"Abu-Nakhla?" Mother asked, astonished.

"I was in the cafe with the others when his son Zuhair came in, smiling in all directions, as if he was giving alms to the poor. We'd never exchanged a word before. I thought he wanted some service from Issa Mattar, who used to tile floors for his father. But no, he came up to me and said his father would visit us this evening."

"They're both bad news, the father and the son," Jamilla stated, and gazed at me until I got up and poured her another cup. "Did he say when he'd come, the villain?"

"He said this evening. Could be any minute."

We liked Jamilla. She had tact and was already on her feet,

though bursting with curiosity to find out what could be bringing Abu-Nakhla to us. "I'm off, good night," she said, her eyes on Mary and her teeth biting her lower lip, as if to stop the words trying to be said. She left.

I didn't need her to tell me, because I knew. Mary's eyes evaded mine. Grandpa and Mother, simple innocents, had no idea about the coming shock. Mary slipped into the room she and I shared.

"Huda," Mother turned to me, "how's the pain? You haven't eaten a thing since you came in from work. We have to have supper. What if he comes in while we're eating?" she asked Grandpa.

"He won't pinch the food from the table."

"I'd serve him poison," she said. "He informed on my brothers after 1948. Because of him they were deported to Jordan. Because of him I was left alone and penniless like a stranger in the city of my birth. Everything was in their name and everything was confiscated. May Allah confiscate the years still left to this criminal. I won't serve any food until he's gone. Huda will forgive me."

"So we'll fast," Grandpa said with a smile.

A knock on the door put an end to her wavering. "Abu-Nakhla," she whispered.

Grandpa stood up, as though preparing for confrontation, but when he opened the door he was the traditional Arab host. He smiled warmly at the guest, as if he'd been awaiting him impatiently all day long. "Ahalan! Ahalan wasahalan!" he sang out. "How are you? Well, please God." Although there were two unoccupied chairs, he motioned to me to vacate my seat and move to another, to show greater honor to the guest. The guest knew that this was a hollow pretense, but would have been offended if Grandpa had behaved more coolly.

On Mother's face too there was a faintly servile smile, which angered me more than Grandpa's false manner. He had been raised in a culture that lauds the common man who manages to evade the powerful by means of guile and deceit. Moreover, Abu-Nakhla had never hurt Grandpa himself, but rather treated him with respect. There was a rumor in the wadi that Grandpa Elias's great green eyes were not merely the eyes of a typical Egyptian. People haven't forgotten that he escaped from his native Egypt and crossed the desert alone, with my father in his arms. If he was spared by the robber bands of those days, it must mean that he had otherworldly powers. This view was supported by his prolonged solitary state until my father married my mother. Grandpa heard and said nothing. It suits a loner to be a little feared, and Abu-Nakhla was famous for his caution.

But my mother's behavior struck me as curious. It was true that Abu-Nakhla had ill-treated her brothers. Her brothers fled across the Jordan during the disturbances before the 1948 war, and my mother, who was on a visit to Jerusalem, was out of touch with them. After the war they tried to get across the border and return to their homes. In those days Abu-Nakhla was busy smuggling and taking refugees through the minefields and military outposts. He brought them to Haifa, but robbed them en route. Many knew about their arrival, and he got ahead of other informers and turned them in to the authorities. They were all deported. This story was deeply etched in my mind. Mother's longing for her brothers, her bitterness at having become penniless overnight, the pain of the loneliness and the humiliation of having to serve others, all these fanned her intense hatred for Abu-Nakhla. And here she was smiling at him obsequiously!

I sat and watched the guest. I had to admit that he was more impressive to look at than Grandpa, not only because he was younger. He had on a red tarboosh with a swinging black tassel. His fine suit fitted his sturdy and supple figure. His shoes gleamed like the two enormous gold rings on his fingers. A diamond pin adorned his perfect tie. There was nothing vulgar about him, neither in his appearance nor in his voice or movements. He was like a prince who indulged in raids of robbery and looting for the pleasure of it. He immediately sensed the hatred that seethed in me like poison, and smiled as though he was getting admiring looks. Only one thing could have shaken him—a haughty look of contempt.

He sat on the edge of the chair and delicately tugged with both hands at his trousers to preserve their crease. Then he looked around with a satisfied, approving smile, like a master indicating to his flunkies that he is ready to be served. He saw Mother going into the kitchen to make the coffee and said to Grandpa, "Where's Mary? You've turned on the light, but no light can rival your granddaughter's beauty."

Grandpa grew tense, and I realized how far I'd grown from my roots. It is not customary for a strange man to compliment a girl for no reason. Abu-Nakhla is not a careless man, and must have known the effect of his words. He stopped smiling and met Grandpa's burning green eyes. His expression became grave and respectful, as though to convey that it had not been mere flattery suggesting disrespect. Grandpa's face showed that he was now more worried about the real cause than the compliment itself. Abu-Nakhla is a wealthy man with business connections extending from Haifa to Nazareth and Acre. He owns shops and apartment and office buildings, but is deeply involved in drugs, prostitution and smuggling. He does his best to cultivate a decent facade for his shady enterprises, and perhaps he is genuinely trying to cross to the safer side of the law, but his son Zuhair is especially drawn to the labyrinths of crime. Though forty, he's a flashy bachelor, clever and bubbling with the raw energy of wild youth. It's an open secret in the wadi, though not to Grandpa and Mother, that he's attracted to Mary. I know he's been trying to win her by every manner of courtship.

Grandpa came to this country barefoot, hungry and fearful for his life, and here found food and shelter and raised a family. He preferred to live in humble anonymity. Privately he did not mourn the loss of Mother's property, and jealously guarded his quiet existence, not necessarily from Christian humility so much as from a deep fear rooted in his mysterious past. From our earliest childhood he hinted to us that a bad secret was breathing down his neck, and seemed anxious to cover up his tracks, until we were old enough to be told about it. Such a man, no matter how poor, does not care to become related to a type like Abu-Nakhla. Also, he's a Christian and Abu-Nakhla is a Moslem, but this fact alone wouldn't have barred the match. He did not bring us up to feel that we were set apart by religion.

Now both men were seeking to retreat. Abu-Nakhla realized that he'd said too much in his opening move, and Grandpa regretted having appeared tense, and was happy to pretend that nothing had been said. I trusted them to do this. Both were experts at pretense, Abu-Nakhla in his tough, bold way, and Grandpa with his Egyptian gracefulness. So while Mother was bustling in the kitchen, Grandpa sat down on his bench, slapped his thigh and gave Abu-Nakhla a playful wink. "Before the coffee, we may as well have a sip of excellent Zakhlawi," he said, and drew the arak bottle out from under the bench.

"My ulcer's playing up," Abu-Nakhla drawled. "But who can resist a Zakhlawi?"

The "sip" extended to five little glassfuls each by the time Mother emerged from the kitchen with the coffee and Jamilla's cookies.

Grandpa said, "Throw away that foreign American cigarette. Let me roll you one with my own tobacco."

Abu-Nakhla pushed his tarboosh forward until its edge touched his eyebrows, giving him a fetching playful look. Even Mother averted her eyes as though from an evil temptation. But he took a tiny cup from the tray and gave her a royal smile.

"Umm-Huda, I've come to bring you good news. I'm removing the trash from the roof, throwing the filth back into the pit it came from. What do you say to that, Umm-Huda?"

"What is there to say. Thank you and again thank you. May you enjoy good health."

"And what do you say, Huda?" He turned to me. "It's good for a girl to be quiet, but not so much as to be dumb."

"We're really grateful," I said stiffly.

"We'll never forget it, Abu-Nakhla," intoned Grandpa, who was now aware of the guest's new intentions.

Abu-Nakhla's eyes went hard and his generous smile disappeared. "I'm losing a fortune to make you comfortable."

"Allah will reward you," said Grandpa.

"Leave Allah out of it," stated Abu-Nakhla, with an air of dismissing a biased judge. "People who wait for Allah's rewards walk barefoot."

His world is so far from the world I've joined. I only knew that these were the opening shots in a hard bargaining session. Was it a new tactic to evict us from our flat, or was he trying to let the room to us at an extortionate price? My imagination caught fire. I'd take that room, and it would all be mine—the spacious roof and the single room, far from the street noises. I'd be able to sit by the window and look toward the sea.

"How much do you want for the room?"

Abu-Nakhla's fingers stopped playing with his beads. "What did you say?"

"The room upstairs, how much would it cost me?"

Abu-Nakhla turned to Grandpa and pointed to me with his thumb over his shoulder. "What's the matter with her? Looking for a room? She should find a husband."

Grandpa's bargaining position was shaken. "She's just dreaming, ignore her."

"Or maybe you've been lying to me all these years. Living here practically for free, protected by the Jews' courts. Maybe you're really rich, and only protest your poverty to me."

"We've never cried!" Mother protested. "We pay you what the law says."

"The law! It set up the weaklings and crushed the lions—that's your law. Wallah, these laws are like the evil eye. Tfoo! Tfoo!" he spat and stood up in a rage, his eyes wandering in disgust, not looking at anyone. But he quickly controlled himself and sank back in his chair, wiping his forehead with a fragrant snowy handkerchief. "Allah preserve us from the cursed devil," he muttered and turned to Grandpa. "I'm losing my temper on account of Zuhair. Another accident. Wrecked the car and survived by a miracle. I ask myself when will he calm down, get married, give me a grandson. You think money's everything. There were times I thought so too, Umm-Huda. Your brothers, that for years you've been accusing me of informing on . . ."

Mother writhed in her seat. "Whoever told you . . ."

"No one had to tell, Umm-Huda. I informed, yes, I informed. I admit. Those were savage days. The Jews' spies were no fools. I had to toss them a bone now and then."

He just happened to toss them the bones after stripping the flesh and fat off them, I thought to myself. Mother wept as she always does at the mention of her brothers.

Abu-Nakhla spoke to her. "Strange are the ways of Allah—maybe I was only His messenger."

"Allah's messenger?" Grandpa's eyes twinkled, his humorous Egyptian nature coming to the fore.

"Just so. Look how far her brothers have come in Jordan—one a television announcer, another a big shot in the Foreign Ministry, and the third—what's the third one doing, Umm-Huda?"

"Lectures at the university," she enunciated proudly.

"University! And how far would they've got in the Jews' state? How far have I got? A crazy son who hops from whore to whore, wrecking cars as he goes."

"He'll settle down," Grandpa said, feeling obliged to calm and console the man. "Let's come to the point," he hinted, like a tired man who wishes to retire to bed.

"You owe me money," said Abu-Nakhla.

"What for?"

"For removing the animals from over your head and bringing to the roof a young man anyone would pay a lot to have for a neighbor."

I was amazed. "You've already let the room?"

"What did you think? You thought I was going to turn it into a dovecote? Money's money, daughter." He turned again to Grandpa. "I've let the room for half the rent I was getting from those animals who bothered you. You should compensate me."

For all his wisdom, Grandpa was essentially a countryman, and the sharp and polished Abu-Nakhla was too much for him. Now he looked at the guest like one who's riding a donkey while eyeing an aircraft. "That's not what you came here for, Abu-Nakhla. Even poor people hold some things more dear than money. Silence is golden, Abu-Nakhla, and I thank you for it."

After he left Mother asked Grandpa reproachfully, "What did you have to thank him for?"

"Woman, he came to ask for Mary's hand and Allah sewed up his mouth."

"Mary—to that crooked son of a crook?"

"He kept his mouth shut, woman, and we'd better learn from him. Meantime, let's eat, we're starving."

At night, in the dark shell of our room, I heard Mary's heavy breathing. I was tired but knew that healing sleep was out of reach and tomorrow I'd go to work like a sleepwalker. Mary turned over in bed, thumped her pillow noisily and returned to her former position.

"Mary," I said, "Abu-Nakhla wouldn't have dared to go so far with his hints for no reason."

"Huda, don't smear yourself in other people's stink. Just look after yourself."

I did as she told me. I put my body to sleep limb after limb. I lay like a log, while my thoughts were sharp as knives.

## Chapter Two

I walked to the lower city as though a fierce wind was blowing in my back. I stepped carefully down the steep sloping alley toward the noise and bustle of Independence Street. Behind me was the mostly Arab wadi and before me the mostly Jewish street. The Turkish sellers of fruit and vegetables praised their produce in Hebrew, cursed in Arabic and weighed juicy apples and women's bottoms with their quick eyes. Most of the customers were office workers who had slipped out to shop. The stall holders never forgot their origins, their poor families, their dropping out of school, their position from childhood to the present, and pounced on the money with greedy fingers. Too late they discovered the dismaying truth that money alone could not make them into the people they dreamed of becoming. They slung foul language at girls who looked cheap, and who paid them back in kind, but their tongues stumbled and searched for words from a different world at the approach of a woman who looked respectable.

On mornings when I felt strong enough I took a shortcut to work through the market. I loved the abundance and brilliant hues of the mountains of produce, and the noisy vitality after the desolate nights. Squatting always in the same place among the colorful stalls was a mint seller who wore a winter coat even in summer. He kept the mint in a moist gunny sack, but I always felt that the scent of mint came from him rather than from the sack. Twice a week I stopped and bought a bunch for flavoring the tea at home. He would respond to my greeting with a slight smile and rummage deep inside the sack, supposedly searching for the freshest bunch. But when I felt tired I took the long way round and avoided the market. The effects of sleeplessness were visible on my face and strange stall holders would mistake me for a drug addict. The mixture of Hebrew and Arabic that served them for a language would overtake me, until I felt that the vendors at the end of the market were ready for me before I arrived. Once I tried to smile at them, but the smile was feeble and they misunderstood it. Their comments and laughter were like hunting cries. None of them, not even any of the Arabs, guessed that I'm an Arab.

That morning my senses must have been dulled, otherwise I'd have taken the long way. I realized my mistake as soon as I entered the market. The comments, jokes and stares felt like a barrage of stones. In my imagination I skimmed over the smooth road and Abu-Nakhla's boys ran after me, puffing in my ears and laughing at the blouse that clung to my skin. As I ran I saw the Moroccan mint seller holding up a bunch like a bouquet of flowers, and I wanted to shout to him that I did not need mint, I needed to huddle in his winter coat and moisten my lips on the damp sack lying before him. He grinned at me, showing four teeth around a hollow darkness, and I was shocked—he too, this worn-out old man? I was offended and was about to scold him, but he went on smiling darkly. He was not really smiling. His mouth was open in an effort to draw breath. And none of the vendors had taken any notice of me. I had been running, or imagining that I was running, for no reason. The Moroccan waved at me to attract my swimming glance, but I didn't have the strength to bend down and take the mint. I was also afraid to open my bag, my hands were so shaky. I struggled to get out of the place before I found myself sprawling among the cigarette butts and rotting cabbage leaves. I closed my eyes and opened them again. The dizziness had not passed. The fingernails of my hand gripping the handbag strap dug into my palm, and aided by this pain I reached Independence Street.

I entered the office and saw an expectant smile fading on the faces of Adina and Shirley. I motioned with my head at the manager's door, and Adina said, "Boaz has gone to Tel Aviv and won't be back today."

I turned to my desk and saw the surprise they had prepared for me, a wrapped package tied with a colorful ribbon. It was a book of poems by Yehuda Amichai, inscribed by Adina and Shirley with birthday wishes. I sank into the chair, feeling the weight of my years. An accompanying note bore three lines copied by Shirley:

> *Forgetting a person is like*
> *forgetting to turn off the light in the yard,*
> *leaving it burning all day.*

I glanced at Shirley. Did she know everything about Bahij? I dismissed the thought immediately. A lightbulb burning in a sunny yard is so pathetic. So was Bahij in my memory. Or was it I who was like that?

"Go into Boaz's office," Adina advised me. "You can lie on the sofa for a bit. I'll call you if there's a pressure of customers."

I thanked her for the suggestion but declined, though the air-conditioned atmosphere was making me shiver.

Once Bahij stopped the car and said, "Would you like to see a flood?"

"In this cold?" I wondered.

He was not impulsive, but sometimes he liked to seem adventurous. My eager response to his ideas satisfied his limited desire for excitement. I huddled in my coat and smiled, thinking to myself, only a madman would go out in this terrible downpour.

Suddenly I wanted to put him to the test. Bahij hated the cold. As soon as the cold weather set in, he padded himself with long johns and two warm undershirts. I stood at the wet parapet of the bridge, captivated by the furious roar of the brown Kishon. The rain soaked through the kerchief on my head and ran from my curls down on my cheeks and lips, like a stranger's tongue. From the corner of my eye I saw Bahij struggling to open the umbrella outside the car while he sat inside. Finally he came out and slammed the door shut with his foot, and his expression told me that he was cursing. The wind yanked the open umbrella inside out, twisting its ribs till it looked like a shot bird. He was compelled to drag it along the pavement, the gale wind tearing phrases from his mouth, "Madwoman!—Why're you standing there?—Look at yourself . . ."

He did not see himself. That's the point. All along, we saw only each other. With my kerchief a rag, my nose a gutter, my ears a pair of wind tunnels, my toes squelching in my shoes, I did not see myself but only Bahij dragging his umbrella. Down below in the rising flood an iron post from some washed-away fence stuck out of the water, which flowed on either side of it, carrying branches, vegetables from distant fields, animal carcasses. A branch snagged on the post and trembled, as though afraid of being swept out to sea. When the current flung a whole tree trunk against the post it loosened the branch's grip, and a moment later it let go and submitted to its fate.

I looked at Adina and the burning cigarette between her fingers. This morning I felt like that branch that clung to the post, but I longed to submit to the current and reach the generous sea. Grasping at something I don't understand, I'm unable to see what is happening around me. Even the gift didn't move me. Today Adina had spared a moment's thought to me, even suggested that I rest for a moment in Boaz's office. She's forty-one, very attractive, but when her lips tighten on the cigarette her face reveals the weary lines of approaching age. The telephone on her desk rang and she answered in her pleasant voice, unmarred by her smoking and her secret. "Yes, sir, of course, it can be arranged. . . . It isn't pleasant, arriving in Paris at such a late hour. You can switch to El Al. It's a good decision, sir."

A good decision. What about her decision? Her son never knew his father, who was killed when she was carrying him. Now the boy wants to be a paratrooper like him, in the same battalion. For that he needs her consent and her signature. He's got to live his own life, she explained to me yesterday. He mustn't live my anxieties. She makes me mad. She still waters the plants on her husband's grave, and he has remained young and fresh and loving. On bad days she shelters behind dark glasses and the tears are audible in her voice. She gets all anxious and nervous when Boaz, the director, goes on reserve duty. And the boy is her only child.

Shirley again offered to make coffee, and Adina responded with a weak smile. I understood that she'd made up her mind. But what can an Arab woman say to a Jewish mother? I kept quiet. At ten the travel agency was packed. Even in the autumn Israelis are eager to go abroad. Some come into the agency driven by their appetite, not even knowing where they want to go, and consult us like diners in a restaurant who can't read the menu. Others, mostly young people fresh out of national service, want to see the world for the price of a trip to Eilat. In my first months here they directed only the Arab customers to me, the Arabs being the easiest to deal with. An Israeli Arab entering an office feels like an outsider venturing into the sphere of authority, and behaves with awe. He's too bashful to ask even basic questions, and wants to show that he has the means and the will for his purpose. After a while Adina began to send me Jewish customers too. She's very good at spotting the difficult customers. When I was depressed she tackled the bothersome ones and looked after them indulgently. I respected her greatly and envied her, but didn't try to act like her. I had run out of smiles for such people. To moderate my admiration for her I reminded myself that she need not be pitied. She had known a man, had suckled a baby and enjoyed his laughter. She's a Jewess and wears the halo of a war widow. Boaz the manager behaves like an adolescent in her presence. But deep inside I was aware of my unfairness. I shall never be able to repay the warm sympathy she gives me. Even today, with the dark glasses forming a barrier between us, she took pains to spare me the awkward customers.

At three Boaz rang from Tel Aviv and Adina said everything was all right. At five she locked the office and said to me, "Come, I'll take you home."

I tried to decline, but went with her to the car park. The shadow of a tall building lay over the cars. She started the motor and her voice merged with its rumble, "He's going into the army next week."

I kept silent. On Jaffa Road we ran into a traffic jam and she lit a cigarette from the wrong end. The car filled with the stench of the singed filter. She crushed it quickly and lit another one. She dropped me off at my house. On the stairs I thought about the room on the roof and Abu-Nakhla's hidden intentions.

Mother was watching television, but she rose and walked backward to the kitchen. "I'll make you something to drink," she said, her eyes widening at the sight of a lioness rending a deer, probably in an African nature reserve.

"Later," I said.

"I'll make it," she insisted, her gaze lingering on a flock of birds spreading like a cloud of smoke. Recoiling unconsciously from the sight of a crocodile, she turned to look at me. "You're still feeling unwell?"

"Don't make her into an invalid," Mary scolded.

She was down in the dumps. Another day of searching in vain for a job, I thought. The labor market's in a bad way. Countless girls comb through the wanted ads. Nor was Mary's sleeping and waking pattern suitable to the circumstances. She went to bed late, woke up at ten and did not start functioning properly before midday. She's perceptive and intelligent, and knowledgeable though without formal education, but these were not the qualities that impressed her interviewers. They saw her lips painted blood-red, the long earrings dangling on her chiseled cheeks, her bold, youthfully provocative hats, and wondered if this was not an opportunity to realize a secret dream. Some suggested meeting her "for a coffee" outside the office, some even drove her back to the wadi, but they evaded the question of employment.

Mary felt offended by these experiences, though she quickly recovered and by evening she would look forward to the next day with its promise and possibilities. Today she was somehow different. Her proud slender neck seemed shorter, her back less straight. I knew the dress she had on. It had two little flower appliques sewn over her breasts. Now one of them was missing, evidently torn off, leaving a couple of white threads dangling like torn roots. I could see a blue bruise on her left shoulder under her dress. Zuhair's name came into my mind, but I didn't dare to think further. I sat down and laid my handbag on the table. Mary immediately shut her big black eyes and stuck her hand into my handbag, like the playful child she used to be who filled our house with her mischievous spirit. Her full lips babbled like an infant's, "What did you bring us today, auntie? What's this, chocolate?" she giggled.

"A book," I said.

She drew the Yehuda Amichai out of the bag and exclaimed, "Ma, today is Huda's birthday—her colleagues gave her a present."

"She's not a little girl any more," Mother said, her eyes pools of sorrow. She turned her head away when Mary showed her the dedication. She couldn't read Hebrew, only Arabic. She had finished two years of secondary school, but married a man who was almost illiterate. She would recall those days to comfort herself. "After 1948 there were no men left, so I took what I could find." I was about four when he died, and know his face only from faded photographs, nevertheless it upsets me when she speaks about him like this. A kind of fastidiousness prevents me from reminding her that his mother, Grandma Munira, was born in a palace—perhaps because the only noble person I knew among my forebears was Grandpa, who was born poor in Egypt.

"Very nice, your friends," she said with an undertone of resentment, as though Adina and Shirley had conspired to expose my increasing years, like an interest-bearing debt that cannot be redeemed.

"Maybe we should have a party for her?" Mary proposed, half seriously.

Mother made a grimace. "You and your crazy jokes."

Jamilla came in, bursting with excitement. "Abu-Nakhla's already let the house on the roof," she exclaimed. It would take coffee to calm her down.

I was curious. "How do you know?"

"I've seen him—something like this," she said, indicating about a meter above the floor.

"A dwarf?" I asked.

"Something like it," she said, and clearly wouldn't add another word until she'd had a cup of black coffee. But Mary was listening attentively and made no move to go to the kitchen to make the coffee. Jamilla kept shaking her head, as though she'd gone dumb. Then both Mother and I grasped the meaning of her silence and shouted together, "A Jew?"

But Jamilla held her tongue and Mother was obliged to go to the kitchen. When she returned with the coffee she rolled her eyes to the ceiling and muttered, "A Jewish dwarf—God break your bones, Abu-Nakhla. What is he thinking of, starting a circus upstairs?"

I couldn't make it out. "A Jew coming to live in the wadi?"

"You heard Jamilla," Mother said. "He's a dwarf. What does a dwarf care where he lives?"

Mary laughed. Both she and Grandpa are quick to see the comical aspect of things.

Suddenly we all froze and our eyes shot up to the ceiling. Then

Mother glanced at the television—perhaps the extraordinary sound had come from that. But no. There was no doubt where it came from. Mary was the first to recover. "It sounds like a trumpet."

We heard an empty barrel being dragged, followed by footsteps. "These are not the footsteps of a dwarf," Mother said. "They're the footsteps of a strong man."

Just then Grandpa came in. Mary said to him, "We have a Jewish neighbor upstairs."

"So he's a Jew," he replied with his Egyptian nonchalance.

"Plays a trumpet," Mother threw in.

"A trumpet?" he repeated, his eyes on Mary. I saw that he spotted the missing flower from the front of her dress.

We sat at the table but Jamilla sat on the side and watched television. Grandpa very slowly munched the flesh of an olive, sucking the pit like a child unwilling to give up a sweet. "Are you fasting?" he asked me.

"I've no—"

The blare of a trumpet broke in. Grandpa spat the olive pit into his hand in excessive alarm. The sound was like a long, agonized exhalation, like the sigh of the wind through broken blinds. I don't know much about music, but I felt that the melody came from a different world, from a person who was utterly alien to me. There was also something embarrassing about it, as though it was a hand sneaking up to me in my sleep and I was not firm enough to repel it, nor did I wish for such firmness.

"So, Jamilla," said Grandpa when the trumpet went quiet and the noises of the wadi returned, "your cat has a competitor now."

Indeed it was like a wail of longing, reaching across endless spaces, hoping for nothing, not even an echo.

"The moan of a lonely man. He's sad, this orphaned dwarf," said Mary.

"You're mad, mad," Mother said smiling. Unlike Grandpa, she had not noticed that a violent hand had plucked a flower off her daughter's breast. Suddenly she jumped up and ran to turn down the television. "He's coming down!" she said.

Mary rushed to the window. "Jamilla," she called and pointed to the street. "Is this the man you saw?"

Jamilla rose reluctantly and looked out. "Yes."

Mother got there ahead of me and I had to stand on tiptoe to look over the shoulders of the three.

"He isn't a dwarf at all," Mary said in some disappointment.

Aging Jamilla, who had never known a man, who was secretly attracted to Grandpa—perhaps in the course of time she'd come to think of men as giants, and considered anyone shorter than Grandpa to be a dwarf. I said to myself that it was all a lot of non-sense, but in reality I was curious, though in recent years I thought I had no curiosity left in me at all. Mary, Mother and Jamilla left the window and I stayed on. The man walked past the lighted front of a shoe shop. He looked very muscular, which instantly repelled me. He seemed to be showing off his physical strength, being dressed in nothing but a black T-shirt, short shorts and sandals.

"So Abu-Nakhla will suck the blood of another unfortunate," Mother said.

"Don't underestimate him," Mary said. "Anyone who owns a trumpet can afford to go out in the evening dressed better than this." Unconsciously, she put her hand on her breast, where the flower was missing. "It's an occupational disguise."

"You mean Shin Bet?" asked Jamilla.

"They're not that stupid—they've got enough Arabs for that right here. This man's a burglar. He took the room upstairs for storage. Tonight we'll hear him coming back with his loot."

I couldn't tell if she was serious.

"No doubt about it," said Grandpa, amused. "A burglar who advertises his presence and opens his business with a fanfare."

Jamilla rose to leave, and advised us to add another lock on the door, to be on the safe side. Grandpa lay on his bench and smoked his narghileh. Mother turned up the sound of the television. I went into the bedroom. The night-light was on over Mary's head, but she was not reading the book in her hands.

"Zuhair?" I asked carefully.

Mary turned off the light.

"You no longer believe that I care, Mary. You used to tell me everything."

"You want a confession? We really are screwed up. When we're in trouble we go to the priest, to a man who has no experience of life and doesn't want any. Our lives are as full as a cesspit, and we turn to a man who hasn't got a life. You're like that yourself. You've decided to be a nun, so be content with messing up your own life."

She fell silent. I heard her crying into her pillow. I didn't have the courage to get up and comfort her. But she was right, I haven't any advice to give, not even to myself. I crossed my arms behind my head and reconciled myself to another imprisoning night. I thought about Amichai. He writes that he renounces the knowledge that he has absorbed in his life, as a desert renounces water. I said to myself that no soil on earth ever voluntarily renounced water. Only man willingly foregoes a vital need. I thirst for things I daren't think about in my waking hours, then they appear distorted and repellent in my nightmares. Mary fell asleep and I was afraid to drop off too. Then I longed for sleep, even if it brought the touch of Abu-Nakhla's boys' bodies. I slept but they did not come. I woke up and listened to something. My heart was pounding though I didn't know why. Then I clearly heard the footsteps on the stairs. He's reached the roof. Maybe he is a burglar standing between me and the stars. A coward's fancy occurred to me—suppose I go upstairs and help him sort his loot. I fell asleep again before daybreak.

## Chapter Three

I opened my eyes and the room was full of light. My pains had melted away during the night. Fearing that it was an illusion, I felt my body, slowly and gingerly, like a walker in a flowering field. But no. My limbs felt light, my body even smelled good to me. I smiled inwardly. If I were alone in the room I'd have laughed aloud. Down below cars hooted and peddlers cried, and upstairs lived a dwarf burglar. Though I'd seen that he was not a dwarf, it was only his receding back that I saw, and I could still give him various imaginary forms. I regarded him as a cute trick played by vile Abu-Nakhla, much as though he'd let the room to a goat or a dolphin. In the morning I did not find his bulging muscles repellent. Dolphins are brawny too, but the Giver of Souls gave them a good soul. And in childhood stories dwarfs are nimble and busy folk. I said to myself that they too need to sleep. The dwarf burglar upstairs had returned late at night, and must now be sleeping his funny dwarfish sleep. I wanted very much to laugh. The joy broke out on my body, like the sweat used to do in the early days of Bahij.

I listened carefully. The dwarf was awake. The ceiling trembled slightly under his feet. The enchantment was dispelled, as if it upset me that he'd risen before me. I said to myself that this man was somehow connected with Abu-Nakhla, and none of that man's connections was any good.

Mary slept against the opposite wall, in the dress from which the flower had been plucked. In her sleep she'd thrown the blanket down to her waist, and the bruise on her shoulder showed like a patch of color in a painting. She is beautiful—dewy fresh, a mouth like a child's. Her eyelashes are long, her hair is a black fog, and her skin as silky as a smooth pond. She's so volatile when awake and so calm in her sleep. My exact opposite.

There was lively activity upstairs. A door opened and slammed, then reopened. He must have forgotten something and come back for it. He was about to go out. I threw off the blanket and went into the living room. Grandpa had already gone shopping and Mother was sitting on his bench. "You're up early," she said.

"Yes," I said and escaped to the bathroom. I was ashamed to stand by the window and look out while she watched. Now I wouldn't be able to come out immediately and run to the window. But intense curiosity made me want to see him in daylight. I grabbed a towel and came out rubbing my face with it, as though I remembered something. "Mother . . ." I said and went to the window.

"Yes?"

My mind was blank and went even blanker when I looked out of the window. He was wearing long trousers now with an ordinary shirt, and sandals. By now he was far from the house and I couldn't see his face. Like most short people, he was very straight-backed, and was carrying something that but for his suspicious exit in the night I'd have taken for books. His walk was supple and confident, like an athlete or a burglar, and he looked around him in a leisurely manner, suggesting a deep interest. Of course, I thought, such a man must get to know his new surroundings.

"I know about Abu-Nakhla's son," said Mother.

I lowered my eyes, as if I'd been found out.

"She's a good girl," Mother went on.

"She's more than that. I wish I had her head."

"What use is a big head on weak shoulders? She's a poor orphan."

So she hadn't noticed me peeping out of the window. Some devil prompted me to ask, "Is she pregnant?"

She jumped up and shook out her skirt, as though shaking off bugs. "How can you suggest such a thing about your sister?" she said, resting a hand on the table, her chin up in the air. Her posture aroused my pity, it was like a general flourishing his sword on an empty platform.

"It's not a disaster, Mother."

"I don't want to hear. And that's not what's killing me."

"What's killing you?"

"You."

"There's no danger of me getting pregnant."

Instantly her arms were around my shoulders. She drew me almost forcibly to the bench and made me sit beside her. I was glad there was a towel between us, but she must have read my mind and pulled it away, flinging it over a chair. Her body heat was amazing, the warmth I'd outgrown so many years before.

"Do you forgive us?" she asked in a pleading tone.

"What for?"

"We mustn't ruin Mary's future."

"What's all this to do with me?" I asked, though I guessed what she was getting at.

"If you say no, we'll understand and obey. You're the elder and you have the right . . ."

"She won't marry Zuhair."

"What are you talking about?" she cried. "They're Muslim and we're Christian."

"Mary doesn't care about such things."

"I'm talking about Wahid, the nephew of my sister-in-law Nuria."

"From Kafr Namra?" I laughed. "What nonsense you get into your head! Mary with a villager who knows nothing except fitting window blinds . . ." I had to restrain myself from running to wake Mary. "Can't you see the books she's reading?"

"Nobody's ever sewn a dress from books."

I grew suspicious. "Who else knows about this foolishness?"

"Your grandfather . . ."

I stood up. "You shouldn't have kept it from me. I'd have told you at once that you're making fools of yourselves. It's like pairing a princess with a horse."

"Mary's not a princess. She's a woman who needs a husband to support her. You even buy her bras for her. How much longer?"

"Don't tell me you've already invited his family."

"They're coming tomorrow."

"Mary will throw them out without ceremony. Poor fellow. You shouldn't have done this to him, Mother." I looked at her face and saw nothing but pity, pity for me. "Don't tell me Mary knows about it?"

"I married your father. He wasn't better than Wahid. Even less than him. Much less. There was a time when I also thought I deserved better. Every person is born with a rope, Huda. Some with a short rope and some with a long one. Mary knows the length of her rope."

I was sure that Mary went along with this joke in a moment of good humor. I went back into the bathroom and turned on the shower. The cold water took my breath away. I turned it off and yielded to the warm towel. My blue lips smiled at my body in the mirror. My nipples thawed and turned rosy, then stiffened and looked like infant mouths. I stroked my breasts as though they were in a cradle. Drops of water glistened like dew on the dusky thicket under my belly. My face flushed hotly and my mouth went dry with excitement. If I could, I'd have bent low and licked the dewdrops. I felt ashamed and told myself I was as mad as Mary. The dewdrops became tiny pearls, until I dried the spangled darkness. I passed my wet hands over my face and closed my eyes.

Suddenly I opened them and looked at the corner, as if expecting to see the dwarf burglar squatting beside the laundry basket, gazing at me with his face resting in his hands. There's no one there, I said to myself, but nevertheless went and stood in that corner as if waiting for something to seize my legs and climb up my thighs.

In the bedroom the blanket was now over Mary's head, leaving her legs bare. They looked like the legs of a prematurely nubile girl, rather than a woman's. They will no doubt appeal to the rustic Wahid more than her head.

As I was leaving Mother said without looking at me, "There's nothing to offer in the house. Maybe some fruit . . ."

"I'll buy pears," I said. She loved pears, and I embarrassed her by catering to her weakness.

Boaz was in the office. A big man with a belly spilling over his belt, he had again cut his face shaving this morning. With men he was sociable and easygoing, but with women he was shy. His jokes were all at his own expense. He mentioned his wife so frequently, either in affectionate banter or open admiration, that she seemed to be a kind of third eye or extra nose on his face. Adina was in love with him in her subdued way, and he treated her with happy bashfulness. Their rapport created a pleasant atmosphere, and I of course envied them.

Now he looked at me when I came in and scolded Adina and Shirley. "What's all this nonsense about her being ill? Look at her, just look . . ." He almost added an actual compliment, but held back and placed a pretty little package on my desk. "Just something for your birthday," he said.

I unwrapped the perfume. "My mother thinks birthdays are only for children. A woman of thirty should be hiding her shame."

"Shame?" he growled. "What should I say then? Your birthdays and my piles always remind me that I'm old."

Adina's face expressed her protest. He was fifty-one but she saw him with her forty-one-year-old eyes.

Shirley was freer. "You're a real man."

"Depends what for," he joked. "Try taking me to a discotheque— they'd haul me off to emergency after five minutes." He turned to Adina. "You signed?"

"I signed," she replied in a low voice.

"Total idiocy," he exclaimed and fled to his office.

Adina's face was scarlet. Those were the harshest words he'd ever said to her. Suddenly he emerged from his office like a schoolboy who's thrown a stone and then realized the damage he's done. He saw her drooping head and the words started and stopped in his mouth.

"Enough, Boaz," she whispered.

"One more thing. A son is not a wife or a husband. Ask me. I'm an expert. My son's in the corps."

"I beg you."

"Every time there's some action across the border I think they're doing it deliberately to hurt him. I run away from my wife, really run away. I go to the sea in the dark and I think, I wish he'd get a bullet in the leg. Let him lose an ear. You know how many parts of his body I've traded to the sea, just so he'll come home alive? What do you need all that for?"

He stood beside her desk and the words died on his lips. His shirttail came out of his belt and revealed a bit of his belly covered with coppery fuzz. I looked at that vulnerable belly and wished I could overcome the sorrow that gripped my throat. Huda, I said to myself, this is a Jewish sorrow, and you're an Arab. Boaz's son in the corps and Adina's son who will be a paratrooper may sooner or later kill Arabs. And Boaz and Adina will breathe a sigh of relief and give thanks when they return home, even at the cost of the lives of the cousins I've never met.

Boaz never showed me a photograph of his son as a baby. In his office hangs a picture of the son in an army jeep, goggles pushed up on his forehead, his curly hair golden, in his eyes a look of weary maturity and on his lips a boyish smile. One mustn't fall for boyish smiles. His officer's insignia give him a forceful charm and the barrel of the submachine gun is a daunting emblem. He looks perfect and timeless, as if he was born thus, framed on the wall of his father's office. By contrast, my cousins grew from letter to letter, from photograph to photograph. My favorite is Hissam, the youngest. Pudgy limbs in the cradle, then a schoolbag on his back on the way to school. The photographs have become blurred from Mother's kisses. I never heard him cry, never smelled his sweat when he came home from play, never heard him moaning in fever or laughing happily. Only stiff smiles and eyes on the camera. Mary and I have grown up without cousins in Haifa, and have no relatives in the country, except the families of our uncles' wives, scattered through the villages in Western Galilee, and we've hardly been a source of pride to them, or a place of pilgrimage. We've hardly ever met them, either in the holidays or at family celebrations. Mother took care to attend every funeral, because you don't need an invitation for that.

I looked up from the paperwork on my desk. Boaz had gone back to his office, Adina had on her dark glasses. Shirley was chanting in her little voice, "What a fucked-up world . . ."

I nodded to her. She seems a pleasant, quiet girl, but there's something ruthless about her rebelliousness. Her father is a well-known gynecologist, and she really doesn't need to work at the travel agency for her living. When her parents objected to the Moroccan man she was dating, she left the university and her home in order to help him finish his studies. But in the meantime she fell out of love with him, or maybe she never was really in love. She's good-looking and the phone calls she receives are not all from customers but also from admirers, and she doesn't put them all off. She talks about "her Moroccan" like a breeder of thoroughbred horses who's raising a racehorse. "He'll go far. He'll get his Ph.D. with honors. He's got brains, not like my dummies." Her dummies, namely her parents, bought her a car, pay her rent, stuff her fridge with delicacies, and don't seem to mind that their daughter is financing the Moroccan's studies. They're waiting patiently for her to come to her senses, and in the meantime make sure she doesn't suffer for her folly.

One day, after I witnessed a telephone chat between Shirley and an admirer, a delightful talk that concluded with a sound like coo-ing doves, I stiffened my nerve and asked her about the Moroccan. "Is he still living in your place?"

"Why not? His room's got a door and my room's got a door. You hear what you want to hear and you don't see what you'd rather not."

"All the same . . ."

"You mean his pride? They were nine children at home in a crummy village near Kiryat Shemoneh, with a paralyzed father who never even sniffed the earth. The only walk he ever took with his mother was to the social services. Over there you learn a lot about that shit you call pride."

"An Arab man wouldn't do it."

"Your Arabs have a screw loose," she said dismissively, the way her parents talked about her Moroccan.

It was all part of the world that was strange to me. I wanted to learn more and more about it, from her and from Mary, in order to understand why everything fell apart between me and Bahij. At times I wonder what good it would do me. There comes a time when you have to accept that it's too late to learn to drive or to swim in the sea.

We closed a little late. I wanted to get home as early as possible, but this time Adina didn't offer to drive me. I took my bag which was weighed down with pears, walked to Jaffa Road and up the steep alley. Breathing so heavily that I had to slow down, I asked myself why I was rushing home. Even Mary's match did not arouse my curiosity. Nothing will come of it, anyway. A fish doesn't jump into a frying pan.

I stopped beside a grocery and thought, I get in a state when I have to tell the tiniest lie, but how good I am at lying to myself. I know why I'm rushing home. If I were proud of the reason I'd also be proud of the excitement. These last few years I haven't had much to feel proud about. The truth is, I'm hurrying home because of the strange Jewish dwarf-burglar whose face I haven't seen.

Grandpa wasn't home. He spends these hours in the cafe with the elders of the wadi. You'd think that in old age, at the end of the road, every minute would be precious, yet old people, the enemies of old age, kill those very minutes. To a thirty-year-old it seemed that these old people exist from meal to meal, from meeting to meeting.

Mary was under a kind of house-arrest. Mother wouldn't let her go out and none of Mary's tricks worked. "That Zuhair," Mother grumbled. "Allah shorten his life's rope. He's already driving a new car. He came and hooted and I swear to you the foolish girl was getting ready to run to him, like a sheep to the butcher."

The match was not yet made and already Mother treated Mary as a married woman whose liberty was at an end. Mary paced up and down in her cage, pouting, wearing a transparent negligee which showed her waist and emphasized her thighs.

"Get dressed properly," Mother begged her. "Grandpa will be here any minute."

"I'm hot," she wailed. "I'm suffocating."

"So go naked." Mother wrung her hands, sank into a chair and sobbed. "The only thing he knew how to do was to die in time," she complained about Father.

Mary pulled me into our room and closed the door. "She honestly believes I'm going to bury myself alive with a primitive peasant. Your Bahij was an academic and still smelled of the village like sweat. This one can hardly scrawl his name. The only thing he knows is fitting blinds." She was so furious that her whisper sounded like a funny whistle.

"You didn't have to agree."

"Mother nagged and nagged—she kept saying, look at Huda, just look at her. I broke down. Not everyone has the courage to be unhappy."

"You've got Zuhair, then. Yesterday he damaged your dress, beat you up. What else did he do to you?"

She fell silent and I became confused, as if I was being interrogated. Perhaps the blue stain on her shoulder was not a bruise but the mark of a passionate suck. Perhaps I preferred to regard him as a violent man rather than one who loses his head in love. "How can you?"

"He's crazy about me. I told him I was getting married and he threatened to kill himself."

I thought, so even Zuhair knew. I was the only one kept in the dark. "Pimps don't commit suicide," I said.

"He's willing to marry me."

"So you'll be Abu-Nakhla's daughter-in-law. He betrayed our uncles to the Jews. I'd like to kill him."

"So go and kill the whole world. Who didn't screw the Palestinians? They're expert at putting themselves in a position to be screwed."

She was right. But the other killers were only on the news, whereas Abu-Nakhla was a red tarboosh and hawkeyes and hands that stirred the whole wadi.

"Wasn't it you who recited the other day a poem by Dalia Ravikovich?" I asked her.

"That's the trouble with poems and stories. You read the works of these people and think you're as great as they are. They're terrific liars, those writers and poets. They peddle drugs, opium, make your head float up to the clouds so you forget that your feet are stuck in the mud. In life everything's different. This is what someone like me can have—on the one hand Zuhair, on the other a blinds contractor."

"You've figured it all out."

"Huda, I know what I want, but you only know what you don't want."

Again she was right. I saw that I was a bankrupt advising a capitalist how to succeed in business. Do happy people also consider themselves experienced? It seems to me only the unhappy ones take such pride. In this contest, which neither of us wanted, she won as she always did. It gave her much satisfaction and wiped out the misery with which she had pulled me into our room. Her black eyes glittered trying to meet my defeated look.

Upstairs there was a noise of something heavy being dragged. I stopped myself from discussing it with Mary. Curiosity leads to trouble. I had to restrain my imagination. A grin appeared on Mary's face. She's so unlike me. She can shake off even a difficult conversation and smile. "He's neither a dwarf nor an orphan," she said. "I talked to him."

"You did?"

"Mother was dawdling downstairs, chatting with Jamilla, to make sure I didn't leave the house. I felt I was suffocating and went up on the roof. Huda, you won't recognize the roof. He's been up there less than two days and he's already washed and painted everything. His name is Alex and he's a new immigrant from Russia. A nice guy."

I didn't say anything. She considered every man a nice guy at first. She had the soul of a child. Despite everything, she was not yet infected with suspicion.

"He invited me to have coffee," she said. "He's got lots of books in Russian and English. He does his own cooking, and you can see he's not exactly rolling in money."

"So now you have both a Muslim and a Jew." I tried to hide my envy, but felt my face growing hot.

"No, Huda," she replied seriously. "You remember the computer course I took?"

"That nothing came out of."

"Every person, man or woman, has this kind of computer in his brain. When two people meet the computer starts to work. You know what it does?"

I had to laugh. "What?"

She laughed too. "The computer comes up with one of two words: 'Maybe' or 'No.' If the computer says 'No,' the brain shuts down and all your wishes and dreams go to sleep. You're like a switched-off unplugged radio. But if the computer says 'Maybe,' the radio comes on, and you start tuning to station after station. Sometimes you make a face, as if to convince the computer that there's nothing doing, nothing interesting on any station. But you keep going. It's something about the body or the voice, something he did or didn't do that grabbed you. There's a lot of appeal in that 'Maybe.' It's like going to an unfamiliar city and expecting to find something there."

"And what did you find in him?" I asked.

"My computer right away said 'No.' Meaning, no broadcast and no radio receiver. You understand?"

"No."

"You're pretending to be thick. You understand perfectly well, but you want to drive me crazy. He's like you. Awfully serious. Wears glasses like bottle bottoms."

"He wears glasses?"

"Yes. And you can see he's very strong. It's hard to describe. It's a kind of strength you don't see often. Muscles like granite, strong nerves and the willpower of a person who never gives up. He even moves like that. Everything done slowly and correctly and intentionally. It's not for me."

I was silent. Mary looked at me intently and said, "You're ruining your computer. Right now it's yelling 'Maybe, Maybe' like a mad parrot, and you're stopping your ears. But that 'Maybe' is already echoing inside you like a stone in a rolling barrel."

She uncovered her shoulder to look at the blue bruise and stroked it as if it was a bird's wing. So it was not the mark of a blow. I left the room quickly.

The moment Grandpa came in the trumpet upstairs woke up as if to welcome him. This time it went on longer, as if to test our reactions from day to day. Grandpa stood beside the table and looked up. "That's nice," he said. I didn't recognize the melody. It must have come from Russia.

I peeled an apple but lost my appetite in the process. Later, when I lay on my bed waiting for Mary to fall asleep, I saw how mad it was. In the morning I wake up to his sounds upstairs, and at night I think about him and wait for him to come home.

I attended a Jewish school and didn't learn Arabic literature till later, when I was carried away by Bahij. I recalled reading an Egyptian story about a prisoner who is held in an underground cell and hears a knocking on the concrete wall. He is convinced that he's next to the women's wing, and that one unhappy soul among them knows about him and is sending him a message. In his desperate loneliness he responds by knocking on the wall too. So he sends his longings, his powerful emotions, his overpowering love, until he discovers that there aren't any women on the other side of the wall.

And I, in the mobile cell of my loneliness, peering out and seeing other people's freedom and joy, while I breathed air and swallowed my tears and bit my knuckles, it was not loneliness I was afraid of then but mainly insanity. If I were alone at home I'd have knocked on the ceiling with a broomstick, though I knew there was no one on the roof.

## Chapter Four

I didn't fall asleep until I heard his weary footsteps on the stairs. He walked about his room for a while, making his bed or a hot drink, and the sounds merged into a quiet sleep free of nightmares. In the morning Mother woke me and Mary, all tense and excited about the matchmaking visit. "Get up," she cried. "The house is empty and dirty and I don't know where to start."

Mary opened her eyes a crack, groaning and protesting against this abuse, and turned to the wall, curled up like a puppy. Mother approached her apprehensively and touched her. "Mary, my love, you must get up early today. We have to tidy the house."

"Our house looks better than their hovel in the village."

"You haven't been there for years. They live in a villa with Italian marble and German taps. At Abu-Saad's funeral I looked at their women and felt ashamed of my clothes."

"You went to a funeral or a fashion show?"

Mother gave a cautious chuckle. When Mary talked like Grandpa there was a chance that the day would pass peacefully. She slipped her arm under Mary's waist as though to tickle her. "Don't you dare!" Mary shrieked and sprang from the bed to avoid Mother's hands. Mother cheered up at the sight of her stretching her long body. Mary stepped delicately to the door as though tripping down a runway, then turned around, came and rubbed noses with Mother. "What do you think, Huda," she asked, "should I take a course in fashion modeling?"

"You must," I replied. "It's the only course you haven't tried yet."

"Oh Mary, don't talk like this," Mother said in alarm, the fear showing in her eyes. Oh how that fear hurt me, the fear of the pauper who's found a treasure. She never looked at me like that. My appearance never awakened her anxieties. I don't remember her ever telling me after I grew up not to come back late in the evening. As though she was certain that no sexual predators would ever take an interest in me.

"Huda," Mother said pleadingly, "tell her. They'll think she's really like that."

"I really am like that," Mary stated. "And if they don't like it they can drop dead."

"Daughter," Mother went on caressing her with her eyes, "they're a little different from us. Their way of speaking, their thinking, are a bit different."

"With the Italian marble and the German taps they'll have started thinking like everyone else," I said. But thinking of Bahij, whose mind was divided between modern plumbing and the rope and bucket, I became unsure.

"You're both trying to drive me crazy. As if you've conspired to spoil everything."

How easy it is to forget. The day before she'd approached me in trepidation and said she'd understand if I objected.

"You've nothing to worry about, Mother," I said.

I wasn't lying. I'd been observing Mary and wondering. Behind the stiff neck I saw a neck bowed to receive the yoke. Her resistance seemed ready to crumble. Freedom, I thought, is a weighty burden which not everyone can bear, especially not women, most especially not Arab women. Only the night before Mary had talked grandly about the computers, but she herself, like so many others, did not follow those "Maybe" and "No" signals. She also considered innumerable factors over which she had no power. Perhaps she found it easier to avoid making the decision about her life and left it to others. She was still tripping barefoot about the room, but her provocativeness was pathetic. She was no longer stepping like a fresh runway model, more like a weary tightrope dancer wishing for a safety net.

"Nothing's irreversible," I said. "It can still be called off."

"God forbid!" Mother exclaimed.

There was a different look in Mary's eyes then, a look I'd have preferred not to see. She was as spiteful as a defeated person can be. She implied, without uttering a word, that I was envious of her, and I protested and felt hurt because she was right. I had rejected Bahij like a vile insect, and now I grudged her a blinds hanger who barely finished primary school.

When I left for work Mother called after me, "The pears were wonderful. Perhaps some grapes for the guests . . ."

"I'll get them," I said over my shoulder.

I returned early, as though to make up for my misconduct. Grandpa was also at home, shaved and dressed in his best suit. I put on my professional travel-agency smile and gave the stage set some final touches. I moved chairs, arranged the roses I'd bought on the way home on the table, put Grandpa's narghileh in the corner.

Grandpa raised his hand like a novice actor and asked, "What, is that also forbidden? The narghileh is a respectable object."

"It isn't modern," Mother said.

Grandpa blew imaginary dust off his jacket. "Modern! They eat pita and olives just like us and they don't travel by helicopter."

Seeing the grin on his face she protested, "And I have to bear all the troubles on my shoulders."

I understood that there was some real trouble brewing. Going into the bedroom I found Mary crouched before the little mirror, tears running down her face and a thick black mustache drawn with a pencil on her upper lip. The contrast between the masculine mustache and the tears was perfect. I sat on my bed.

"Suppose I go out like this to meet them?" she threatened.

I kept quiet. We both knew she'd yield in the end. I asked her, "Do you want a Valium?"

"I know where you keep them. I took two."

"You must be feeling woozy," I said coolly.

"They say if you drink some alcohol on top of it you really take off. How about pinching me a little of Grandpa's arak?"

I gripped my fists between my knees. Mary returned to the mirror and added more lines to the black mustache.

"Why didn't you paint on a red mustache with the lipstick?"

I should have kept quiet. Only Grandpa's jokes are never tasteless, and his humor does not annoy because it comes from a generous and kindly spirit. Mary wiped her tears and the mustache with the back of her hand and said, "You know what I used to dream, how I'd meet the man I would marry? We're both in white tennis clothes, me in a short-short skirt and snowy panties. After the game I go up to the net and shake his hand. In the dream it doesn't matter who won and who lost. He keeps my hand in his. Everything vanishes—the crowd, the sky, the court and the net, there's just the two of us standing there, my hand in his, and my body and soul know all the answers. Huda, these dreams are also part of reality. Why is life like a diseased stomach that vomits all the beautiful dreams? It isn't fair."

"What isn't fair here?" I demanded, defending myself against something that threatened to break through the fence I'd learned to live within.

"I didn't cultivate dreams like you did. Someone or something came up with this stupid dream and fucked up my brain. I fantasize and it all looks and sounds real. I can even hear the thump of the ball, I see the sweat on man's forehead, and feel how my hand swoons and wakes up in his palm. Then it all bursts, like bubbles of piss in the toilet bowl."

"Dreams," I said, "are merchandise like any other. People choose their dreams according to their means."

Mary pointed crudely with her thumb at the ceiling and said, "I bet the man up there doesn't think about expensive shops or cheap shops when he needs something."

I went into the living room and greeted the guests as they came in, aware of Mother's anxious look. Grandpa tore open two packs of Marlboros and offered them to the men. I didn't know any of them. They didn't look like villagers. They were the potential groom, his father, mother and his teacher brother Assim. I knew at once who the groom was. His hair was damp, as though he'd just come out of the shower. His movements were heavy, and he watched the others closely, apparently ready and willing to follow their directions. He was forty but looked fifty. His teacher brother was older but looked younger.

The groom did not hide his disappointment at my appearance. In the brief moment he thought I was Mary he stripped me, felt my limbs and covered me with pity. His mother bit her lip. I was too small and thin for them, not at all to their taste. I'm familiar with this disappointment, but I've never grown accustomed to it. When I was an adolescent Jamilla used to urge Mother to fatten me up, so I'd look "like a woman."

I sat down beside Grandpa, shook away the smoke with my hand, as if driving away flies, and said, "Mary will be out in a moment."

The mother's sigh sounded like air escaping from a pierced balloon. Wahid immediately took his eyes off me, confused, as though he'd meant to go into a cafe and accidentally entered a barbershop. His mother cried in relief, "You must be Huda, the elder sister."

I nodded at the teacher brother, who smiled back, the married man who shows that he is unconventional. Grandpa again offered the expensive cigarettes.

Mary knew her timing. The dress was familiar, the delicate makeup, the light shoes, the dark cascade of hair, yet she was a different person. There was no trace of rebellion and cheek. She was all shyness and modesty, as though she had only this minute shed the robe and veil of a devout Muslim and for the first time joined the company of strange men. Mother looked at me questioningly but I had no answer. When Mary playacts only Grandpa can guess how it will end. He was smoking intently. Perhaps Mary surprised him too.

The guests stood up—the same guests who'd remained glued to their seats when I entered. Mary went up to the father and shook his hand, her head bowed and her hair quivering like the coat of a cringing dog, her eyes lowered and her lips mumbling shyly. Then she shook the hand of the teacher, who lost his free married-man smile. She glanced up briefly at the paralyzed Wahid, and without touching his hand fled to his mother. The woman was instantly overcome. She embraced Mary tightly and wept, as though her only daughter had just been restored to her. In her ample bosom Mary's cooing "Auntie, Auntie . . ." was almost submerged. The woman could not stay on her feet and almost collapsed together with Mary. Mother hurriedly pushed a chair at her, and the woman put Mary on it and sat down beside her, without letting go of her hand. "I'm taking her," she said in a choking voice, and turned to her husband. "Abu-Assim, this child is ours."

The intended groom groped for his seat like a blind man and sat down carefully. He looked so extraneous and alien in the place where he had hoped to belong. I noticed that Grandpa was looking tense. His eyes wandered to the narghileh in the corner. The wide-awake teacher offered Mary a pack of cigarettes with an understanding smile. Mary looked up at him in surprise and responded with the bashful grimace of a ten-year-old. The stunned guests evidently did not notice the odor of tobacco on her breath.

"Stop smoking!" Mother ordered.

The astounded men were not prepared to forego their mental prop. Only Wahid hastily stubbed out his cigarette. If I were not jealous of Mary I'd have enjoyed her playacting. I had never had so much love lavished on me. In my self-pity I recalled Amichai's words, "The girl from my childhood they killed, and my father was dead." What would have happened if Father were alive?

Wahid's mother was still clutching Mary's hand. I thought, Take her and choke on her! You've no idea what a land mine you're embracing. You'll step on it and it will explode, and explode again after your legs have been torn off, and go on exploding till there's nothing left of your body but the head, for aches and grief. I saw her dissolving by degrees until her head rolled on the floor at Mary's feet.

I sipped the cold lemonade Mother had handed around. Why was Mary using this particular tactic? Surely her sexual computer was shrieking "No! No! No!" All she needed to do to scare off the groom and his attendants was to be her usual self. On their speedy way downstairs they'd have landed in the arms of Jamilla, who was waiting below, consumed with curiosity.

I looked again at Wahid. He had hardly uttered a sound. When Grandpa asked him how his business was he replied only, "Thank God," as though trapped in a bubble of silence. How come Mary's waywardness didn't prompt her to poke fun at him? She had been mistreating such people since she was a child. Even the wadi kids were afraid of her tongue. In my mind I contrasted his clumsy form with the light feline shape of her imaginary tennis player. Yet instead of crushing him she was fluttering her long lashes at him and looking up like a timid hen. The look seemed to thrill him.

The explosion did not take place. Mary turned her face to the mother with a wordless plea to relieve her of the tension. The mother let go of Mary's hand and patted it, as though saying, You're right, daughter. Then she sat up and ordered, "Speak, Abu-Assim."

And the father spoke. At first he did not know whom to address. When he turned to me I looked blank, and when he turned to Mother she appeared to disown responsibility. She was still stunned by Mary's behavior. Finally he addressed Grandpa. "We have known each other for many years."

What a lie!—but then Grandpa is a tolerant Egyptian. "We're one family," he replied. He could have added that the funerals Mother attends prove as much.

"We hear nothing but good about you in the letters we get from my sister-in-law in Jordan." Indeed, they learn about us from the illicit correspondence with Jordan, while we live a spitting distance from their village. If they'd only remembered us once, at Christmas, at Easter. . . .

"We honor you and your daughter-in-law, your devoted upbringing produced these beautiful flowers." He looked at me and Mary, skimming briefly over my face, as if I were a thorn in a bunch of flowers. "You've good reason to feel proud."

Grandpa pressed the side of his nose and said, "You like narghileh smoke, don't you?" He stood up, towering in the small living room, and turned to Mother as if including her in a secret rite. "Just a few coals. Give our guest a taste of real tobacco."

Mother went into the kitchen and he set the narghileh between him and the surprised father. "This mixture is my secret," he said, putting his hand into the pouch and kneading the tobacco as if it were living flesh. "Today people are abandoning the narghileh. I've always looked for someone to pass my secret to. It would be a shame to take it to the grave." He sat down and looked at the kitchen door, implying that nothing more needed to be said before the coals arrive. And we all sat in silence, as though there was nothing more important this evening than the ancient narghileh. When Mother returned he took a generous pinch of tobacco from his pouch, laid the coals on top, took a few gurgling puffs to test it and handed the mouthpiece to the father.

"Now then," said Grandpa, "there is nothing above us or below us."

"What?!" the mother exclaimed, galvanized as if the burning narghileh embers had flown into her lap.

"No money," the father said, a little dazed by the effect of the smoke.

"No money and no property," Grandpa announced as though it was good news.

"Impossible," said the mother.

"What's impossible?" Grandpa smiled. "You think we have some only we're hiding it? I wish we had. For Mary I wouldn't even hide my soul."

Honesty is plain to see, especially in an evening full of lies. "So you've gobbled up the future of the poor girls?" the mother asked.

Mother turned pale as though she'd been slapped.

The teacher brother said hopelessly, "Maybe a way can be found all the same."

The mother stood up. "What way are you thinking of? They're out to rob your brother and you're wasting words." Her eyes rested on my face. "They've already buried one girl, now they're ready to bury the other."

"Please," the father tried to calm his wife. "Don't fly off the handle. We're guests and we shouldn't offend. Calm down, woman, calm down in the name of Jesus."

Her hands were on her hips. "Why are you putting this disgusting pacifier in your mouth?"

Grandpa leaned forward and took the pack of Marlboros, thought a moment and offered it to Wahid. Wahid took a cigarette and Grandpa put the pack away.

"One moment," Wahid said.

"No point in waiting even half a moment," his mother declared. "We're going."

There was a loud knock on the door. Zuhair, I thought, and for some reason it struck me as fine timing.

Another angry knock.

Mother's mind ranged close to my own. "It can only be Abu-Nakhla."

Grandpa was more practical. "Who is it?"

"Open the door," said a strange voice in Hebrew.

The groom's mother sat down again. It seemed that the appearance of an unexpected Jew in a gathering of Arabs can momentarily relieve inner tensions. Mother opened the door. On the threshold stood the non-dwarf. My face felt as if it was being dipped alternately in boiling and freezing water. The young man fell silent at the sight of the gathering. His eyes were enormous behind his thick glasses, and seemed to be searching for something to latch on to. Mary shrank behind Wahid's mother, so that the neighbor would not reveal that he knew her.

"Yes, please?" Grandpa said politely.

The neighbor's arm rose and dropped as though suppressing a rage. "Somebody broke my lock and stole from my room," he said.

"Come in, come in, tfadal." And as the neighbor stepped into the room Grandpa burst into laughter. I froze. I saw the neighbor's wrestler's chest swell. His neck, shoulders, arms and legs were a mass of muscles. For some reason I thought about Grandpa's belly. There's nothing more vulnerable than a laughing man's belly. I saw the big eyes narrowing behind the thick lenses.

"Why is he laughing?" he asked, looking for assurance that a madman had crossed his path.

Grandpa, who is usually so careful, doubled up with laughter. Perhaps it dispelled the tension of the earlier conversation. "This is the man we decided was a burglar himself," he said in Arabic. "Wallak, ya ibni, that's your occupational hazard."

Good thing he's a new immigrant and probably knows no Arabic, I thought. The neighbor looked at us and asked, "He is drunk?"

"Yes," Mother replied quickly. "We have guests and he's had a lot to drink." She took him by the arm as though pacifying a dangerous thug. "Come, son, sit with us a while. Have something to drink." She pushed him into a chair and stuck a glass of lemonade into his hand. "Now tell us what happened."

I looked for Mary and didn't see her. She must have slipped away to the kitchen or to our room. The nearsighted fellow was looking at me strangely, perhaps taking me for Mary.

"Are you sure your room was broken into?" Mother asked.

"In the morning I study," he explained to Mother, who stood over him and didn't let up. "At night I work in port. I'm a docker."

"What are you studying?"

"Electronics at Technion. Electronic engineering." Like many new immigrants, he was used to explaining simple things repeatedly.

"The boy is honest and speaks the truth," Grandpa said in Arabic.

"Today I come back from Technion, door is open."

"Maybe you forgot to lock it."

"They broke . . . the . . ." he turned to me.

"The lock."

"Yes, the lock. Completely broke. Nobody heard?"

Grandpa stood up, gently moved Mother out of the way and took her place. "No, son. We didn't hear, and even if we had, we wouldn't have lifted a finger."

"Why?"

"Because we're cowards, son. Sometimes it's better to be afraid. What did they steal from you?"

"Money. Half month wages."

"You shouldn't leave money in the room."

"What I must do now?" he asked me.

I remained silent.

Seeing his expression, Mother shook her head. She was probably seeing him humping heavy sacks on the docks and earning those half wages by the sweat of his brow. "Why are you alone like this?" she questioned him gently.

"Mother and father in old-age home. Old. Mother sick." He stood up and looked at me again, then said goodbye.

"One moment," Mother stopped him and went to the kitchen. He remained standing, trying not to look at me but looking. Our eyes met and he blushed. My palms were sweating. Mother returned with a plate of biscuits and said to him, "For you."

He took a biscuit.

"No. Take the plate. It's all for you." She pushed the edge of the plate against his chest. He took it and the words stuck in his throat.

Walking backward he said, "I'm not going to police. Thank you, thank you."

It is possible that in my imagination, which I'd allowed to roam free for some days, I had already taken him up, before I had even seen his face or heard his voice. Now everything was in his favor, both what he said and what his words implied. I'm not saying I fell in love with him. At my age you probably don't fall in love at first sight, but that computer Mary referred to was wide awake. I relished the ideas that came into my mind and the sensations in my body. And here I'd been thinking that they had dried at the source.

The second act of the matchmaking was at its height. Mary had come back to the living room and was wavering about where to sit down. Wahid stared at her like a believer gazing at a miracle. She chose to sit down beside him and he blushed scarlet, writhed as if trying to screw himself into the seat and looked at his brother in a silent plea to speak for him.

The shrewd mother spoke to him in a soft voice, "Wahid, don't you think it's time to go?"

"To go where?" he asked.

In different circumstances I would have controlled myself, but my mood had lightened following the neighbor's visit and I broke into a short laugh, instantly suppressed.

"Home," said the mother angrily. "They take us for fools!"

"God forbid," Mother protested. "We see you so rarely. This is like a feast day for us. Umm-Assim, I beg you, sit down. We haven't even served you with anything. Mary, bring in the refreshments."

They ate and drank in silence. Now and then someone tried to start a conversation, but the mother's shadow lay over everything. Mumbling short parting phrases, they got ready to leave. The oppression grew. From habit, I feared Mary's reaction. She is not one to swallow an insult in silence. Then I reminded myself there was nothing to fear. I'd be delighted to see her pay the vile woman back with interest. The case was lost anyway, and it was not a great loss. Wahid backed toward the door, looking at Mary with desperate courage. I too looked at her face and at first could not believe my eyes. Two pearls trembled on her cheeks. She raised the pristine gaze of a hurt baby to the doorframe over the heads of Wahid and his mother who was pulling him away.

When the door closed after them I flew into a rage. "You miserable, miserable creature!"

Mary rose and her tears turned into tears of fury. "I swear by the Holy Virgin," she hissed, "I'll make her into a cringing bitch and feed her nothing but stinking grass and piss to the end of her days."

Mother took pity on her and embraced her trembling shoulders. Seeing the smile on Grandpa's face she screamed at him, "Stop!" and went on comforting Mary. "Let them go, and good riddance. There'll be other grooms who will beg—"

"What are you talking about! He will be my husband and she will be my mother-in-law. That's what will happen. I shall tie her in the yard with an iron chain till she dries up, she and her chicken shit. This I swear."

I believed her without an oath. At that moment I did not think of the price she would have to pay.

## Chapter Five

On Friday afternoon an argument broke out between Mother and Grandpa. "You should have tried harder," Mother reprimanded him. "You let them get away."

"It was important to let the mother feel she was in control."

Their way of arguing was like a dialogue between two branches stemming from the same tree. Usually Mary and I listened as if to a background hum. Only this time it touched directly upon our selves.

"And if Mary should end up like Huda?" Mother said. "She let Bahij slip through her fingers."

"Because her fingers are worth more than he is."

"And in the meantime he's married and making a good living, and her life is draining away."

Grandpa paced up and down as if caged. I had rarely seen him so agitated. Now and then he pulled up his trousers by the belt. Then he stopped in front of me, looked at me and said, "Huda is still my baby."

Mother was torn between laughter and tears. "Baby . . ."

We were accustomed since childhood to being discussed in our presence. They would say quite openly the best things and the worst, and sometimes they hurt a lot.

Grandpa returned to his bench, sucked on the narghileh mouthpiece and remained silent, as though absorbed in the bubbling of the water in the glass bowl.

Mother softened her tone. "You could have done something with that puffed up woman."

"You mustn't put a strain on dealings with a relative."

"You call that witch a relative?"

"She'll be Mary's mother-in-law."

"Like my brothers will come back from Jordan."

"They won't give up what they have in Jordan. Over there nobody yells at them 'Out, dogs!' And Mary has already decided."

Mother and I looked at Mary. Her face was frozen. Mother felt it was all going above her head.

If I wished for a different ending it was no longer from jealousy or envy. I loved Mary and admired those qualities in her which I lacked. At that moment it seemed to me that she was about to kill the fine and important part of her for the sake of the less important part. I tried to catch her eye but she avoided me. I had nothing to offer her, not even a pauper's counsel. I said, "Mary?"

"There's someone at the door," she said.

It was the neighbor, come to return the plate. He was shaved and his shirt was freshly ironed, and he seemed more confident than the other evening. I'd thought a good deal about that plate, fearing he would bring it back when I was out.

"Come in, come in," Grandpa said, inviting him to sit near the bench.

He put a blue knapsack on the floor and sat down with the plate on his knees, looking at me and at Mary. By now I was certain that he wouldn't reveal that they had met. Mary played his game with greater skill.

"My name is Alex," he said.

"This is Huda and this is Mary and this is my father-in-law," Mother told him.

Alex frowned and his eyes narrowed behind the thick spectacles.

"It means the husband's father," I explained.

"Ah, thanks . . . And where is father?"

"Dead," I said.

Alex gave the plate to Mother, saying, "It was very nice. I was sure it was enough for week, but it finished in one night."

"I don't know where Abu-Nakhla found this boy," Grandpa said in Arabic, smiling.

Alex turned to me for the translation. I said, "Grandpa says you're sincere."

"What does it mean, sincere?"

"It's when you say what you think without censorship," Mary explained.

He must have caught her mischievous undertone. "Who needs censorship inside," he said. "There is too much censorship outside." He waited for us to translate "censorship" for Grandpa, and bent down to the blue knapsack and took out a bottle. He gave it to Mother, saying, "Please."

Mother recoiled. "Absolutely not."

"What is it?" Grandpa asked.

Alex turned to him and showed him the label. "Vodka, good vodka." Suddenly he grabbed his short black hair. "Sorry, sorry!"

"What about?" asked Grandpa.

"I forgot. They say Muslims do not drink such things."

"We're Christian." Grandpa smiled at him and reached for the bottle with a nod of thanks.

I noticed that Alex was sweating. I wondered if he always did. I don't like men who sweat. Bahij's skin was pleasant to the touch.

"And the trumpet?" Grandpa asked. "I hope it wasn't stolen."

"I was lucky." He added apologetically, "I disturb you."

"No, no, it sounds nice," Grandpa reassured him, placing the bottle on the floor beside the bench.

"In Russia I played at weddings and parties, also funerals. To make a little money. I learned to play in orphanage."

"You said your parents are here in an old-age home."

"Yes, I have parents, but I grew up in orphanage. That is long story." Behind the glasses the huge eyes were shining. "On roof I can see the sea."

Grandpa smiled. "So you play your trumpet to it."

"No, then I speak with Assya."

"Assya," Grandpa repeated as though he understood.

"In darkness, at night, I feel . . . I . . ."

"Longing," I said. "You feel longing."

"Yes, yes, thank you. Longing," he said, looking at me. "It is very sad to stand on roof and think about something far . . ."

"You're telling me," Grandpa said.

"You are not new immigrant."

"Everyone has a long story of his own. I wasn't born here either. Glasses!" he called to Mother. "We'll have a drink."

Without a word Grandpa filled two little glasses. The liquid was as clear as tears. He must be thinking of Assya now, I thought. I felt hot and my face was burning. The little glasses kept going up and down. "You'll get drunk," Mother warned Grandpa.

"I've never been drunk. You know how to drink," he said to Alex.

Alex took off his glasses and wiped his eyes with the back of his hand, like a bespectacled person who has been laughing, but his face was serious. There was a soft look in his naked eyes in their natural size. As if feeling lonely in his myopia, he pointed at us and said, "They don't drink and all the time they don't speak."

"They don't understand, son. They don't understand a man who stands on the roof and whines in a trumpet."

"Wails," I corrected, knowing what he meant. "To wail, like a puppy crying."

"Wail," Alex repeated, "nice word." He put his glasses on and looked at my face. Again I got the impression that he was seeking another face, as when you expect a particular person to phone and someone else rings instead.

He stood up and said to Mother, "This evening some guests will come. A little party? It will not disturb?"

"No, no," Mother replied politely.

His legs were steady as he backed toward the door, opened it and left.

"I'm tired," Mary said in our room that night.

"I'll read by the small light," I said. I opened the Amichai book and read a couple of lines again and again:

*And my door stays open*
*like a tomb from which the dead has risen.*

I don't believe in the resurrection of the dead. It's a dream of the living, not of the dead. It's best not to open tombs. I often wanted to write to Amichai. I suppose many girls did. Shirley writes to every successful writer and poet. Amichai doesn't write about a happy world. His poems are like a row of tombstones, of dreams that he himself can't tell where and when have died.

"So he has Assya," said Mary's voice.

"You're not asleep?"

"Can't."

Her sleeplessness is torture to me. She keeps turning from side to side and thumping her pillow as though to rip it up.

"Try my system," I advised—I did so much want her to fall asleep. "Don't fight it so frantically. Lie still, relax your limbs. I literally freeze my body."

"That's because your body's frozen anyway," she said. "Can you also freeze the thoughts that run through your mind?"

"I try not to think," I said in an aggrieved tone.

"I try not to think," Mary mimicked me. "I try not to feel, I try not to love even in my dreams. What are you alive for?"

Out in the street a police siren shrieked. On a distant roof a cock crowed. Jamilla's cat yowled as if trapped in a burning box.

"I don't know what I'm alive for."

Instantly Mary flung off her blanket and came toward me with a wicked look and an outstretched finger. "Are you cold?"

I screamed even before her tickling finger touched me. "Get away, enough!"

She settled on the edge of my bed. "How's the pain?"

"Gone."

"I'll make us some tea."

We sat cross-legged, leaning against the wall, and sipped our tea.

"I can hear women on the stairs too," Mary said when Alex's guests began to arrive. "I don't like that kind of woman's laugh. A party sort of laugh."

When Bahij threw a New Year's Eve party in the students' dorm in Romema, he asked me to come and help prepare it. In those days I used to rush to do his bidding as if it was holy work. A crate of whisky and several crates of Danish beer were stacked in the kitchenette. We laid the table in the living room under Lenin's piercing gaze and Fidel Castro's shaggy beard. There were posters of Palestinian fighters behind barbed wire. The Arab guests were male students, but I was the only Arab woman. The others were three Americans and one German who had two streaks of green dye in her hair. She kept stroking her thigh the whole time, as if nursing a sleeping cat. Bahij spoke fluent English. The fumes of hashish and beer turned my stomach. After three hours of running back and forth I fled to the kitchen and drank black coffee on an empty stomach. Bahij came in drunk and pulled me into the living room. With his hand on my shoulder he announced, "We forgot to thank Huda for all her work."

The German girl continued to stroke her thigh. The words fell from her mouth like heat-struck flies. "I wonder why the Arab man is better looking than his sister. Honestly, I have seen very few good-looking Arab women."

Bahij did not correct her, did not say that I was not his sister. At two in the morning I'd had enough. Bahij explained that it wasn't done for the host to leave the party. One of his friends volunteered to drive me to the wadi, on condition that I helped him keep the steering wheel steady on Ruppin Road and make sure the car didn't tumble into the ravine, and would also tell him at every intersection if the light was red or green. Other conditions were added en route, but I rejected them. He stopped the car near Solel Boneh and refused to enter the wadi. He leaned back and smiled with drunken understanding: "Now I understand why Bahij escapes to alien orchards." He bent over me and I misunderstood the movement and leaned so hard against the door he was opening for me that I fell out. He staggered around the car and tried to help me up. I stood up and he fell on his face. My knees hurt and he sobbed.

Up on the roof the trumpet was like a flag leading a procession. Someone was playing an accordion and Russian songs swelled on waves of nostalgia. Now and then a cheerful song fought for its life, but quickly perished. The mood upstairs was not jovial. They all reverted to an all-embracing melancholy.

My shoulder touched Mary's shoulder. "Are you serious, Mary?"

"What about?"

"Burying yourself in a village with such a mother-in-law and such a lump."

"I've no choice. I'm not like you. You were born with the bit between your teeth. I can't persevere in a job like you and support myself. I look at you when you wake up in the morning. The faces in a hospital recovery room look better, but you still go to the office. Not everyone can gather up his crushed limbs and force himself to keep going, or smile like a flower when inside everything is stinking and sour. I'm incapable. I find that most of what we do is simply stirring the muck. Cheating and pretense. In every job I started there were weird things. You remember the insurance company? The boss got hysterical over every mistake and every smudge. He was obsessive about clean sheets of paper, when everything around was rotten. Clients staged break-ins and exaggerated accidents and I printed their lies in pretty letters on neat sheets of papers. Sometimes the boss himself helped them to prepare the lies. When I woke up in the morning feeling foul, I'd ask myself why get up and pretend that I'm enjoying a job which is nothing but the art of deceit. I don't have Grandpa's optimism, which helps him to believe that today's shit is the fertilizer for tomorrow's roses."

"So this is an escape, this move to the village?"

"You're the escape artist. I'm just changing direction. Better to be a queen in a village than a mouse in the wadi."

"And you'll be capable of . . . ?"

"Sleeping with Wahid? In the dark, Huda, in the dark it's possible. After a shower. Smells drive me crazy. His mother will have to throw the goats and chickens out of the yard until he builds me a house of my own."

"You're asking a lot."

"You saw his liquid eyes. You can do anything you like with a man with liquid eyes. You've heard of Pierre Trudeau. He didn't get to be Canada's prime minister for nothing. He's one hell of a man. And his wife? Mother would say she's the vulgar sort, but he ran after her for years."

"Because of his liquid eyes."

"Go ahead and laugh. Not that there aren't other men, a rarer kind. They live and die on their feet, and they're really dangerous. If you've got the patience of a rock they may kindly allow you to be their slave."

I was shocked. "You've spent too much time with Zuhair. You've grown used to vulgar men."

She listened to the noise on the roof. "Their songs melt the soul, damn them. Huda, you must come with me to the sea."

"You're mad. It's almost winter."

"So we'll just lie on the sand and look at the water. Maybe a big wave will come and swallow us up."

The tremor in her voice gripped my stomach. "You and your foolishness."

"Next Friday I'll come and drag you from the office straight to the sea."

Up on the roof the sound of a woman crying spread like a turbid puddle. Fast Russian phrases rolled. Light footsteps ran across the roof, followed after a moment's hesitation by other feet. The crying woman screamed and some people laughed and others shouted in alarm. There was a thump on the railing. Mary gripped my hand and whispered, "The woman's going to jump down to the street." Again there were footsteps rushing around and sounds of wrestling, wild laughter and angry exclamations. Then a loud peremptory voice.

"That's Alex's voice," I said.

"You're trembling."

"Someone's really going to jump."

She took my face in her hands and turned it to her. She spoke into my eyes, "Huda, you're not just trembling."

Her hands fluttered on my forehead, rubbed my cheeks, sneaked into my dressing gown and rubbed my shoulder hard.

I opened my eyes and saw that the light was still on in the room.

"You scared the daylights out of me," she scolded.

"She jumped?"

"People don't jump that easily. Cowards are cowards, even when they're drunk."

"She's stopped crying."

"She probably stayed with him. Sometimes women cry because they want someone to comfort them."

I pushed her hands off my body and sat up. "We have to go to sleep. Go to your own bed." She didn't move. There was a rustling on the stairs, then some words in Russian down in the street which knows almost nothing but Arabic. "I want to sleep," I repeated.

Mary ignored me. "I'm not so sure she did stay with him," she said. Suddenly, when she'd got back into her bed and covered herself with the blanket, the trumpet blared. "Like a sick dog," she said sadly.

It was more than that. It was as though a chimney was spewing thick smoke, not choking the throat but deepening the darkness, spreading night upon night.

## Chapter Six

Mary probably exaggerated the power of the lymph that flows in the eyes. I don't believe Wahid is capable of rebelling. He's mature, staid and prudent. He was not likely to break off with his parents, certainly not with such a formidable mother. Mary obviously appealed to him, maybe more than appealed, but when a man like him thinks about marriage, he looks for a hard-working woman, neither too stupid nor unduly clever, healthy, fertile and above all docile. Such a woman would surely suit him better than a romantic girl. Mary had known other men. In her illusion of equality, which a noisy democracy fosters in many hearts, she imagined that life is a magic garden where people run around unfettered by tradition and status. Or maybe for some incomprehensible reason she sobered up and leaped to the other extreme, adopting the old established attitude separating marriage from love. Sometime later I realized that she genuinely wanted to marry Wahid. On that failed matchmaking visit she was doing her best to capture the mother's heart, but failed miserably.

Mother took the defeat harder. Nor was she willing to forget the past. A few days later I heard her saying to Grandpa, "That lot? When they came to visit our house they sat on the edge of the chairs and sweated in their shiny velvet dresses." She was referring to her father's house, which loomed like a mountain over the horizon of the past. Since 1948 she had made no attempt to find out what happened to it. It was registered in her brothers' names, and was confiscated when they were deported. In the course of the years it grew in her imagination and ours into a dream palace. But the family relations scattered in the villages of Israel preferred to forget that past. I suspect that it was not only to honor the dead that Mother took care, almost compulsively, to attend every funeral. Death is a defeat. The men and women who ill-treated her were being carried help-lessly in hard wooden boxes into the soil, which swallows everyone indiscriminately and pitilessly. The visit of Wahid's family had kin-dled a new hope in her heart. She hoped through Mary to forge new links to the past.

Not so Grandpa. His laughter did not dim after that visit. He came from the banks of a vast river that flows through a mighty desert. He had very little faith in human will. To him, fate and God were one and the same thing. Confronted with them you could do one of two things—grind your teeth and avail nothing, or smile and regard life's shifting fortunes as a great joke.

That evening he sat at the table and looked at the fine lines form-ing around Mother's eyes. "Isn't it a shame to waste the food?" he said gently. "Don't tell me that the bread and the cheese have also become enemies."

"I can't swallow anything. And why aren't you eating?"

Later that evening Abu-Nakhla came in. Unlike the previous time, he skipped the niceties and went straight to the point. He put his tarboosh on a nearby chair, a sign that he meant to remain seated until he concluded the business for which he'd come. "I've talked to Jamilla," he started. "I gather it didn't work out with the family and you failed to sell Mary."

"We didn't intend to sell her," said Grandpa.

"All right." He didn't care what they called it, so long as the deal went forward. "She's pretty, I admit, but Zuhair's overdoing it. A man shouldn't lose his head over a woman."

"He'll settle down," Grandpa said. "Young men are apt to forget themselves."

"Zuhair young?" Abu-Nakhla frowned. "He's forty."

"You have to believe," sermonized Grandpa, the hater of ser-mons. "God is great."

Abu-Nakhla laughed aloud. "Don't tell me you've begun to pray."

"I didn't say I was a priest," Grandpa replied patiently.

Abu-Nakhla is corrupt but not an atheist, nor a skeptic like Grandpa. He believes wholeheartedly in God, but regards him as a kind of income-tax inspector. So long as he isn't caught or punished, he is innocent in the eyes of heaven. Allah is great and mighty and eternal, but undoubtedly has no time to worry about such trivialities as Abu-Nakhla's doings. Nevertheless, it is advisable to be cautious, the ground is not always safe under one's feet— needless talk about Allah might draw the tax inspector's attention. After a brief silence he returned to the subject at hand. "I've come about Zuhair and Mary."

We feigned amazement, but Abu-Nakhla wasn't taken in. "We Muslims," he went on, "are not like the Jews and the Christians. Our house is open to all and we don't force anyone to kiss the cross or the mezuzah. I don't know how Mary bewitched my son. He doesn't sleep and doesn't let others sleep. All right. I don't begrudge you. Maybe thanks to her he'll grow up and Allah will bless them. One more thing, we won't ask for money and a dowry. On the contrary, I'm not short of money and I won't be stingy with my son. They can have a villa anywhere they like, even the most expensive neighborhood of the Jews. Even on the Carmel." He took out his beads and clicked them as he observed our faces. "Umm-Huda, you will admit that I never wasted my money on foolishness. I've always lived modestly. Money was saved and kept piling up. Here's your chance to restore everything to your daughter and her children." He looked at Grandpa, who was gnawing his narghileh mouthpiece. "We're both old men, you and I, and know how to forgive and forget. What's a Muslim? What's a Christian? We're all human."

Grandpa regarded Abu-Nakhla primarily as a kind of representative of the authorities, and like all Orientals, viewed the authorities as a menacing force, like a flood or a fire. "What can I say?" he replied.

"Give thanks to God, bless the couple and wish them happiness."
He leaned forward and looked at Grandpa in disbelief. "You hesitate? What is there to consider? You're paupers and I'm leaving everything to Zuhair and your daughter." He turned to Mary and graced her with his princely smile. "Now it's all up to you."

"I'll do what Grandpa and Mother say," she whispered.

I rebelled. She isn't a coward. It isn't fair to place the burden on other people's shoulders!

Abu-Nakhla gave me a pallid smile. "You hear? She'll do what Grandpa and Mother say! She didn't ask them when she ambushed my son in corners and addled his brain."

"Abu-Nakhla!" Grandpa shouted.

The guest silenced him. "Leave it. It's between me and your granddaughter. Mary, listen. I say it again, you're as beautiful as a spring morning. But we both know how short morning is. Look, just look at your sister. She also turned up her nose once. Now even a worm of a man wouldn't piss on her."

"Abu-Nakhla!" Grandpa shouted again.

Abu-Nakhla ignored him. "Mary, you and your family had better understand me. I'm no crazier than you are about this deal. But I said, if Zuhair wants you so much, maybe that's what fate ordained. You're not exactly the chaste virgin I dreamed of for my son. Maybe you people are right. Maybe you're only a craving of his, like a new car. He likes shiny toys."

Mary fled to our room. Grandpa writhed on his bench as though struggling with invisible chains. Abu-Nakhla looked at him and grinned. "Don't think I underestimate you," he said to placate him. "If I were lying I'd have bitten my tongue and swallowed it. Ever since I can remember death has appeared to me in many strange guises. I've never really feared him, but I've treated him with respect." He stood up. "Egyptian, that's the respect I have for you. I've always suspected that you're only another guise of death. I didn't mean to insult you, any more than I'd dare to insult death.

But the children have grown up, and not the way we expected. It's like a cucumber growing from a seed that you thought would sprout a palm tree like yourself. Still, it's the new generation and we have to accept God's will. Don't get up, I haven't come here to wrestle with you." He went to the front door and turned the handle. "I'll let Zuhair sort out his own mess with your daughter. I won't meddle in this business any more."

Mother was alarmed. "He'll destroy us. You've got to restrain him."

"Me?" Abu-Nakhla asked, standing in the door, his tarboosh almost touching the lintel. "Maybe I was wrong, Umm-Huda. Maybe death is as miserable and as shitty as my son. Let your daughter restrain him. I've tried everything and failed. Good night."


That night silence came down on our house. Nobody dared to ask questions and no one would answer those that were left unasked. Even Alex crept upstairs on tiptoes at dawn. Jamilla didn't come and even her cat kept quiet. Mary thumped her pillow ferociously and kept turning from side to side. In the darkness her cigarette was a wandering firefly. Nevertheless, by morning she was sound asleep in her rumpled bed, her fine face as calm as the face of a shipwreck survivor who's found a firm plank to float on.

Four hours later she came into the travel agency, met Adina and Shirley and sat in an armchair, leafing through tourist brochures, fresh and dynamic and attractive in her tight trousers and floppy shirt. I envied her. She knows how to sleep and forget. While dealing with a customer I glanced over and saw her taking a cigarette from Adina's pack, chatting lightly with Shirley and shaking her loosened hair at Boaz, who came out of his office and took her for a customer. "I'm Mary, Huda's sister," she reminded him with a stunning smile.

"Ah, yes, yes. Hullo. Welcome," he mumbled, laid some papers on Adina's desk and withdrew to his office. In Mary's presence the bashful grew more timid, and the bold bolder.

"I've come," Mary said to Shirley, "to buy Huda a swimsuit."

I'd forgotten the promise, and at that moment the idea struck me as pointless and absurd. Shirley was astonished. "Now? It's almost winter. But that's Huda. She always puts things off." When I finished with the customer I excused us by saying, "Things are always cheaper at the end of the season."

The three of us went shopping. There was a great selection, but everything seemed designed to emphasize precisely what I try to hide. In the years after Bahij I felt I was gradually withering. The shopkeeper stretched the swimsuit to demonstrate its elasticity and good quality, and I felt as if his fingers were touching my flesh and not the garment I had not yet bought. "Go on, take it," Shirley urged me. "It'll suit you. You've got a terrific figure."

There was no mockery in her tone and I was afraid to look into her eyes. The shopman grew enthusiastic. "You must try it on. Over there behind the curtain."

I didn't go. I put my hand on something green and said, "This one, please."

Outside Shirley complained to Mary, "Going shopping with your sister is like visiting the bereaved."

And when you cling like a branch to a post stuck in a stream, said I to myself, your very existence hinders the current of other people's lives.

Mary gave her a mischievous smile. "Now everything's going to change. Huda's fallen in love with the trumpeter."

I ought to have denied it and scolded her. I kept silent. I even enjoyed Shirley's prolonged stare.


In the evening Wahid showed up at our house. He looked like a man who's run as hard as he could and having reached his destination doesn't know what to do with himself. He sat and smoked in silence and sipped the coffee noisily and did not look at any of us. Mother's warm smiles did not help him break his silence. He'd come straight from work and smelled strongly of sweat. I saw that he had a gold tooth in his mouth. Suddenly he stood up, went to the window and came back, grumbling, "The police gave me a ticket."

Mother and Mary hastened to the window. "This is an awful place," Mother apologized, as though it was her fault.

Not to appear indifferent, I also went to the window. I saw Alex leaving the house. He stopped for a moment by the car and looked at the ticket. Then he glanced up and saw me, and his hand rose a little as if he meant to wave to me. I forgot the guest and looked after him till he turned the corner and disappeared. Something in my expression made Wahid think that I was doubting his word.

"It's a ticket, I tell you," he exclaimed.

"Never mind," Mother said to comfort him, and put roasted almonds and biscuits on the table. "Go and get dressed," she whispered to Mary.

Mary was still dressed in tight trousers and the loose shirt and her face was clean of makeup. She looked at Wahid with big eyes and asked, "I'm dressed all right, aren't I?"

Wahid blushed. Grandpa hurried to help him out and said, "I'm sorry the last visit ended as it did."

Wahid addressed Mother. "I haven't come to apologize." He fell silent again, as if the words were fluttering wildly inside him, unable to break out. Mary sat down facing him, radiant with the glow of a promised paradise.

Grandpa again tried to raise the guest's spirits with Oriental chitchat. "We thank you for coming. You're a welcome guest in our house."

"Umm-Huda," the guest struggled with the words, "Umm-Huda, I want to marry Mary."

Mother's face beamed. "We'd be delighted, truly delighted."

Grandpa stood up and they shook hands. After a moment's hesitation they embraced. While they were clasping each other Mary spoke up. "It's out of the question." There was no smile on her face.

"Why? Why?" Wahid cried out.

I almost burst out laughing. His hoarse voice sounded like a wailing child who has found himself under a dripping gutter and doesn't know how to escape it. He sank into the chair and stared at her. Mary passed her tongue over her lower lip, slowly, as if estimating the taste of her prey, and looked devastating. But her voice suggested closeness, as if she was tackling an intimate matter with a person of undoubted importance. "I respect your mother and father, and I don't want to enter your house as an enemy. I haven't the strength, I haven't the strength for that."

I need not have feared that she would overdo it and demonstrate how powerless she was. She knew the right measure.

"I've thought about it," Wahid growled. "What do you take me for. I wouldn't let them insult you."

"You yourself are perfectly all right," she enfolded him in her low voice.

"I make a good living, thank God. You won't have to dirty your hands working. We'll live anywhere you like. Doesn't have to be the village."

That's how Bahij too talked in the beginning. He was ready to promise a trip to outer space. He was completely unaware of the falsehood of his promises. All the same, his promises sounded different. Wahid sees himself as inferior to Mary, for all his mother's prosperous manner.

"It's not a question of house and property," Mary said to him. "A wife can always be discarded, replaced . . ."

Wahid's mouth fell open. "Me, discard or replace you?"

She ignored his astonishment. "But a child or a mother can't be replaced. I am very flattered that you came, but I don't want to start life like a thief."

"And if Father himself came and said what I'm saying?"

Mary gave him a sad smile. "You know that a mother-in-law is a second mother."

At that moment Wahid was ready to strangle his mother with his bare hands. He looked to Grandpa to rescue him. Grandpa was cautious and played Mary's game. "She's right, son. A bride must respect her mother-in-law's will."

"Then she will have to come herself," he announced and got up to leave.

Mother tried to detain him. "Stay a little longer. Have supper with us."

He declined politely. His throat was so tight he would have been unable to swallow a grain of rice.


In my bed that night I hugged my knees in distress. We girls were raised and trained to get married. They didn't bring us up as people who live in a community, but rather as soldiers trained to carry out a mission. Plotting, cunning, booty, triumphs, defeats and false morale—all were legitimate in the struggle for the coveted goal, a husband to support us. That was the essential happiness, as our forebears saw it. But we live in a different age, one in which love has become a kind of new religion. The trouble is that in this religion there are no priests or prophets, no divine revelation or scriptures. Individuals must find their own gods, interpret the omens and make their way through life without any clear guidelines. We all go out into the desert in search of this love, and most of us get lost in the wilderness. I felt so tired. The empty roof weighed on my chest. If Wahid had enfolded me with the same fervor with which he enfolded Mary . . . I shudder to think how I'd have reacted. I, who rejected Bahij . . .

I fantasize and live in dreams. What have I to do with a roof and a trumpet I have never even seen, and the sturdy figure which had stopped and glanced in passing at my face in the window? Why do my fantasies cling to him, of all people? Even the blindest love has an element of choice in it. And here there is no real love, no blindness, nothing but choice, and it has no foundation at all. Since Bahij I've deliberately clung to nothing but fantasies. Once I convinced myself that I was in love with a pimp who came into the travel agency to buy flight tickets to Germany for himself and two of his prostitutes. Business is great over there, he told me jovially, it's work like any other, and certainly more interesting than selling airline tickets. He had knife scars, hard eyes, and a display of rings on his fingers. He must have noticed the darkness behind my forehead, or he wouldn't have dared to speak to me as he did. I was drawn to him because I knew that if I'd run into him alone in an alley I'd have passed out in terror. Another time my heart went out to a slightly retarded street cleaner in the wadi. He came every day from the Bedouin tin shacks near Jalama, dressed in a torn robe and nothing but plastic slippers on his cracked black feet, even in winter. He swept and raked the street diligently and sensibly, and would suddenly drop everything and run after a piece of paper tossed by the breeze, like a dog chasing a startled bird.

I didn't know what was preferable, the life without illusions that Mary opted for, or the fantasies which were driving me out of my mind.

In the meantime, half asleep, I listened for the sounds of Alex returning from the port. First I heard the heavy footsteps. Then the sound of other feet overtaking Alex on the stairs. Then our front door was shaken by powerful banging.

"Open up, I tell you!" Zuhair was yelling drunkenly. "Mary, I'm not leaving this place."

Mother leapt from her room and shackled Grandpa with both her arms. She rose on her toes and spoke into his blazing green eyes. "You're not going near the door," she begged. "He must be armed. He'll get tired. The police will come, the neighbors will drive him away."

"I'll break his arms," Grandpa groaned, almost in tears at the sound of Zuhair's blows and curses.

Mary trembled. "He'll kill me, he'll kill me," she mumbled. "You don't know him . . ."

At that moment I was more afraid for Grandpa than for Mary. I knew he'd bar the bully's way with his body.

Zuhair kicked the door.

Mother pleaded tearfully, "Zuhair, my son, I beg of you, leave us alone and Allah will reward you."

"I'll break down the door if you don't open it."

"What do you want from them?" said Alex's voice in Hebrew.

How did I forget him? I froze. His voice sounded to us like a fanfare of deliverance. Then a different fear gripped me. They were both standing in the dark, one violent and armed and the other tired, weak-sighted and probably unaware that his rival was a dangerous man.

"None of your business," Zuhair said to Alex.

"Go away, go," Alex ordered him.

I could see him plainly—short, his thick spectacles peering at Zuhair's face in the dark. I wanted to call out to him to be careful, that he was facing a murderous man, but as in a dream my shouts emerged as stifled moans.

"Piss off, punk," Zuhair said.

"What's that in your hand?"

"A knife. You want me to fuck your mother? I told you to piss off."

Alex's voice was heard no more. There was a short struggle and some dull groans.

"He murdered our poor neighbor," Mother said in terror.

The silence outside the door gripped my throat like a fist. We stood in the living room and listened to one pair of feet going down the stairs. My facial muscles seemed to have gone to sleep. I approached the door as if impelled. Mother let go of Grandpa and spread out her arms. "No, daughter, no. There's a corpse outside."

"But maybe he's only wounded and needs help," said Grandpa.

I opened the door and saw nothing. The light from the living room showed drops of blood on the landing and the stairs. I fled inside. "He's carrying him down," I said and ran to the window. On the pavement outside the entrance stood three of Zuhair's men, smoking and looking up. Lights were on in some windows and heads were peering out. "He's taking the neighbor down to his gangsters," Mother sobbed.

But it was not Zuhair who came out into the light of the street lamp. Alex was holding a bloody knife in his right hand while his own blood dripped down to his fingers. Zuhair was thrown over his left shoulder like a rolled-up rug. Alex didn't have his glasses on. He gazed at the thugs surrounding him without seeing them clearly. "Where's the police?" he asked, like a man who'd lost his way. One of the thugs laughed aloud. His friend silenced him with a slap and said to Alex, "You killed him?"

He was shorter than the three of them. His eyes searched for a breach in their wall. The street lamp must have looked to him like a dazzling puddle. Up the street a police siren pierced the silence, probably summoned by a neighbor on the phone. The thugs fled and Alex turned like a blind man to the approaching siren. The police car stopped with screeching brakes and two policemen spilled out as if popped out by springs. At the sight of the knife and the blood they drew their guns and again a silent scream froze in my throat. But Alex didn't see the small details. He noticed the open door of the vehicle and flung his burden inside, saying, "Take him." The heavy silence warned him that something was wrong, and he stepped back like a blind man sensing danger. The two policemen advanced toward him with their guns aimed at his chest. Drop the knife, Alex, drop it, the shout came out of my mouth as a low mumble.

"It isn't him!" Mother yelled from the window.

I grabbed her shoulder and trembled all over. Alex and the policemen looked up at us. I wanted him to hear my voice too but couldn't utter a sound. The other windows remained silent. The Arab street kept silent in defiance and with gritted teeth. Another Jew beating up an Arab. And although I was wholeheartedly on Alex's side, and would have stood between him and the cocked guns, I felt the Arab street's pain.

"What's going on here?" one of the policemen asked Mother.

"He came to smash up our house. He threatened to kill."

"This one?" he asked, pointing at Alex.

"No, the other one."

Only then did Alex understand what was going on. He dropped the knife and approached the policemen, pointed at the vehicle and said, "I didn't kill anybody. It is only stinking drunk."

The policemen pounced on him. A gun was pressed to his temple and another to his back. "And the blood on your hand?"

"What blood?" Alex wondered. He raised his fingers to his eyes, spread them and closed them, surprised by their stickiness. He hadn't noticed that he was wounded. "It is my blood," he said.

He was pushed into the vehicle. It roared away and then silence returned to the street. Jamilla's cat jumped out of the window and licked the drops of blood.

## Chapter Seven

Mother was afraid to open the door and kept talking about Abu-Nakhla and the three thugs who got away. She was convinced that they would come back to wreak vengeance on us. Mary sat with her elbow on the table, chin in hand, staring at the wall over Grandpa's head.

"You've ruined us," Mother wailed aloud. "And with someone like Zuhair! Then you have the nerve to put conditions to Wahid."

"Leave the girl alone," Grandpa said.

"I could bury myself. I'd be ashamed to look the wadi people in the eyes."

"So don't look," he advised her.

When I went to the door she screamed, "Where are you going?"

"To look for the neighbor's glasses. They must have dropped on the stairs. Maybe they broke."

"His glasses? That's what's on your mind now?"

"Mother, he saved us. He took a risk and got wounded and now he's in the hands of the police."

"Jews are released right away. Who asked him to get into a knife fight in front of our door? Now the whole wadi will gossip about us. Zuhair would have got tired and gone away."

I was angry with her for talking like this about Alex, when just a little while ago she saw him as a savior. But I kept my mouth shut. There was no lightbulb on the staircase so I opened the front door wide to get the light from our living room. I found only bloodstains on the landing, but looking up I saw the glasses lying folded up on the third step, beside the wall, so they wouldn't get stepped on accidentally. Presumably he was accustomed to taking care of his glasses first of all. I went inside and shut the door and laid the glasses on the table. Mary recoiled, as though I'd dropped a dead bird beside her. I was offended. I took them to the bathroom, washed them and returned to the room, huffing on them, drying and polishing them with toilet paper. Seeing Grandpa's green eyes on me I blushed.

"We do owe him thanks," he said softly.

"He felt that Huda's crazy about him," said Mary, as if speaking to herself.

Mother gaped at her. "Huda?"

I didn't care to object. It occurred to me that I owed him at least that much. I sat opposite Mary and sheltered the glasses with my hands. Mother approached me. "Huda, he's a Jew."

"So what?" said Grandpa.

Mother was bewildered. "She's Arab! Her uncles are refugees in Jordan. He's a Jew—don't you understand what sets them apart?"

"No more than what set me and Grandma apart. I was a pauper and she was a privileged lady."

"Umm-Huda, open up," Jamilla called through the door.

She came in with her nephew, the lawyer Halim, a respected and popular personage in the wadi. He was very fat. He was in house slippers and a long coat over his pajamas. Usually he was nattily dressed and walked about the wadi with his head high. Nowadays many Arabs in Israel have straightened their backs, but the fat lawyer had held himself upright even in the early fifties, when some Arabs felt ashamed to be Arab. His house was like a village doctor's courtyard, packed with humble peasants broken by injustice. He joked and smiled a lot, but his smile was different from Grandpa's. Grandpa's smile is winning and hides any unruly or violent impulse. Not so Halim.

His presence infused confidence in our house. "Who is that Jew?" he asked.

"Abu-Nakhla let him the room on the roof," Mother replied.

"Is it that Abu-Trumpet, who's been driving us all crazy?"

Abu-Trumpet! Mary pricked up her ears and suppressed a grin. I knew she'd like that nickname.

"What's between him and Zuhair?"

"The villain was drunk. He must have got lost and ended up at our door."

Halim looked at Grandpa, wordlessly asking for the truth.

Grandpa said, "He and his father are demanding Mary."

Halim sank into his chair, almost breaking it apart. "What do you mean, demanding Mary? She's not some package of hashish they forgot at your house." Evidently he hadn't heard the gossip in the wadi. He turned to Mary, "Has Zuhair bothered you in any way, daughter?"

Mary didn't want to answer. Mother called from the kitchen, "She's already engaged, and this gangster will ruin her." I wondered how far she would go with her exaggerations.

"She's not actually engaged yet," Grandpa corrected.

The lawyer's patience snapped. "All right," he said to Jamilla. "We'll have coffee and leave. They're as scared of me as if I was a police officer."

"Not at all," Mother protested.

"Mary, do you want me to handle this business? For free, of course," he reassured Grandpa. "I can chop their hands off, both father and son."

"We don't want any trouble," Mary whispered. Then she raised her head and her voice, and fully in command of herself said, "Not every victim shares in the act of aggression."

The lawyer clearly didn't believe her. "As you like," he said and sipped his coffee.

"Daughter," Jamilla pleaded, "he wants to help you."

Grandpa remained silent. Mother objected, "What is she supposed to tell him?"

"My cat wanders outside at night, he could tell."

Mother was in agony but couldn't get really angry with Jamilla, because there was no malice in her words and no one doubted her great love for Mary.

"So you won't file an official complaint," Halim said in summary to my sister.

Mary shook her head. Halim stood up.

"And the neighbor?" I asked.

He seemed more surprised by my expression than by the question itself. "When they know who he is, they'll apologize and release him. When they hear that he risked himself to protect Arabs they'll tell him that's going too far. They'll urge him to file a complaint. By now he's probably at the hospital, for a checkup and treatment."

If only I could go straight to the hospital and take him his glasses! He probably hadn't even eaten anything after working in the docks. Until he came to live in this house I used to be content with my fantasies. Now I found myself thinking and considering, yet these thoughts and considerations seemed insane. After all, I knew nothing about him. I'd not even had a proper conversation with him. His past was a closed book to me, filled with mysteries. His parents were in an old-age home, yet he grew up in an orphanage. He was obviously a man who knew what he wanted and decided on the path he wanted to follow, and yet he stood on the roof and wailed with his trumpet at the sea, and sent his longings to one Assya. Why did he leave her? And what made me think that he would consider me as a substitute for that Assya? Above all, I realized that I was changing. I never took the initiative where men were concerned. I'd always assumed that that's the way we are by nature. Yet here I was ready to take the initiative, though readiness alone doesn't amount to initiative. I still didn't know what to do and how to begin. It isn't enough to have a rich imagination, as I have. It also takes daring, and a willingness to fail and to survive defeat.

But the decision had been taken, as though someone had taken it for me. I knew it when I realized that I wouldn't go to work that day, not until I saw him. Morning came, the sun flooded the busy wadi, people were going to their daily occupations, and my nervousness intensified. Finally I couldn't sit still any longer and drew Mary to our room, where she listened to me gravely and murmured, "This is madness."

I thanked her mentally for not laughing at me, but almost laughed at myself. Bold Mary calling me mad! "I have to," I said to her, distressed. She was quite recovered and now she grew lively, as though all her troubles were dwarfed by my problem. She said, "You can go to the police station on Independence Street and ask about him. If he's detained he can probably be released on bail. You can do it yourself. And if they won't take an Arab woman's bond, go to your office and tell them. Your Boaz will help you."

"And if he isn't detained?"

"It's like Halim said. He may be in the hospital. He probably lost a lot of blood. Who knows how bad the stab was. I can come with you and help."

I refused. I was eager to do it by myself. When I met him I wanted him to see only my face and know that I alone acted on his behalf. That too was a kind of initiative.

Mother called through the door, "Huda, Mary, why have you shut yourselves in? We have a guest. The neighbor's come."

Mary jumped up at once. I couldn't rise. My knees went weak. Something strange was happening to my face, as though its features were falling apart and rolling around like pebbles in a box. I felt them with my hands. Eyes, nose, mouth and ears were all in place. Nevertheless, I looked at Mary in alarm. She smiled and said, "Close your mouth. Even an idiot looks almost normal with his mouth closed." She hugged me and kissed my cold cheeks, then pushed me away and chortled, "Huda, it really suits you. You look terrific with this face. Come on."

I went out first. He was sitting with his back to me, facing the window. His good hand was quietly drumming on the table, and his injured arm rested on his knees. I went up to him, put the glasses in his hand and whispered, "Good morning."

He seized them and put them on, smiling like a child. "It is whole. It did not break."

I didn't want to correct his Hebrew. He was smiling at me without seeking another face in mine. "Thank you, thank you very much." He went on looking at my face. I drank in his smile and gaze and mumbled something, I forget what. He pressed the spectacles gently to his eyebrows with a fingertip. "It is first thing I bought in Israel," he said.

Despite the muscles bulging through his shirt and shorts, he was clearly exhausted. I thought about the loads he had humped on the docks the previous night, then the fight and the loss of blood, and his muscles no longer repelled me.

"Accident. In Russia I did much sport. Mathematics, trumpet and sport," he said quickly, as though to hold my interest, and laughed. "It was good there. Very good. At meals I read mathematics like novel. I loved sport very much. Then I fell on my head, like this, legs up and head on ground. Six months I lay in hospital in dark. Did not see anything. It did not hurt, no pain at all." He struck his thigh with his uninjured hand and went on, frowning, "Yob-tvoi-mat, it was not so bad like specs I got after. People saw it and fell down laughing. Thick round glass with white iron frame like old man specs." For a moment he looked at me as though I was responsible for them all, and turned to Mother for understanding. "It was very bad with girls. They laugh badly. I understand if they do not want to look, but to look just to laugh? Good thing I had trumpet. I played sad music even in weddings."

"And Assya?" Jealousy impelled me to ask. "Did she laugh too?"

"We were friends from very young, almost children. She said never mind. But if your sister says that it does not help. It is maybe more annoying. And she also had specs."

I was overjoyed not to be wearing glasses. I caught myself flirting my green eyes at him. Mother vanished into the kitchen. Grandpa sat on his bench, seemingly sunk in thought, but I knew he was observing Alex and that they were all as surprised as I was by the childish frankness of this muscular fighting man. Yet he broke down the barriers with his frank talk about the faraway country, his longing for an irretrievable past, and appealed to the hearts of both Mother and Grandpa, till they forgot how alien he was. At first his excessive openness made me uncomfortable. Had he said the same things to me alone, I'd have been flattered by the confession. I am obviously still drawn to intellectuals who imply more than they reveal. And yet, having solved all of Bahij's mysteries, what did I find? A darkness of mental disorder which much of the intellectual sophistication was designed to cover.

"Do you remember Pierre in *War and Peace?*" Alex asked me.

I remembered Pierre, but I'd begun to read the book in Hebrew, then went on with Bahij in Arabic, and then both Bahij and the book broke off in the middle. Before I could reply Alex went on, "You remember that one woman wanted to kiss him, and she shouted at him to take off specs. Oukh, that woman made me so angry! I would not take off." He stood up slowly, looking faintly embarrassed. Maybe he wondered, as I did, what had made him bring all that up now. Another man might have drawn attention to his wounded arm when he stood up. After all, he'd been wounded because of us. But Alex hid his arm behind his back, as if ashamed. "I am going to my room. Must wash and go to Technion."

"Studies can wait today. First you must eat breakfast with us," Mother said and blocked the door when she saw that he meant to refuse. I thanked her in my mind. Mary and I, influenced by a different culture, couldn't do that. She pushed him almost forcibly back to his chair. "You've got to sit and eat." Grandpa rose to help her. He took Alex by his good arm and made him sit down.

"Do you like kubbeh?" Mother asked.

"What is that?"

"Meat and pine nuts and stuff. It's usually eaten in the evening, and only when there's an important guest."

"Oh," Alex said.

"Huda, come and help me," Mother called from the kitchen.

I got up reluctantly and joined her in the kitchen. While preparing the unusual meal I strained to hear the conversation in the living room. Grandpa said to him, "I see they took care of your arm. Was it serious?"

"The policemen said very serious. They took me to hospital. He will have to pay for it. What did I do to him? Just told him to go away. For that to stick a knife any place?"

"He's a criminal," Grandpa said. "An ordinary criminal."

"He wanted to stick it in my chest."

"Did you say all this to the police?" Grandpa queried.

"I told, but I did not sign."

"What do you mean, you didn't sign?"

"They wrote it and said I must sign. I don't sign so quickly. I hear he is landlord's son."

Grandpa was controlling his anger. "He tried to kill you and you don't sign? He should have his hand chopped off."

"When necessary to chop, I chop myself. I don't leave it to any police. I'm not stupid."

"Not stupid?" Grandpa repeated, and added in Arabic, "A one-eyed donkey's a genius next to you, ya ahbal."

"Please," Alex said, "I don't understand Arabic."

"And I don't understand you," Grandpa replied.

"You think I understand you? Why did he come to your house with knife in his hand? Who did he want to kill? And why did you not go to the police and make complaint against him? What he did to you and what he wanted to do to you was much, very much— but you want me to make complaint against him."

"Wallah, the fellow's a shrewd bastard," said Grandpa in Arabic.

"In Hebrew, please, Hebrew."

"I said you are clever."

"In orphanage you have to be clever. If not, you're very stupid. There is no middle. Why did you not go out to him?"

"Aren't you going to serve our guest?" Grandpa called to the kitchen, pointedly in Hebrew.

Mother and I set the table. I saw Mary watching him when he scratched his wounded arm over the bandage. "It hurts?" she asked. His laughter filled the living room and his wounded arm waved like a white flag through the air. "Little, little," he said. "But criminal and his father will have to pay much, very much for this little."

Grandpa's green eyes continued to study the neighbor. "Huda," he said to me in Arabic, as if telling me how to lay the table, "this man's like an umbrella on a rainy day."

My hands were full. Bowls of kubbeh, salad with mint, labaneh in olive oil, goat's cheese and a heap of warm pitas covered the table. Alex did not need much urging to come to the table. Mother crossed her arms under her bust and said proudly, "It's all in your honor."

We sat at the festive table as if it was a holiday morning. Alex devoured the food with both his good and injured hands, as well as with his nostrils, eyes, teeth and jaws. If he'd jumped on the table and danced among the plates we would have cheered him on with laughter—the laughter that was so lacking in our meals. Nevertheless, I couldn't help recalling fastidious Bahij's fine table manners. Grandpa chewed quite noisily with his mouth open, but picked up his food delicately like a feeding bird. Alex was shielding his plate with his uninjured arm, gobbling his food and glancing at the serving bowls as if afraid they'd soon be empty. A streak of olive oil glistened on his chin. Mother hastened to refill his plate again and again. I buried my eyes in my own plate. "Look out, everyone," Grandpa muttered in Arabic, "don't let the guest nibble your fingers."

All at once he stopped chewing and looked sheepishly at our faces. His mouth was full and he swallowed quickly with the help of a few sips of water. "Forgive me," he said. "This happens to me always—especially when there is much food on table. Like in orphanage. When they put much food on tables everybody jumped on it. If you did not jump you were left hungry. So please forgive," he concluded. Suddenly he rose and went to the door. "Thank you very much." He was gone before we could gather our wits.

His footsteps on the stairs were like slaps in Mother's face, and she was the first to find her voice and scold Grandpa. We knew that even though Alex did not understand the words, he caught their tone. Perhaps he also suddenly became aware of our silent curiosity and astonishment.

"It's my fault," Grandpa admitted. "Allah apportioned man twenty years on earth, but man yelled for more. So Allah took twenty years from the donkey and another twenty from the monkey and gave them to the man. Since then man lives and rejoices till he reaches twenty, then he works like a donkey . . . It seems I've already finished the twenty years of the stupid monkey. I'd go upstairs and ask his pardon," he added, looking at me, "but I might make things worse."

## Chapter Eight

I phoned in and told Adina I wasn't feeling well and was staying home. She wished me well and urged me to see a doctor. Mother was ashamed to meet the neighbors and didn't want to leave the house. Grandpa went to the cafe, looking gloomy and heavy. Jamilla came up excitedly and told Mother that there was some dried blood in front of our door. Mother shuddered and looked at me and Mary, but we shirked the task of washing it off. I went to the bedroom and lay on the bed with Amichai, contented that Mary was not there and I had the room to myself. After about an hour Mother came in looking for her. At first she wouldn't believe Mary was not there, and almost searched under the beds. "The wicked girl, she's run away. Where to?"

I told her not to worry about Mary, she'd be all right.

When she came back she wouldn't tell Mother where she'd been. She closed the door behind her, sat on her bed and said, "Your man's been sick upstairs."

Amichai fell on my stomach. I stared at her without saying a word. I would never have had the nerve to go up to him as she did.

"I've asked him to come on Friday," she added.

"What?" I yelled.

"I'm telling you he isn't feeling well and needs to be cheered up."

I panicked. Events were moving quickly, forcing me into an unaccustomed pace. And where were they leading? A figment of the imagination, pointless fantasy, daydreams, they were turning into facts which compelled me to gamble away everything for the sake of some wisps of haze in the distance.

"Don't you want him to come?"

"I don't know what I want."

"Then leave it to your sister to know what's good for you," she said confidently.

"A Jewish husband?"

"Who's talking about a husband?" she replied, waving her hand dismissively.

"Look where you got to with a man who's not a husband."

"Zuhair is a mistake, like Bahij was a mistake. But we're still only a half looking feverishly for the other half. Huda, you mustn't be shy. The shy ones buy vibrators and masturbate all their lives."

"No," I said. "This isn't for me. Jews and Arabs are strangling each other and I don't have the strength to fight their stupid war."

"Where are you going?"

I didn't reply. I took a pail of water and a rag and went out on the landing. The whole time I was inside I'd felt as though the blood was calling me, like a reminder of an outstanding debt, or perhaps an enticing treaty proposal. It's only a patch of dried liquid, I said to myself. Alex himself probably didn't notice it. It could just as easily have been Zuhair's blood. I wanted to break the spell. Blood can be washed off and forgotten. Only sadists speak of blood covenants and the blood of martyrs and virgins, the blood that sanctifies the altars of those believers whose God craves victims.

Mary grabbed the pail from my hand and closed the door. "I'll swab," she said and slapped the rag over the floor without a broomstick. When she dunked the rag in the pail the water turned red. My knees went weak. The water rippled and swirled in the pail and turned into a whirlpool that threatened to engulf me. I sat on the stairs, watching the pail, careful not to let my feet touch the wet floor which was turning pale like a body whose life is draining away. Mary was neither repelled nor concerned. Her movements were purposeful and energetic, her handsome supple body full of life.

"Don't come down," she ordered me. "Wait till it dries."

Suddenly I felt that Alex was standing in the doorway of the roof looking at the back of my head. Excitement welled up in me. I won't look around, I thought, until he speaks to us. I was surprised that Mary was unaware of his silence. I forced myself to turn around and my lips spread in an open smile that came from inside me. The rectangle of the empty doorway was shining brightly white. My smile withered and Mary saw the disappointment and puzzlement in my eyes. "He's lying down," she said.

"You buried my son and you're chatting on the stairs!" Abu-Nakhla's voice roared in the stairwell's narrow space.

We fled into the flat. He marched in uninvited and addressed us all with masterful anger, like a teacher whose pupils have run wild. "You should have been deported to Jordan too, you scum! You've allied yourselves with the Jews." He pulled out a chair and laid his tarboosh on the table. With one hand he smoked and with the other mopped the sweat on his brow with his snowy handkerchief. "Where's your father-in-law?" he asked Mother.

"He's at the cafe, and you should be ashamed to burst into a house where there are only women."

"Ashamed? My son is suffering down there with Jewish policemen who're only too happy to jump on an Arab's guts. Mary, go get your grandfather. You, Huda, go upstairs and tell the Jew to come here."

"No one's stirring from here," I summoned the courage to say. "And I'm asking you to leave."

Fearful of his intentions, Mother added quickly, "We've got a lawyer now. Jamilla's nephew, Halim."

"A lawyer, eh? What else? Mary, go call your grandfather." He stopped for a moment then said to Mother, "Your daughter knows."

Mary cowered under his glare and slipped out of the house.

"And you," he commanded me, "go upstairs and get the Jew."

"You get out of here!" I shouted.

He turned to Mother. "Tell your daughter to run when she's told, or else your stink will spread all over the wadi." Then he coolly pulled his beads out of his jacket pocket.

Grandpa arrived out of breath, followed by Mary. She turned to go to our room but Abu-Nakhla stopped her. "Mary, you stay here."

Grandpa was astonished. "What do you want from her?"

"I want you to release my son."

"What's she got to do with it?"

"She enticed him to rape her," he said and did not even rise to defend himself. He calmly watched Mother struggling to restrain Grandpa. Perhaps it was his calm that froze Grandpa. "Mary," he cried hoarsely, "go to your room." When she closed the door behind her he said to Abu-Nakhla, "I could kill you."

"I know. Sit down, sit. It's no slander. Sit, sit, why're you standing? It's true. Zuhair saw what he saw, smelled what he smelled, tasted what he tasted and went out of his mind. He wants your grand-daughter, and I came to you and asked you man-to-man to give your blessing to their marriage. I was willing to have my only son marry a girl who's lost her virginity, and you turned up your noses."

Grandpa collapsed on his bench. "Mary and your son Zuhair?"

"I wouldn't lie in such a matter to a man like you—I swear by the Prophet and his precious book."

Grandpa's green eyes clouded over. His voice moaned "What do you want now?"

"Only to release my son. I'm willing to silence the whole affair. I'm willing to compensate her for both their misconduct. I'm will-ing—"

"What do you want?" Grandpa repeated.

"That you will not testify to the police against him, and persuade the Jew not to file a complaint."

"You brought the Jew here, you talk to him," Grandpa said in a low voice. He rested his head against the wall and suddenly began to beat it against the wall, as though trying to break into it.

Abu-Nakhla went up to him and touched his shoulder. His face and voice expressed real sorrow. "Don't distress yourself. It's a dif-ferent generation, they're following a different God, not our God.

And nothing's happened. Your granddaughter will marry the blinds contractor and we'll forget all about it in another few months. All I want is my son. You must persuade the Jew."

"I'll call him," Mother gave in.

Abu-Nakhla breathed a sigh of relief. "You've always been a wise woman, Umm-Huda."

I dreaded leaving Grandpa alone with Abu-Nakhla, but longed to flee to my room before Alex came in. His head appeared behind Mother's face, which was awash with tears. Abu-Nakhla rose to meet him. He was pale, and the cautious, cunning look in his eyes scared me. Aware of his short stature, Alex walked around Abu-Nakhla like an animal measuring its enemy, and there was a cruel look in his face. He didn't wait for an invitation but sat at the table, rested his injured arm on it and came straight to the point. "The one with knife is your son?"

Abu-Nakhla, ever quick and adaptable, sat down facing Alex and replied simply, "Yes."

"He's big fool."

"I agree, son."

Alex dismissed with a toss of his head his rival's false humility. "He is buried very deep in ground."

"Huda, explain to him," Abu-Nakhla asked me.

I hadn't imagined that this would be the first real exchange between us. Using roundabout words I tried to explain our situation, but his conceptual world was different from ours and he couldn't understand the connections between virginity and honor and gossip. "If your sister wants to drop that shit, yob-tvoi-mat, it serves him right." He turned to Abu-Nakhla as though waiting for the next move.

Abu-Nakhla blew his top. "Wallah, these Jews don't know the meaning of honor!"

"Speak Hebrew," said Alex.

"All right. I ask you to forgive my son."

"If I forgive everybody, I would be in ground long ago."

"I'll agree to anything. Just say what."

"I want your son never show his face near this house."

"He'll move out of the wadi altogether. Is that all?"

"What you think I am?" Alex gave a crooked grin. "With such arm I can't work at least two months."

"I'll give you two months' wages."

"And price of blood I lost."

"You'll have it."

"You took very much rent for room upstairs."

"You can have it rent free for a year."

Alex nodded.

"So it's all fixed?" said Abu-Nakhla.

Alex slammed his uninjured arm on the table and tapped hard with his forefinger. "Money," he reminded Abu-Nakhla. "We talked about money."

Abu-Nakhla's eyes glittered. "A Jew! A Jew!" he cried with relief, hatred and admiration.

"I will kill you if you call me zhid!" Alex said.

I fled to my room. Mary looked up at me, but I had nothing to say to her.

In the morning I tucked my head between my shoulders as if huddling against the cold and avoided the eyes of the wadi folk. Walking down the steep alley to Jaffa Road I heard sandals slapping behind me. I didn't turn around.

"Good morning," he said, out of breath.

I nodded, expecting him to pass by and continue to gallop down the street. But he matched his pace to mine, and I did not hide my displeasure.

"You think I am pig, eating until I vomit and making money from your trouble."

I made no protest. His shadow on the road was almost as long as mine.

"He wanted to kill me, so he and his father must pay."

Not with cash on our table, I thought to myself.

"I am going down to police to finish this business."

I allowed myself a smile that provokes men. Alex was not provoked. It seemed to me that he was indifferent to honor because of his short stature.

"Money is money," he said. "For studies I need, and to buy something for parents every week. I also sell semen."

I smiled at his Hebrew. He probably didn't know the meaning of the word. But what did he mean, what did he have to sell, except the strength of his muscles and his sense of justice. I glanced sideways at him and said to myself, it's only in my fantasies that I can feel attracted to this man.

He must have realized that I didn't understand. "There is gynecologist who buys. Some women need it."

I was filled with revulsion, as if a disgusting dog had attached itself to me, one of those that can't be offended or driven off. But he was looking ahead, his chin raised, without a trace of humility.

"Police station opposite your office."

I was alarmed. When did he follow me and find out where I worked? How did I miss him? I turned and said goodbye.

"I like you," he said, as if offering a cigarette. "You very beautiful. But if you don't want never mind."

For some reason I remembered at that moment that my eyes are green. Perhaps because I wanted to crush him with a look. "I don't want."

"Then why you smile?"

I didn't realize I was smiling. A Mary-like thought occurred to me—did this stud bull even know how many offspring he had?

"Your sister said you invited me to go to sea on Friday."

"She's talking nonsense," I almost shouted. "I said nothing of the sort."

He smiled. "If you don't want never mind." He turned to go to the police station.

*Chapter Nine*

The bay was behind us and the car sped down the Acre road through the exhausted, desiccated and dusty autumn landscape. The few words exchanged merely underscored the tense silence. Wahid was driving and Mother sat rigidly beside him, the big chocolate box on her lap. Grandpa, Mary and I sat in the back. This was the first time since the creation of Israel that Grandpa had left Haifa. From time to time he roused himself and looked around him. Some of his agitation got through to us when he clapped his hands and exclaimed, "Everything's changed, I don't recognize anything." He sounded downcast, as if the landscape had failed to recognize him. His eyes devoured the minarets of Acre, then when the car turned into the Safed Road and he saw the shabby housing estates with their rundown courtyards he said again, "It's all changed. I don't recognize anything."

Realizing that he was repeating himself, he glanced at Mary, who was sitting between us, calmed down and once more withdrew into himself. Mary obviously didn't hear what he said. Her gaze was fixed in the space between Mother and Wahid. I wondered when she would explode, how long she'd be able to swallow the black road which was piling up inside her like a folded ribbon. When will she open her mouth and scream, Enough, we're going back! But she only wrung her long hands, like an atheist frightened into desperate prayer, and the clear varnish on her fingernails gleamed.

Inarticulate Wahid was making a huge effort to play the cordial host. When the car stopped at the railway level crossing he pointed and said to Mother, "That's Napoleon's Hill."

Mother thanked him with a little smile, glanced at the undistinguished hill and reverted to silence. Having previously journeyed only to funerals, she was now unable to shed the mourning manner.

Ostensibly the car was carrying a well-dressed family out for an evening's drive. Mother and Grandpa were impressive to look at, and Mary, with her face of an ancient Egyptian princess, was heartbreakingly lovely. In reality, though, we were like innocent convicts who've won a new trial. Wahid's mother had firmly refused to submit and come to us, arguing that propriety dictated that we return the visit. The second act would therefore take place on her patch. We were going to fight the second battle with empty ammunition boxes. Mother proposed that we return the flat to Abu-Nakhla and give the lease money to Mary for a dowry. Grandpa was resigned, but Wahid was shocked and rejected the offer with chivalrous courtesy.

If I use the imagery of war, it is because the old-fashioned matches always opened with the two camps blackmailing each other. The side that gave in and suffered losses could find satisfaction in the fact that it had had something to lose. But we were being carried to Wahid's village with nothing in our hands but the shame of our inability to help Mary. Her self-confidence evaporated even before we left the house, and she had stopped speaking about the subjugation of her future mother-in-law. The incident with Zuhair undermined her position. She realized how precarious it was when the next meeting was set to take place in the village. If the mother chose to shut herself in a room and refuse to receive us we would go home covered in humiliation.

Mary leaned forward so that Wahid would be unable to see her in the rearview mirror and whispered to me, "I'm actually trembling for the sake of this chump!"

The closer we got to the village the more confident Wahid became. It was evident in his posture and the way he held the wheel, and the fact that he began to address all of the car's passengers and not Mother alone. He must have felt he was bringing Mary home like booty. He was bringing a bunch of paupers from a miserable wadi to his country estate. Now he turned around and smiled with a glimmer of gold tooth. "Mary," he ventured at last to speak up, "you've nothing to fear. You just leave all the worrying to me."

Grandpa reached for something to hold. "Look out!" he cried out in alarm. "Watch the road, man."

The car left the shoulder and returned to the road in a cloud of dust. "Don't worry," Wahid laughed. "You know how many hours I drive every day?"

Mary frowned as if trying to place that laugh. I could have told her. It was in secondary school during the breaks. It was the empty laughter of adolescent boys, which some men never outgrow for the rest of their lives. Grandpa never laughed like that. Mary would have to live with this laugh. I'd always admired her ability to retreat at the last moment and not feel committed by her own word. Perhaps that was what drove Zuhair out of his mind. But now she even stopped whispering to me, and her eyes filled with the desperation of a captured bird. I wanted to tell her that she was still free to fly away, but I kept quiet because I couldn't say where she could fly. I'd fled from Bahij, but instead of soaring to freedom I trudge on the ground with tranquilizer pills and listen to the trumpet blare of an alien world.

Wahid relaxed in his seat and announced, "Here we are."

We looked around us. A narrow road without sidewalks, grand villas higgledy-piggledy with wretched little houses, television antennas and chickens in the yards, a modern fashion boutique next to a grocery from the turn of the century. Well-dressed men walking past a shepherd in torn boots. An old woman in black balancing on her head a gigantic bundle of twigs, making way for three women who looked as if they had just stepped out of a fashionable beauty salon in Tel Aviv. Manicured gardens in the twilight and sewage flowing in the street. And it was all very quiet and peaceful, as though the village had been accustomed for thousands of years to walk on two vastly uneven legs.

Wahid's family house stood in a narrow alley which twisted and turned arbitrarily. The car parked in the front yard belonged to his brother Assim, who lived, Wahid told us, on the upper floor. It immediately disappeared behind Wahid's parents and the brother and his wife, his sisters and their husbands and numerous children. Wahid stopped but did not open the door, and I thought he wanted to impress us with the large crowd that had come to meet us. Mother really was impressed. Such meetings had always taken place among tombstones and forgotten graves, in mourning clothes and through tears. Here she was being met with bouquets of smiles. Nervously she fingered the chocolate box on her lap and turned back, seeming to ask me for a hint how she must conduct herself. Grandpa shrank back as though alarmed by the rushing mass. Mary was afraid to look. She leaned forward again and whispered, "Is she there, tell me, is she there?"

"Yes," I assured her. "She's even smiling."

It turned out that Wahid did not open the door because he was paralyzed. His father and brother came forward and opened the car doors. In the back of the crowd women ululated joyfully. We were received with handshakes and hugs and kisses, like the last remnants of a lost tribe. I tasted my own salty tears. This whole warm, cheerful crowd was ours. All these old people and children, the men and the women, were our relatives. Yet from childhood we had walked alone. I felt my arms growing longer and embracing them all in my thirst for affection. Only someone who's grown up as an orphan in a teeming neighborhood, with a mother who shut herself up in a palace of dead memories, can understand how I felt. Grandpa had never talked about family, because long before he fled through the desert he had no relations left. To this day he's like a ship without a home port. He would not even share his memories of the dead with us.

Dazed, we were led into the spacious living room of Wahid's parents' apartment. Those who had no seats stood around in rows and looked at us. Grandpa was blinking, as if dazzled by camera flashes.

Mother froze upright in her chair. My own smile froze, fearful of what Mary might do. I glanced at her and saw a truly impressive woman. She seemed to be in complete control, even of the fluttering curls on her forehead. Her smile expressed regal restraint and she looked altogether like a flame that may only be seen. Assim walked through the room, handing out cigarettes, as though to close the men's open mouths. I myself was captivated by her beauty and the enchantment she cast on all who saw her. After a little while she smiled without the regal restraint, moved her hands freely, exchanged loud kisses with the women, and took big gulps of the drink that was handed around. I began to fear that she would get carried away with her playacting.

"Smile," she whispered to me, "smile as if I'm telling you an innocent children's joke."

I obeyed, but hissed through the affected smile, "Mary, don't play the fool. This visit . . . everything depends on it."

"Silly, it's not just a visit."

I went on smiling till my jaws ached.

"Wait a little," she smiled at me. "Listen, this is a regular betrothal, not just a visit. I'm sure my idiot's already got a diamond ring in his pocket."

In such matters her instincts never failed, but this time I was unsure. The journey from Haifa had taken about an hour, and Wahid, the simple fellow, had sat in our house for a long time before we set out, and I couldn't believe that he'd kept the secret all that time. "A diamond ring," I grinned, "no less."

The smile never left her lips. "A diamond ring, and presents from his father." The curls on her forehead shook. "And from the loathsome snake."

Poor Mother and her chocolate box, pauper Grandpa with nothing but an ancient narghileh from Ottoman days to show off to his guests. Wahid's father rose and clapped for silence. Very deliberately he turned to an inner door and all eyes turned with him. A long moment passed and he stamped his foot and said irritably, "Where is he?"

Mary's knee touched mine. "They're waiting for Wahid," she whispered almost without moving her lips. Her head was high and her expression that of a cultivated person politely watching a vulgar show. "Go fuck such an idiot," she whispered, this time in Hebrew. "On our wedding night he'll probably trip on his shoelaces."

Grandpa heard the whisper and lit another cigarette. "Enough," he begged, but a green light twinkled in his eyes.

Wahid appeared in a white suit with a blue shirt and a red tie, his hair stiff like black cement. He was sweating as if he'd just passed under a tap, the sweat dripped from his eyelashes and the tip of his nose, and already his collar and underarms were wet. Mary jumped up, ready and willing to catch him in her arms if he stumbled and fell before handing over the ring. We were obliged to rise too. Grandpa looked for a place to stub out his cigarette, because standing up he could not secretly step on it under his seat. Wahid, who was used to hard physical work, mustered the strength to display the ring to all before putting it on Mary's finger. My sister did not raise her eyes to him, but looked as if she was witnessing a miracle and was seeking God to give thanks to. She did not have to search for long. Her future mother-in-law's mighty bosom thrust up like the tower of a fortress, and Mary approached her in the silent living room as though the grim-faced woman was the only person present. Mary stopped before her and bowed, a very slight bow but an unmistakable one. Then she tremulously took the woman's hand and buried her face in her rolling corpulence. For extra effect she butted the vast bosom with her forehead, as though struggling to contain her tears. The woman's stiff stare resisted for a brief minute, but Mary continued to butt, like a calf seeking reluctant udders, and the fortress fell with a sob.

The thrilling ceremony was followed by an amazing feast. Mary hardly touched the colorful spread. Wahid, shyly complying with

the calls of the men to feed his betrothed and plump up her fine figure, handed her a plate with a pigeon stuffed with rice. Mary took a
bite and desisted.

After the meal most of the guests left and we sat in armchairs in
the big living room for a businesslike discussion. We had to agree
on a date for the wedding and where the young couple would live in
the beginning. Mother sat restlessly on the edge of her chair, her
lips dry and her nose pointing up, anxious not to miss her chance
to speak. "Do you remember," she said to Wahid's mother in a raw
voice and with a crooked smile, "when we came with my brother to
ask for your sister's hand?"

It is pleasant to remember one's youth, but the hostess replied
cautiously, "Yes, I remember."

"It's the same village," Mother went on, "but it was very different
then."

The hostess no doubt recalled it well. In those days a village was a
village and a city a city, and a gulf of two centuries separated them.
But the bridegroom's mother's memory was selective. "Yes, it was in
the summer. There was great rejoicing, and I remember that we sat
outside, under the mulberry tree."

"Because there wasn't enough room inside," Mother said pointedly. Grandpa cleared his throat, but Mother was carried away by
vindictive venom. "There were only one-room hovels in the village,
there was no electricity and the women carried water in buckets on
their heads."

Wahid's mother twisted a chocolate wrapper between her fingers.
She herself had carried water on her head that day, and walked barefoot. She could hardly dispute Mother's recollection that she'd cut
her foot on a piece of glass that morning and had to bind it with an
old handkerchief and receive her guests with her foot bandaged and
stuck in an old house slipper.

"Those were hard times," Wahid's father sought to divert the dangerous conversation to a safer track. "People were poor, but decent."

Mother's nose went even higher. "We came in Father's car. Who had cars in those days?"

Grandpa laughed. "British officers, and merchants who smuggled goods."

Wahid's mother shook out her skirts. "God preserve us! My father, rest his soul, was a law-abiding man. He fed us with calloused hands."

"And my father," Mother said, thrusting out her lower lip, "was born in a villa and died in a villa."

Grandpa slapped his knee and said, "And my father was born on a torn reed mat in an adobe shack, and was so swollen from eating beans that he burst!" His green eyes held Mother's gaze till she retracted her claws and remained alone on the ruins of her memories.

Assim sympathized with her, perhaps because he'd never carried water on his head. "Mother was always telling us about your house in Haifa. Once you invited the whole family for one of the holidays. Right, Mother?"

His mother responded graciously. "True. I sewed myself a new dress, but I still felt ashamed of it." She smiled.

I breathed a sigh of relief and Grandpa gave Mother a conciliatory smile. I heard Mary whispering aloud to Wahid, "I'm afraid to go back to our house." I looked at her and saw what Wahid saw. Her eyes were glazed and her lips trembled.

"What happened?" asked Wahid and his father together.

"I'm ashamed to tell you," she said in a low voice, deeply distressed, and looked at me. "Huda, can you?"

All eyes were on me. I remained silent, unsure what she was after and what I was supposed to say. My silence seemed to confirm her hint that she was in some danger. I didn't know why Mother turned pale, but there was an Egyptian twinkle in Grandpa's eyes. I realized that it was one of Mary's tricks and threw it back at her. "Mary, you'd better tell them yourself."

"There is a gangster in the wadi that even the devil is afraid of," she began hesitantly.

"The one who robbed the family men on the border," Grandpa explained, "and then betrayed them to the Jews."

"That fiend Abu-Nakhla," Wahid's mother breathed.

"Yes," Mary went on with her eyes downcast. "But he's an angel compared to his son."

Wahid's face was the color of his tie. "What's that scum got to do with you?"

Mary's lashes fluttered like the wings of a weary butterfly. "He . . . he . . . he . . ." She broke down.

Grandpa stamped out his cigarette under his chair, as if the Italian marble floor annoyed him, and said, "A beautiful girl always needs protecting. Mary is an orphan and I'm old, and that young man's eyes rove too freely. He's armed and surrounded by a gang of thugs."

"He dared . . . ?" Wahid asked in a croak.

"And how dared!" Mary exclaimed. "He attacked our door with a knife in his hand. His thugs were waiting downstairs in the street."

"Listen, people," Grandpa helped her. "We almost died of fright."

"Fortunately," Mary said, "fortunately we have a Jewish neighbor upstairs. An Arab wouldn't have dared to fight Abu-Nakhla's son. Even the Jew was almost murdered."

Wahid's mother almost swooned. Wahid, in his white suit, put on an imaginary armor. "I'll break his bones."

Mary instantly refused the fate of a young widow. "Don't you dare!" she exclaimed. "I don't want him to hurt you. You've no idea what a vicious criminal he is."

Wahid was already flourishing his sword. "I'll kill him . . ."

"Daughter," said the groom's mother, "you can stay with us, from tonight."

"Oh no," Mary recoiled. "What will people say?"

Grandpa supported her. "The father and son are already spreading filthy rumors about her."

Assim finally got the message. "In that case, why wait? Hold the wedding at once."

Nobody objected. Only Grandpa needed time to adjust. "Perhaps in two months' time?"

There was general agreement, and it was decided that after the wedding the young couple would live with the parents, until the third story was built over Assim's flat.

Wahid drove us back to Haifa. As we drew near the wadi he looked left and right like a detective. Stopping in front of the house he got out, checked the entrance and stood guard. A trumpet fanfare rolled down the dark staircase.

"What's that?" asked Wahid.

"It's the Jew who saved us. He plays the trumpet," said Mary.

Wahid came up with us and waited until we opened the door, and wouldn't leave until he'd checked the place and made sure that no one had invaded the flat. He sat in his car downstairs for twenty minutes before driving off.

Alex had noticed our return. The fanfare turned into a short sob, and then enveloped me in a wistful nostalgic melody.

## Chapter Ten

"He did so much for us," said Mother, "and how have we repaid him? Listen to him playing the trumpet in the dark. Maybe he's hungry. I wish we'd brought him something from the feast they slapped on over there. You only pinched some cigarettes for yourself. How could you, before all those eyes?"

"There were opportunities," said Grandpa. "Like when Wahid came in and nobody knew if he was going to make it to Mary's finger."

"Go on, laugh, ruin it all. Wahid will cherish Mary. She'll never want for anything with him." Her voice rose. "Interesting—you knew about Zuhair the whole time, you saw your granddaughter playing with the fires of hell, and you didn't open your mouth. But now . . ."

I also wondered where his tolerance and permissiveness came from. Inevitably I thought about Munira, my paternal grandmother.

"I know Mary. Zuhair was just an illness, but Wahid is . . ."

He didn't finish the sentence, but my mind followed his and finished it for him: Wahid is a disability. I looked at Mary and quickly turned away. I didn't really want to know.


But in the following days Mary did not behave as if she was disabled. Wahid came every evening, neat and well-dressed, and his presence did not miss any of us, till he almost won Grandpa's heart. He would sit in the living room and hold an awkward conversation with us, while Mary got dressed and made up in the bedroom. She was never ready to go out when he arrived. He would bring her back late, tired and irritable. She withdrew more and more into herself, and her usual enlivening chatter ceased for several days. She hid the blue and red love marks on her body, like a soldier ashamed of the wounds suffered in defeat. This was her usual way of coping with developments that displeased her. "Now he's playing on our nerves at Abu-Nakhla's expense," she grumbled about Alex while undressing in the dark, unlike her usual habit, growling as she undid her bra, as though the sound of the trumpet prevented her finding the clasps. "Go, go on up," she urged me. "He's calling you. Go up to him!"

"I'm not Jamilla's cat." Jamilla told us her cat liked the sound of the trumpet. Every time it played the cat wanted to go out and up on the roof. And so it seemed, until it transpired that Alex was feeding him.

"Why don't you go up to him?" she said again one night. "You could say that the trumpet is keeping you awake."

I made no answer, annoyed that I hadn't thought of it myself. Now that is initiative, I said to myself.

"Tomorrow's Friday," she said. "We missed two Fridays. Tomorrow we'll go to the sea."

"Mary, you're already engaged."

"That's why. With Wahid I'll never see the sea. He'll expect me to go into the water in a long gown, and will swell like a turkey if any man looks at me. I'm entitled to have a little fun before burying myself. Tomorrow I must go to the sea. Once on the beach you'll have plenty of opportunity to arrange things with Abu-Trumpet."

I kept my mouth shut. In such matters it's no good lying to her. She turned over in bed, huffing and puffing irritably, thumping her pillow, but finally settled down. The music of the trumpet hovered softly like a black bird over the sleeping wadi. My heart ached. It suddenly struck me how much I need Mary and love her, and now I'm going to lose her. Already with her being out with Wahid for hours the evenings have grown very dull. Ever since I can remember she has been invading my bed, invading my soul, her laughter soothing the scrapes and bruises of time. There was always a generational and cultural gap between us and Mother and Grandpa, and even with our different personalities Mary and I drew very close and our friendship ran deep. I sat up in bed. I wanted to sneak into her bed and clasp her body and cry. I stopped when I heard her moving. Her clear voice revealed that she hadn't gone to sleep at all. "Have you noticed," she said, "that ever since Alex began to play his trumpet all your crazy illnesses have disappeared, and you're really well?" Then she turned to the wall and went on speaking as if to herself. "So maybe there's something to be said for the trumpet. They say music makes plants grow faster and cows give more milk."

I didn't go to her bed and did not hold her body. I lay back on my solitary bed and examined myself. Indeed, my body felt light and supple and did not hurt. The skin under the nightdress was soft and fragrant. The trumpet accompanied my passage into sleep.

In the morning I didn't wake her. I stuffed the swimsuit into my handbag and told Mother I'd be late. I meant to steal the march on Mary and tell Shirley myself. Adina was in Boaz's office. She has taken to shutting the door when she goes in. There weren't many customers that day.

"I'll come too," Shirley said. "I'll ask Kobi and we can go in my car."

"There's . . . there's one other person."

"Mary's fiancé?"

"No . . . a new immigrant."

"The trumpet player your sister was talking about?" She didn't expect an answer. Shirley was used to bizarre combinations. An Arab woman and a new immigrant did not strike her as an odd couple.

I came out of the office early to meet Mary and Alex outside. Kobi arrived first, carrying a bag with rackets, towels and swimsuits. He took the car keys from Shirley and brought the car around from the car park to wait for us on Independence Street. Mary and Alex arrived from different directions, though they had left the same house at the same time. My sister was being careful to prevent malicious gossip. I saw Alex and shut my eyes. I felt an impulse to hide behind a mailbox. Short and stocky, with a Mao cap on his head, a worn cotton blanket tucked under his well arm, the injured arm still bandaged and wrapped in black rubber like a bicycle inner tube, he stood on the pavement scanning the passersby. Mary waved and caught his eye and he came over to us, smiling shyly. I was anxious about his encounter with Shirley and Kobi. They represented two ends of Jewish society in which I had no foothold: Ashkenazi Shirley, born on top of the Carmel, who seemed to believe that the Jewish State had been created just to serve her, and Moroccan Kobi, who cultivated the chip on his shoulder and expected everyone to kneel before him and apologize and lavish on him whatever the State denied him in his deprived childhood. Both of them were predatory—Shirley in her sweet way, Kobi in his aggressiveness.

They had an opportunity when we got into the car to observe Alex and smile, just as I'd expected them to do—as if we'd brought a goat with us. If Alex noticed, he didn't seem offended. Perhaps he'd learned to hide his inner feelings. He sat between me and Mary on the back seat, the ragged cotton blanket on his lap, trying not to touch my body with his. He looked at the traffic between Kobi's and Shirley's heads. He seemed lonely in the packed car.

"How's the arm?" I asked him.

He raised it, as if to show me that it was getting better, lost his balance and his thigh touched mine. He perceived instantly what happened to me. My head was on fire. For years I hadn't let a man touch me even by accident. When getting into a bus I held the coin in such a way that the driver's fingers would not touch mine. Alex's muscular thigh was bare below his shorts and sprinkled with black hairs. The fire was followed by a chill. I felt my blush turning into pallor and my lips were dry.

Alex looked down and didn't ask if I was feeling unwell. He must have understood, because he looked embarrassed, as if he'd opened the wrong door by mistake. He moved away from me. "The arm almost all right," he said. "I keep on bandage for Abu-Nakhla. I really can do easy work in docks at night, but he pays so let him pay."

A smile began low in my body and rose through my belly and womb, tickled my back like ants, pinched my breasts, encircled my neck and felt sweet in my throat, but did not reach my lips. At first I did not want to admit it, but then the longing overcame me. I wanted the hairy leg to touch me again, and of course I did not dare to move, but the longing itself was like sunrise.

The few sea lovers on the beach sat in small groups, like clumps of thin vegetation in the desert. The breath of the sea came and went in chilly-looking white breakers of late autumn. I lay on a towel, looking at the blue sky, surrendering my body to the wind. Kobi pulled Shirley up on her feet and they walked like dancers on the foaming water line. Then they went into the sea and the waves beat on their bodies. They stood in the water, locked in a long embrace which had something about it of the eternity and natural-ness of the rocks and the sea. I observed them and saw nothing wrong with the observation nor with what I saw. Kobi removed the top of Shirley's swimsuit and she clung to him, till they looked like a single creature with two heads and no legs. Then their legs reap-peared when they walked out of the water to the golden sand, still locked in their embrace. She strained backward and he bent over her, as if to revive her lifeless body with his breath, until her hair spread over the sand and her knees rose toward the sky. I had never seen such a sight. I knew that I should have felt ashamed, that it was a shame to watch, but I felt no shame. As if it was me lying on the sand and my knees praying to the god of the wind and the sea. I lay on my side, supporting my head on my hand, and continued to watch them, feeling my body ready to explode. Suddenly fearful, I turned on my back and looked away, and saw Alex drawing lines in the sand and Mary smiling sadly. She would never lie with Wahid on the warm sand.

Alex had seen them too, and the lines he was drawing in the sand became deeper and deeper. Suddenly he stopped and gave me a long silent look. I pretended not to understand, though I knew I was blushing. He nodded at the opposite side of the beach and I rose on my elbow, as though seeking something.

"You want to walk?" he asked finally, giving up the pantomime.

I smiled at him and he didn't know how to interpret my smile. I was confused, knowing only that I was happy.

"You want?" he asked again.

Of course I wanted to, but did not dare. The smile I gave him was all the daring I was capable of. Not since Bahij had I smiled like this at a man.

"I am going to swim," he announced, rising. He dropped his glasses on the blanket and ran to the water.

"The water is cold and your arm is wounded," I shouted after him.

Perhaps he didn't hear in the sea breeze. I thought he would recoil from the cold water, but he leaped into the base of the first wave. I knelt till I saw his head on top of a white crest.

Mary removed the towel that covered her. Her skin looked like the surface of a pond with blue blossoms floating on it. Wahid's lips and teeth were everywhere. I couldn't help laughing.

"Disgusting, isn't it?" she grumbled.

"But he's thorough."

She rubbed her shoulders repeatedly, as if to wipe off the marks. "You call this thorough? He skims the surface. I keep offering him everything, like a greengrocer, and he devours the pomegranates and melons and cherries but only with his eyes, and won't do a trade."

I laughed. "A trade?"

"For his banana. He guards it. Once I pulled it hard. Even his yell was a squeak. How he guards his banana!"

"Wait a little," I told her. "The wedding's round the corner and he's old-fashioned. He values virginity."

"Huda, I'm not just not a virgin. I'm pregnant."

I tried to smile. Tried to touch her. "You're pulling my leg," I said, though I knew she was serious. I was like a child beside her, and the only solution I knew for grownups' problems was to deny their existence. "What do you mean, pregnant? You don't get pregnant from the air."

"Huda, I'm not you and Zuhair isn't Bahij, and certainly not air. His father was being truthful and was even very generous. It's true he raped me, but no court will believe me. There was a moment when I could withdraw and I didn't."

"He's a criminal!" I screamed. "A stinking criminal!"

"Forget it, Huda. Don't let your sense of smell and sense of justice get mixed up. Zuhair knows how to strip. His muscles are warm and his skin smells sweet. He doesn't squeal and squeak like Wahid. And don't imagine that he used force once. He's savage when necessary and gentle when necessary. I was the one who squeaked and squealed. Whenever I saw him I turned into a shell and wanted him to come, to come and fill me up. Once on the radio I heard a soldier saying that floating through the air in freefall feels stupendous. Huda, this is even greater. You feel as if you're floating down, you open your eyes and he's above you and you're no longer a shell but a flowing spring."

I shut my ears to the lascivious music. I tore the parachute strings and saw her sitting on the sand, spotted with sucks and bites that disgusted her. "So you're pregnant," I said. "What will you do if everything is discovered?"

"Why should it be discovered?" she questioned.

"You can't buy virginity in the pharmacy. In the villages they still make sure. And you can't hide a pregnancy."

"I'll force my idiot to rape me. Then I'll go mad and weep and yell that he ruined me. He'll be too dazed and confused and won't think about virginity. But it's hard with him. Yesterday I opened his coop. His rooster wept and fainted before me. Last week I tore my bra at home. In the car I pressed against him and then accused him of tearing my clothes. He apologized and bought me a whole bundle of panties and bras. Why shouldn't he believe that he tore my cherry and made me pregnant? Wallah, what a chore it is to spur on someone like that."

I couldn't believe my eyes. She was smiling. She wrapped the towel around her shoulders, rested her beautiful head on her knees and smiled again. Seeing my frozen expression she laughed and exclaimed, "Huda, life's perfectly crazy, but we keep trying to find some logic in it."

"There must be some logic."

"Listen, man went looking for logic and found God. Went on looking and lost God. Logic ruins life."

"I don't understand how you can smile."

"Because I've long ago stopped looking. See where logic has got you. Meantime, Abu-trumpet is lost at sea. Maybe he's trying to swim to Cyprus, or he's drowned." She stood up and said worriedly, "I really can't see him."

Shirley and Kobi came back, their limbs slack and their eyes dull as though half asleep. Shirley sat on the sand and Kobi lay like a crucifix, his swarthy body dozing in the sun. "What's wrong?" Shirley asked.

"He's been gone a long time," I said, scanning the sea. I stopped myself from saying that he jumped into the water when they started to make love. A dark silhouette of a Navy ship sailed on the radiant horizon.

"Wallah, have you seen his glasses?" Kobi said, holding Alex's glasses. "The midget's blind without them. I bet you he's swimming across the sea, thinking he's heading this way."

"What should we do?" asked Mary.

"We should call for help," said Shirley.

"There are no lifeguards and I don't see any boats nearby," Mary said.

They both looked at me, as though it was my problem and my decision. Without taking my eyes off the sea I leaned over and took the glasses from Kobi, put them on the blanket and covered them with the peaked cap. Mary, who's taller than I, suddenly yelled, "There he is! There! I'm sure I saw his head."

"Probably a lump of tar," Kobi said dismissively.

"Why don't you jump in and check," Shirley suggested.

"For that specimen? One weirdo less. Why bother?"

"There, over there!" Mary exclaimed again.

He was so far away that I couldn't tell if he was returning or receding, if he was caught in an undercurrent or if he existed at all.

I cursed him aloud, "God damn him to hell and gone!"

"These Russians are all quite mad," said Kobi. "They can all go right back where they came from, as far as I'm concerned."

Shirley's fist landed on his chest. He sat up and looked at her, to see if it was meant affectionately or in anger. But Shirley was looking at Alex, who was drawing nearer. My knees gave under me and I sat down. "Such trash," said Kobi. "I wouldn't invite him to my grandmother's wedding. What do you need him for?"

Alex emerged from the sea with a childish smile on his face. We stared at him in silence. Kobi lay down again, pointedly indifferent. Alex didn't notice the silence or our expressions. "Good, good," he said, wiping the water off his body with his hands. "Very good!" Then he put on his glasses and saw our faces. "Something happened?" he asked and shook the water out of his hair.

"Hey, fellow, watch it!" Kobi called and sat up.

"Sorry, sorry," Alex stammered, his chest still rising and falling like a bellows. Perhaps this is the fate of all immigrants, that they must keep apologizing right and left.

Kobi stood up and took the rackets. "Come on, Shirley, let's play."

"Don't feel like it."

"I am ready," said Alex.

Mary and Shirley watched the stiff contest between the two males with almost erotic excitement. Kobi was like a frenzied tiger cub. Alex seemed a little heavy compared to him, but his smile held a trace of disdain which at that moment seemed unwarranted.

After a little while I saw the reason for his smile. Language gives no advantage in a ball game.

Limber Kobi took in Alex's provoking smile and positioned himself close to his opponent, as though out of consideration. Alex declined the favor, sent the ball in a high arc over Kobi's head and sprang back. Kobi had to jump to get at the ball and return it without pretending to show consideration for the little man. Dark skinny Kobi pirouetted on the sand, strutting his attractive tall manhood. By contrast, Alex was careful and meticulous, as if taking some disability into account, prepared for failure as part of his life, but unwilling to regard it as defeat. He ran to the ball which Kobi had sent high and sideways, moved a few steps further back and returned it with calculated force. The ball whistled through the air as it crossed the great distance between them.

"Your little friend wants everything on the big side," said Shirley.

Mary defended him. "He came from Russia."

Kobi served and the ball fell powerless some four paces before Alex's feet. "Higher, more power," said Alex, picking up the ball.

Kobi laughed like a spoilt child. After ten minutes of fierce, silent serves, which looked like an exchange of blows, Kobi leapt in the air and caught the ball in his hand. "Enough, enough. I'm beat." He looked at Shirley and added coyly, "We were too wild over there on the sands."

"So rest a little. It's a game, not a penance."

He rejoined her and they merged again on the sand, breast to breast, mouth to mouth, as though we weren't there. Alex drew up his knees and stared at the sea.

"Your wound has reopened," I said.

"I must learn Hebrew," he said to the sea. Perhaps he didn't hear what I said against the roar of the waves.

"Huda knows Hebrew perfectly," Mary told him. "She can declaim all the Hebrew poets by heart."

"I have no money to pay."

Mary smiled. Bundled in her towel she spoke like a shrewd peasant haggler. "Huda will give you credit."

He looked into my eyes. I dared to smile at him but blushed and my head sank immediately.

"One day I will pay everything," he said. "It will be very much?"

I drew a tremulous line in the sand across the blurred ones he had drawn. "Almost for free."

He looked back at the sea. "All my life I did not have enough money. I worked hard just not to steal." He laughed and turned back to me. "Language I am ready to steal, but language you cannot steal, right?"

"Language you pick up slowly and it's hard work."

"I know to work hard. When I was five they said I must wash my own clothes. They did not even give me chair, and sink was high. Somebody had to open tap for me, and I washed clothes without seeing, like pianist playing without . . ."

"Sheet music?"

"Without sheet music. Yes, I knew words but forgot—nice words."

*Chapter Eleven*

"It's quiet upstairs," said Mary. "Abu-trumpet's sleeping."

"Gone to his parents," I said.

"I wonder if they're his real parents or adoptive."

"Mary, when you leave home it'll be awful here."

"You'll have Abu-trumpet. You won't be bored with him. Does it bother you that I call him Abu-trumpet?"

"No. It suits him. I promised to go up tomorrow to teach him."

"And you won't," she said.

I shook my head.

"Don't worry, he'll ask you again."

I believed her. I went to bed with the belief, fell asleep and didn't hear his footsteps on the stairs when he returned from the old-age home.

Like most Arab contractors, Wahid did not work on Saturdays and he came to the house at ten in the morning. Jamilla showed up soon after, and bent over the crate of grapes and figs he'd brought, examining them like produce in the market. She took a fig and bit into it.

Grandpa resigned himself to the idea that Wahid would be Mary's husband and accepted him as fate's decree. Wahid's tongue had loosened a little and he was now capable of uttering whole sentences, with Grandpa encouraging him like a patient, good-natured teacher. But the moment Mary emerged in all her glory from the bedroom he stopped hearing Grandpa. His love for her was filled with fear and anxiety, as though time had lost its continuity and every moment held new dangers. Every evening Mary offered him her body, and the next day he could not believe that she would let him near her, and bore his submission like a white flag.

Jamilla polished off a plate of figs and washed them down with three little cups of coffee. She repaid us with gossip. "I saw Zuhair last night," she began, unaware of Grandpa's angry look and Mother's grimace. "He was hanging around here like the angel of death."

"What was he doing here?" Wahid asked, his chest swelling.

"He was born here," Jamilla told him, "and he'll die here."

"I don't want to see him in the neighborhood."

"Son," said Grandpa, "our wings are clipped. He is king and his father is emperor."

"I want to go away from here," Mary whispered.

Wahid was startled. "Where to?"

"For a week or two. To Tiberias, the Dead Sea . . . I'm tired. I want to breathe some different air."

Wahid's face fell. "On your own?"

"Why?" she asked. "Do you want to run away from me already?"

He couldn't believe his ears. He was as embarrassed as if he'd been caught naked in church. His eyes swept over the living room. "And the family, will they agree? We're not really married yet."

Mother looked at Grandpa, who took a cigarette from Wahid's pack and said thoughtfully, "Wallah, to tell you the truth, I don't know."

"He agrees," Mary interpreted for Wahid.

Wahid was paralyzed and couldn't utter a word. The trumpet came to life. Wahid looked up to the ceiling and asked, like a person waking from a swoon, "What is that?"—though he already knew.

"The Jewish neighbor," Mother said. "You've seen him." She turned to Grandpa. "You should go upstairs and talk to him. We haven't seen him since that time we offended him." But Grandpa didn't like to apologize and preferred to let time take care of it.

Wahid stayed to lunch. After he and Mary went out in the afternoon I felt the roof weighing on my chest. I didn't know how to avoid keeping my promise. I hadn't said exactly when I would come, and this made me even more uneasy, wondering when he would give up and go about his business. A crescent moon appeared in my window and hung between a television aerial and a solar heater. Alex's music was soft and melancholy, willing the moon to rise over the roofs. Mother and Grandpa were in the living room, chatting calmly and quietly, as if they'd begun and would end in eternity. Their intimacy was as natural and matter-of-course as rain. That is love after my own heart, I said to myself, the essence of confidence which I lack so much. The trumpet continued to thrill the evening air and the crescent pulled away from the roof and hung on the tip of the aerial. I lay on my bed without turning on the light.

Suddenly the trumpet uttered a loud cry and fell silent. I jumped up in panic and ran to the living room. I heard the trumpet drop and roll on the roof. Grandpa and Mother were on their feet, staring at the ceiling. The footsteps on the roof sounded strange, as if someone had begun to run, then stopped and started again.

Mother turned pale. "Zuhair," she whispered. "He attacked the neighbor in revenge."

"Shouldn't have meddled with such filth," Grandpa declared from the depths of his ancient wisdom.

"Huda!" Mother shouted.

Somehow she knew that although my feet seemed nailed to the floor and my body was trembling and seeking something to hold it up, my thoughts were breaking through the door and rushing up the stairs. Grandpa came to me and hugged my shoulders. "Calm down, my love, calm down."

I shook off his arm. "He'll kill him, he'll kill Alex and then come to us."

The roof was quiet. At the sound of footsteps on the stair Mother rushed to the window, meaning to call for help. Then came a knock on the door which froze her throat so she could not utter a sound. Grandpa said in an odd voice, "Who is it?"

"Me," came Alex's agonized voice.

I collapsed on a chair and Grandpa hastened to open the door. Alex came in, his face contorted with pain, clutching his buttock.

"He stabbed you?" Mother asked.

"Very hard," he moaned.

We looked at his fingers, his buttocks and legs, but saw no sign of blood.

"Here, here," he pointed with his free hand to the hand clutching his buttock. "Stabbed very hard."

Grandpa was the first to collect his wits. He pushed Alex's hand away and pulled down his short trousers. His anxiety was dispelled and he laughed aloud.

"Why are you laughing?" Alex protested. "It hurts very much."

"We thought it was a knife."

"Why knife? It is something black with a tail standing up. I killed it."

"That's a sting, not a stab—it's called akrav, a scorpion!" The sudden relaxation of tension made me yell at him.

"Thank you for Hebrew lesson," Alex said, grimacing with pain.

Nobody saw me blushing. Grandpa made him lie face down on the bench and called for the bottle of arak. He bent over Alex's head and explained, "We have to rub the place with arak, and it's good to drink some too."

He massaged the area of the sting in the fold of the buttock, just below the underpants, and both he and Alex drank some.

After a while Alex said, "It is not helping. It still hurts very much."

"Not working on the backside or on the head? By now you should be drunk."

"I'm used to drinking."

"It's swelling like a balloon," Grandpa announced between swallowing and massaging.

Alex gave me a sideways glance, agonized yet mischievous. "It was because of you. I waited for you on roof and scorpion got me.

Huda agreed to teach me Hebrew," he explained when Grandpa's hand halted on his buttock. "I want to pay."

Grandpa was almost drunk. "An Arab woman teaching a Jew Hebrew. Not bad. Now when a man teaches a woman to dance nobody knows how it will end. When a woman teaches a man . . ."

"It's the same thing," Mother concluded, and looked at me in speechless wonder.

"You should put ice on it," said Grandpa, who by now needed the bench to lie on himself. "Go up to your room and Huda will bring you ice."

When he left Mother looked accusingly at Grandpa.

"It's all right, woman," he said aloud. "A man with such a swollen arse couldn't dishonor an ant."

"He'd better come and get the ice himself."

"He needs watching a little. Maybe he has a weak heart. Maybe he should be taken to the hospital. Some people die from a bee sting."

He was not really drunk. He was encouraging me to go up on the roof. Mother shrugged. She found it convenient to rely on his judgment as though it were fate. My heart was pounding as I went up the stairs, with a bowl of ice in one hand and a dish of stuffed vine leaves in the other. The door of his room was wide open. In my confusion I stood in the doorway smiling and greeting him, as if it was our first meeting that day.

"Hello," he said. He was lying on his side, supporting his head on his uninjured arm while the other circled around the area of the sting. I laid the bowls on the table and wondered what to do next. If he or Grandpa imagined that I would sit on his bed and put ice cubes on his backside they were mistaken. In addition to the bed the room contained a table and two chairs, bookcases, a gas range and an old wardrobe. The sink was outside, and I wondered where he showered.

"Where's the scorpion?" I asked after a long silence.

"Outside by barrel."

I went to look at it. In fact I wanted to see if Mother hadn't crept up the stairs to spy on me. The scorpion was indeed big and horrible, and already swarming with ants. When I returned to the room the bowl with the vine leaves was beside the bed and his injured hand, abandoning the painful site, was moving quickly between the bowl and his mouth. He didn't like me to see him wolfing down the food. "It is your fault," he said. "Today I played for you. I sat there beside barrel . . ."

"And the scorpion was quicker than you," I said laughing and sat on a chair. "Jamilla's cat is also attracted by your trumpet. You'll soon have a whole zoo on the roof."

"How can we study? You did not bring book."

"You can't study now."

Night had fallen and here I was sitting in a strange room talking with a real man, not a figment of my imagination. The muscles on the mattress did not frighten me. I hadn't been alone like this with a man for years. But perhaps I was calm because I was sitting and he was lying down, afraid to move and stir up the pain.

"It does not bother me," he said. "I can study."

If he can concentrate on studying now then perhaps he can also . . .

"You are afraid of me," he said, and I realized that my eyes had turned to the open door. I said nothing.

"And I am afraid of you. That is not good."

"You're afraid of me?"

"Yes," he said. "You are very beautiful and I am short and ugly."

"I am beautiful?"

He did not hear me. "You don't know what it is like to be new immigrant. Suddenly you are like child. You want to speak but it comes out like mud. I am same man, thinking thoughts of grownup, but when I open my mouth I think people are laughing. Like when I got the horrible specs. I speak Hebrew like child, so people think I think like child. In Russia I talked like I think, quick and natural. Today I speak like . . . nu . . . like that animal with . . .

yob-tvoi-mat! You see, I can't explain simple things. What do I need this for?"

"You meant an animal," I said pedantically. "Describe it."

"I don't want. I can't. I am fed up."

"Then you will remain like a cripple, an invalid."

He took off his glasses and wiped his forehead with his bandaged arm. His naked eyes gazed at me in silence for a long time. My face must have looked to him like a pale blur, but it felt as if fingers were exploring it curiously, gently, in wonder. I sat up straight, like a person conscious of being photographed, and unwittingly smiled at him as into a camera.

He put his glasses back on and the spell was broken. The face that was so charming in its serenity was gone. "She loves water," he said.

"Who?"

"The animal."

"A fish."

He smiled. "Loves water, not lives in water." He looked cheerful, as if it was a guessing game. "She goes in water but breathes air like me. She puts eggs like chicken."

"Lays, you mean, lays eggs," I said. "A water bird?"

"No. Instead of skin she has something very hard."

"Armor."

"Ah, yes—armor, like tanks."

"Right," I said. "That's a turtle. Turtles have armor. It's called a shell."

"Turtle," he said. "I speak Hebrew like turtle."

"Huda?" Mother was calling softly from the stairs.

I started. The ice cubes had melted and were floating like tiny islands in the bowl. "Mother," I called out and my voice sounded full of joy. "I'm coming down."

I went out on the roof and saw the stars, the harbor lights and the crescent moon above the summit of the Carmel. Mother was a dark form in the doorway. "You laughed," she said in wonder.

"Yes," I said quietly.

*Chapter  Twelve*

On our father's side, our origins begin with Grandpa's childhood and boyhood, unless it's a myth, like all stories of origins. Grandpa Elias grew up in an empty shack, some distance from a Coptic village in Upper Egypt. His father, brothers and sisters worked in the sugarcane fields of a feudal lord who lived in Cairo and had a mansion in the village. There was no school in the place, and Grandpa only visited the village itself on holidays. The hovel he grew up in stood on the bank of a canal which drew its water from the Nile, and that was his entire world. He could not even remember his mother's name. She died when he was small, and he was brought up by his sisters.

After one harvest the stacks of sugar cane rotted outside the shack. No one came to gather them. Death hovered on the Nile and the epidemic reached the village. Bodies lay in the paths. One day a cow came to the shack, lowing in agony with its udders bursting. They milked it and drank, then slaughtered the animal and ate it. There was no sense in keeping it or looking for its owners, who must have died in the epidemic. Or perhaps his father knew that death would soon catch up with them too. This was the first time he tasted meat. Then he helped his father bury his brothers and sisters. Seeing him cry, his father said it wouldn't get him off doing the job. When he buried his father he was free to cry to his heart's content. The epidemic had spared his father, but a strange death took him—he swelled up, he lay on the torn rush matting and went on swelling. At night the son slept out of doors because of the ghastly smell. When his father stopped begging for water the son knew his time had come to join his sons and daughters. The next day he bathed in the canal and put on his father's robe.

A year later another family came to work his family's plot, convinced that none of them had survived. When they found him with his green eyes and his father's robe they thought he was a ghost and scattered howling through the canefield. The next day they returned with an improvised cross made of two sticks tied together. He was glad to see that they were Christians like himself, but they interpreted his smile as an attempt to draw them into an evil snare. Two days later the men alone returned, bringing with them the new local priest. They stood some distance away on the quickest escape route and watched the priest, who advanced toward him, drawing courage from the heavy cross he was holding up. He must have been eleven years old then, or maybe fourteen—he didn't know for sure. Whichever it was, the priest himself didn't believe that such a young lad could have cultivated the big plot all by himself. Nor could he, but what he had achieved struck them as unnatural. They were also taken aback by the three goats behind the shack. The village elders said that his father had been a pauper and did not own so much as a plucked chicken. He was afraid to tell them that the goats had wandered over from the plague-stricken village, as the cow had done. The cross in the priest's hands shook and he kept staring into the boy's green eyes to force them down. He ordered the boy to walk ahead and show him the graves. The men followed behind, making a rustling noise. The priest stopped before the graves in horror, torn between the impulse to flee and his duty to the church, which was to hit the boy with the heavy cross and dispatch him to the darkness whence he'd come. "Which grave is yours?" he roared at the boy.

The boy understood the question at once. There should have been twelve graves, the old one of his mother and eleven more of his father, brothers and sisters. Instead there was a row of thirteen graves. "The number of all of you together!" the priest shouted. He raised the cross and drew a great semicircle embracing the field and canal, the shack, the graves and the boy. Greatly daring, the boy kept his eyes wide open and refused to succumb to the priest's arc of death. He had the advantage of knowing the secret of the extra grave. After they had eaten the cow his father was filled with anxiety, and it was he who suggested this way of hiding the bones. For who would think to search for them in the graves at the height of an epidemic which had already devoured the gravediggers themselves? Now, standing before a priest armed with a cross, he did not even recall which of the hummocks hid the cow's bones. He could hardly open all of them to prove that he was not buried there. Standing in front of the cross he repeated stubbornly, "I'm not dead, I never died!" But in the eyes of the law and the church register he was dead. The priest was afraid to pinch him and find out, and he and the men left the plot quickly. No one else tried to claim the plot or to cultivate it. For about two years he was a proper ghost, and on his weekly visits to the village the inhabitants would scatter and hide. Only the storekeeper, seeing real produce and real money in his hand, did business with him and knew the truth, though it suited him to keep his mouth shut.

In time the other villagers realized that he really was a living person, but he remained a singularity. One day some children wandered into the canefield, or perhaps ventured onto the path in order to torment him. Having pestered him enough, they jumped into the canal to swim, and one of them drowned. The boys were convinced that he had dived under the surface and deliberately pulled their companion down to his death. They abandoned him and ran back to the village. A little later, walking down the path carrying the child he'd rescued, he met the family accompanied by men armed with cutlasses and the priest walking in front. They were sure that he had raised the boy from the dead, and he did not deny it. By then he knew well the effect of his green eyes and tall figure, and the extent of their stupidity.

His new standing as sorcerer and healer was much pleasanter than that of ghost. He made a good living. Women consulted the solitary young man on matters of the heart and barrenness. Seeing them leaving his shack with fresh hope shining in their eyes he began to believe that he possessed secret powers. Had there been a school in the village he might have understood that his superiority over them was nothing more than a better brain. His new position intensified his desire for women and money. At times he believed that he was the god of that wretched nook of poverty and ignorance. And that was how he received my grandmother Munira, my father's mother. Like the cow whose bones were buried among the family graves, and the three goats now in his backyard, she too had left the prosperous world and wandered into his appreciative arms. He did not know if he really loved her, though there were times when she was dearer to him than his life, but he couldn't love her humanly, because he was never sure that she would stay with him. She had run to him from the decaying mansion and her dissipated, gonorrheal gambler of a father, herself infected with the damnable disease which he had already experienced, having caught it from the women whose husbands worked in rich houses in Cairo and came home for the holidays, bringing presents as well as the infection. But he hadn't known you could catch it from a father. She knew. That was also why she knew her father wouldn't come after her.

She stayed in the shack and recovered and became pregnant and drove the village women out of the yard. At her side he longed for the touch of the earth, the feel of water flowing on bare feet. For all his conceit, he knew very well how helpless a village sorcerer would be faced with the might of the mansion. He assumed that sooner or later she would also recover from her love for him and fly away. Even when she crouched on the mat to give birth he feared that she would throw the newborn into his arms and flee from the shame, and in time would marry a mansion dweller who didn't know about her disgrace. How would he look after a squalling infant by himself? These fears prevented him from seeing the approach of death. Already there were three black-clad figures sitting before the shack, waiting for the moment to start wailing, and he did not see or understand that the birth had become a death. When he saw it in her eyes he said to her mentally, Now, Lady Munira, you will never escape me. He dug the grave quickly to finish it before sundown, then he straightened his back, looked at the canal and knew that everything was at an end. Himself too. He realized how much he had loved her, and that she'd come to him of her own will and stayed with him from love, not by his sorcery. The three women wailed while he carried her down into the grave, where he crouched and held her on his lap and prayed that the earth would cover him too. He began to sweep it in from the margins, until his feet were buried. Suddenly the wailing of the women stopped and he heard my father cry and something crawling through the thicket. He stood up in the grave and roared. These were not mourners but spies from the mansion who had come to murder an unwanted heir. He ran after them but they fled in fright.

From that moment on my father was never out of his arms. He held him in his left arm while with the right he finished the mother's burial. That night he heard them stealing her corpse, and the following night they came and set fire to his shack, unaware that he'd crept out and was hiding with the baby in the reeds, together with a goat to milk for the infant. The third night they returned with knives. That was when he had to kill a man.

The Nile carried him with the baby and the goat all the way to Cairo. There they lived in a terrible stench. That was what he remembered most of the big city with its many lights. By day he worked as a garbage collector with a Coptic crew with donkeys, the baby always strapped to his body, and by night he slept in the cemetery. The buzzing mosquitoes and the groans of the sick prevented him from listening to the rustle of the murderers' approach. They would know where to look for a Coptic fellah who fled to the city, and they did. He didn't wait till dawn. He had sold the goat before anyone stole it, because in the city milk could be had for money, as well as milk powder, which a Coptic mother had showed him.

Two weeks later he stood on the eastern bank of the Suez Canal, because he'd heard that one could follow the railway all the way to Palestine. By night he walked on the sleepers and by day he slept with the baby among the dunes. On the third day he had no water left for the milk powder, so he chewed dates and fed them to the baby. But the child grew weaker. He, who had grown up beside endless water, had never imagined such an end.

He wondered about God who helped them to evade the murderers only to kill them in the desert. In later years he understood that he had won the things that mattered to him through challenging God and fate, but at the time he begged heaven for mercy. He was about to lay the dying child under a bush and leave the responsibility in God's hands when, in despair, he decided to use his sorcerer's magic to force God to open his eyes and show him a source of water. He stood on the tracks and closed his eyes and forced himself to reach the great calm which is so essential in magic, then he commanded the water. But the water did not materialize.

In the morning he was afraid to look at the baby, not wanting to see him dead. Suddenly he felt someone looking at him, turned around and saw a Bedouin with a bundle on his back. "Where did you find him? He's still alive, Allah be praised," the Bedouin said, as if a brief glance was all he needed, and turned east. He hastened to pick up his son and followed the man. "He's my son," he said to the Bedouin's back. "His mother died."

On the third day of his stay with the Bedouins a strange rumbling was heard rising from deep in the ground. The Bedouins hurriedly moved their encampment from the slope to the top of the hill, where they stood and watched the mighty torrent that rushed through the wadi. He pressed the child to his heart and whispered, "Son, the blessing of the Nile has caught up with us, the river is following us."

And I, Huda, his granddaughter, have inherited his green sorcerer's eyes, but I haven't the power to enchant anyone. Only Alex says I'm beautiful.

## Chapter Thirteen

Alex probably expected me to stay with him on the roof for several hours, maybe even spend the night, as the young Jews do. Saturday night he played the trumpet till late, long after sleep overcame the wadi. Mother and Grandpa did not mind the trumpet. They didn't know much about music, but they respected Alex's ability to produce the sounds. When he was out they were tense and waited for his footsteps. Then they would go to bed like children whose sleep has been exorcised of wolves and demons. Alex's fanfares drove out their fear of Zuhair. Needless to say, I was proud and enjoyed the praise they lavished on him.

Once Mother said in some puzzlement, "Such times we live in! We find protection in the yowling of a Jewish trumpet."

"When it rains, any roof will do," Grandpa responded. As usual, they talked to each other as if to themselves. Mary had gone out with Wahid and I listened to their soft chat while watching television. Mother got up and made a cup of tea for Grandpa. From the corner of my eye I saw her body rubbing against his arm, which rested like a living creature on the edge of the table, basking in the light touch. The wrinkles on Grandpa's face smiled as he noisily slurped the hot tea. I closed my eyes and imagined him older and somewhat ill, sitting in the big tub in the shower stall, with the hot water bucket beside him. That's how he always bathes, as he doesn't like to take a shower. I see him in my mind's eye taking water from the bucket but being too weak to raise it, his arm droops on the bucket's edge. He remains seated in the tub, unmoving, feeling the cold, his body getting smaller and smaller. Mother paces nervously outside the door. There's no sound of splashing, the silence grows weighty and the urge to go in gets stronger, but the inhibitions are stronger still.

"Are you bathing?" she asks.

"I'm cold," he whispers.

"So wash quickly and come out. I've made your bed. Added another blanket."

"I'm cold, woman."

Her voice is shaking, as if she's cold herself, but it's a different chill. "Come out of the water and get dressed."

"I smell. A smelly old man."

"I'm coming in."

Silence.

"I'll wash you."

Silence.

Her tremulous fingers grip the door-handle, she rubs her cheek on her shoulder as she always does when she's agitated, then pushes the door open as if rolling away a great boulder from the mouth of a cave . . .

My eyes were on the book that lay on my lap even in front of the television. I daydreamed and smiled. They took no notice of me. I went to the kitchen and stuffed labaneh into two pitas, put them on a plate, with a handful of black olives, shining like happy children's eyes, covered everything with an embroidered napkin and slipped out. He wasn't there. He must have gone out and I didn't notice. The door was locked and its silent obstruction put me off. It was not like the bathroom door. I left the offering beside it and tiptoed down.

Mother and Grandpa were still absorbed in their murmuring chat. I put the book back on my lap and watched the film they were watching. I tried to join in their talk to cover up my sortie, but remained left out. For years they've talked to each other exclusively and their conversation flows like a river. I asked myself if I was missing Alex and said no. We miss a person who's left an impression and an imprint, someone with whom we've had a powerful experience. Finally I admitted to myself that I was longing for him more than I'd longed for any flesh-and-blood man for years.

I was shaken awake by the rattle of the plate on the roof. I opened the door and hurried upstairs because I knew at once what had happened. Jamilla's tomcat dropped the piece of pita he was chewing and retreated, his eyes glowing in the dark. I ran after him, cursing him for a son of a bitch, slipped on an olive and fell. Crouching, hugging my bruised knee, I shook my fist at him, "Just wait! I'll catch you yet!" But the cat slunk disdainfully to the doorway.

I followed him, smiling to myself despite the pain in my knee. I'd got so worked up because of a man's meal. I felt I was fit and strong and a woman.

Mother was waiting for me in our doorway, her eyes darting down the stairs in fear of Zuhair. "Why did you scream on the roof?" she asked, looking at the plate in my hands. I didn't know how to explain it. "The cat," I said and went into the kitchen. I left the plate in the sink and went into my room. Mother followed me, pointed at Mary's empty bed and asked, "Can I sit?"

I nodded, though I was not in the least receptive at that moment to a mother-daughter chat. We were both confused. In my teens I heard from some of my Jewish friends that their mothers didn't just lecture and warn them, but sometimes held real conversations with them on matters of the heart and even about things that had been done. Shirley informed her mother the evening she lost her virginity. The mother got "awfully excited," Shirley said, beaming. "Oh, I must tell your father. He'll go crazy when he hears that his little girl . . ." Shirley said they both burst out laughing. But Mother didn't know what to say, didn't know how to start. If I'd offered her a different topic for conversation she'd have grasped at it with relief.

"You're not angry with me?" she fumbled.

"Of course not." I read poetry, and in my own eyes I'm no different from any other woman, in Tel Aviv or in London. Nevertheless, I waited patiently for her to lecture me. Perhaps I wanted her to, perhaps I really wished that someone would come and block this impossible road.

"You're already mature."

"Almost old. It doesn't bother me. I'm used to it."

"It hurts me," she said. She got up, took a cigarette from Mary's pack and offered the pack to me.

"I don't smoke."

She inhaled and choked. She rarely smoked. "Should I be happy or worried? Huda, I'm ashamed to ask."

I couldn't go on making her suffer. "There isn't anything, Mother. Maybe I'm just dreaming."

Her anxiety dispelled, she stood up for my dignity. "Who does he think he is? Where will he find someone like you? Huda, a woman's a woman, she can always tell how a man feels."

"You saw me. An empty plate. The cat spoilt what was on it."

"I meant that he's a Jew and you're an Arab. Have you thought it through?"

"Come in, Grandpa," I called, knowing he was listening behind the door. Grandpa came in and sat on the bed beside Mother, rubbing his eyes with his fists, as if struggling with sleep. He even gave a loud musical yawn, but I wasn't taken in. "Grandpa, what do you think about an Arab woman with a Jew?"

"Won't work," he said.

I smiled with relief. "Then that's that," I replied.

He took one of Mary's cigarettes. "I didn't say that. One of you will have to give in."

"He couldn't be an Arab even if he wanted to."

"I know."

"So I must forget that I'm Arab?"

"In time, he'll forget that he was Russian. I forgot that I was Egyptian. But do you honestly believe you could be a Jew? The dogs on both sides will sink their teeth into you. Do you have the strength for that?"

I wasn't blind. In a country torn by antagonisms and living in a state of war it isn't possible to cultivate an oasis of love on the border between two nations seeking to strangle each other. In Bahij's room hung a colored poster showing a Palestinian man and woman armed with Kalashnikovs, their proud faces grim and their eyes filled with revenge. That woman wouldn't hesitate to riddle my body with her assault rifle. In her vengeful eyes I've been a traitor for a long time. Nor are the Jews innocent angels. They're suckled on hate from nursery school. Once grown up, they prepare themselves for war and think a lot about their own death and about killing the man and woman in the poster.

"Mother," I said, knowing the question was unfair, as it was I who had to make the decision, "Mother, would it bother you?"

"If it will be good for you I'll kiss him on the forehead every day. I myself didn't believe I would get married and have children. After the family was deported I lived in Acre and felt like a stranger in a town where there were almost no young men left. Your grandfather stopped me in the street and pointed to his son. I only wanted to have children. I was afraid to be like the empty city. When I was carrying you I didn't suffer from morning sickness, but I used to make a noise like I was throwing up, for everyone to hear. I went out into the street twenty times a day, so everyone would see. In the hospital the nurse said to me, scream, scream if you want to, I didn't scream. The body was suffering but it was so good. The other women screamed to high heaven and some cursed their husbands. I had only one thought in my head—that I might scare you if I screamed. I called the doctor to come and check your pulse while you were still inside. They laughed at me. I said, go ahead, laugh. And the pains—only God could invent such a thing. Like two wild horses in your body, each pulling a different way and they won't rest till they tear you apart. I said, go on, pull, tear. The nurse came and said bear down. Why should I bear down, I asked. For the baby to come out. Me, bear down on the baby I didn't believe would be mine? Let them pull and tear. Another one came in and they started to squeeze my belly and I cried for the first time, careful! Careful! Suddenly I heard you. I rested my hands on the sheet and sat up. You were God, I hope He forgives me. You think pregnancy ends with the birth? That's when the second pregnancy begins, the important one, the long one, which goes on to the grave. The whole world becomes a big womb and you suck and crawl and walk and grow and become a woman, but you'll always be my unborn baby."

I patted her smoking hand. "You were always a good mother."

"You don't understand. If Alex is meant for you, take him away from here. This country is cursed. This soil is not a good womb in which to bring up children."

I laughed. "He hasn't said anything yet. And he has a girl friend."

"She's in Russia, and that's far away."


On Friday he told me he was going to visit his parents in his boss's pickup truck and would come back to pick me up. I nodded, but he wanted an explicit agreement.

"All right," I said. "We'll meet at Solel Boneh. I don't want us to be seen in the wadi."

"Is it dangerous? Is it true Arabs kill the girls?"

"Not all the Arabs and not when things can be arranged between the couple."

"I don't want them to hurt you."

I said to myself, Only you can hurt me. Aloud I said, "They won't. They already know."

He was surprised. I thought he looked displeased to hear that the family already knew something he was still unsure about.

At nine-thirty he waited for me in the pickup beside Solel Boneh's marble edifice. He was tense and drove wildly. At the Nevi'im intersection he cursed another driver. On steep Balfour Street the engine groaned aloud and he slapped the wheel and grumbled, "Not pulling, not pulling. Shitty car."

I looked down and even my dress looked faded in the passing lights. The thrill of expectation dispelled and my spirits fell. I wanted to go home.

"Parents," he said. "Every visit crying. Mother sick, always sick. She takes pills and wants to punish whole world. Father weak. He should hit her."

"A sick woman?"

"She already quarreled with everybody, doctors and nurses and neighbors. Threw father out of room. Crazy, she was always crazy." He held the wheel with one hand and pulled at his shirt with the other. "Look, she tore my clothes. She says it is my fault they put her in old-age home. She wants to leave. She heard I have room and yells I am waiting for her to die among old people. Traitor, traitor, she shouted at me. All the fruits I brought she threw in my face. Father stood outside in cold by tree, afraid to go into room. I am sure he had temperature and did not tell."

His shirt was in fact torn. Some buttons had been pulled out and there were pink scratches on his chest.

"Because of clothes we can't go to place with people," he said. "What will they think of you going with somebody like this?"

"We could've sat in your room."

His eyes turned to me, as though mistrusting my words. I remembered rides with Bahij. "Go up to the university," I said. "There's a nice place on the mountain. You can see the whole valley as far as Nahariyah, like from a plane."

"There are no people there?"

"Only couples in cars."

He parked near a clump of shrubs. Below were spread the lights of Jewish and Arab towns and villages as far as the Lebanese border. I opened the window and put out my head, bathing my face in the soft wind, and thought I could hear the rustling of the stars in the silence. It was years since I'd been here. I loved this quiet observation point, where there were usually no more than three or four lovers' cars. The silence and solitude used to trouble Bahij and he did not hide his fear. Whenever a car approached looking for a place to park he would take his hands from my body and say, laughing, "Here they can strip us naked. They won't even need a knife to scare us. What Arab couple has ever complained to the police about being attacked in a makeout point?" His nervous laugh would extinguish the stars, lower an opaque curtain over the twinkling lights below. The chorus of crickets surrounded us like evil whisperers.

Now I smiled at the stars. I stuck my head out further and smelled the wind which brought the scents of pine trees and the sea. I was in the company of a fearless man who had beaten Zuhair and was a Jew. It's true he's a new immigrant, but even he already felt that the stars and the smell of the sea belonged to him. He sat still and smoked, and I glanced at his profile and back at the stars. My forehead was moist with dew. I was so relaxed. It had been a long time since I had known such pleasure, to the point of forgetting my body, till I forgot that a lonely man was sitting beside me, hungry for comfort.

A rough and heavy hand dropped on my thigh. I froze. My head was outside and my body inside, and I felt I'd been cut in two and didn't know how to put the halves together again. But that was not how Alex interpreted my immobility. His fingers closed on my thigh like a vise and pulled it to him. I didn't dare turn my head. I was afraid to touch his fingers as if they were snakes. I was gripped by something stronger than fear. A tremor began where his fingers gripped me which spread and shook me all over, sending hot and cold waves through my body. I remember that in the midst of these agonies I also felt profoundly ashamed of myself. It was my body which was to blame, not his hands.

His voice was hoarse. "You're still afraid of me."

My head was still disconnected from my body. I was two beings, of which one, abashed and anxious about its femaleness, squawked, "No . . . no . . . It's all right." His free arm encircled my back, grasped my trembling shoulder and pulled my swooning body over to his muscles. My other being had become a lifeless bird in terror of the touch of his hand on my thigh. Perhaps that was why I didn't understand that he wanted to kiss my mouth and my head sank until my face was almost on his lap. He uttered a grating sort of laugh, his fingers let go of my thigh, moved to his fly and unzipped it. His body twitched backward, and out of the darkness, like a dragon, sprang a predatory creature I had only ever seen in pictures.

"You like this?" he said. "You can. I like it also."

I still didn't comprehend, until he directed and moved my mouth toward the menacing dragon in the dark. A fear I'd never known before combined my two beings and I grabbed his thigh with both hands and recoiled back in my seat. The dragon moved in search of its prey.

"What happened? What is wrong?" he asked.

I had almost no control over my voice. "No . . . nothing."

"I thought . . ." He straightened up, returned the dragon to its lair and closed the zipper. I was relieved to see that he did not intend to trouble me again. His face caught the lights of the university and moved away from me. His hands were steady when he lit a cigarette. I was pleased that his voice too sounded firm. "You . . . not men?" He reverted to the broken Hebrew which might have concealed mockery or offended confusion.

I shrugged and said nothing.

"You only have to say what is true. I am short, I am ugly—I can swallow that."

"I didn't say you were ugly."

"No? Sure! I am good looking like mad. So why you jumped back from me?" His fingers lingered irritably on the car lighter. "We will go home."

"No."

He looked at me for a long time. "You want to laugh at me more?" Then he noticed my distress. "You sick? You tremble like in malaria."

"I'm not used to this," I managed to say.

"You are already woman. You must have . . ."

I was not accustomed to holding such a conversation with a man. I turned to look out and let out a scream. A black form stood close to the side of the car, the white of its eyes gleaming in the dark.

"What is it?" Alex shouted.

"Outside, outside," I whispered in alarm.

In a second he was outside and chasing after the form which leapt among the rocks like a wild boar. I feared for him. Then a terror seized me. He'd left me alone. What if another one appeared? I heard him yelling and throwing a stone. I thought to myself, what if he beats up another Arab for my sake, the sake of an Arab woman? He came back grumbling and cursing in Russian. "All his clothes black. Coat black, even his hat black."

I felt better. It was not likely to be an Arab Peeping Tom, not in such clothes.

"We're going back home."

"I'll come up tomorrow and take your shirt to mend."

## Chapter Fourteen

I got out on Solel Boneh Square and he drove off to return the pickup. I fancied I saw the dew falling like a blessing on the sleeping wadi, washing the roofs, flushing the pavements. I felt so light, as if on a floating magic carpet. I passed Caesarea Street and didn't even notice the dark corners which always terrified me at night. I am not a stranger in my neighborhood, my city, my world. I have grown up here and it's all part of me, the sea and the houses and two tail-waving cats and the odor of the pita bakery. I am like a cloud in the wadi, enveloping everything, the dreams of the sleepers and the thoughts of the waking.

When Alex stopped the vehicle and leaned over to open the door for me he saw that I did not recoil from his arm which rubbed against my breasts, and stopped and looked into my eyes. His lips were on mine for a brief eternal moment. My lips did not respond, nor did they reject. My face still felt the bristles of his beard, the smell of tobacco, the touch of his nose. A man's real face was on my face, and I was walking in the wadi feeling so brave. Yet I wanted no one to observe this glow, for fear that it would be taken away from me. I hoped Grandpa and Mother didn't wake up when I came in, and that Mary was back and sleeping.

I opened and locked the door very softly. I tiptoed to the bathroom and stood before the mirror, looking at my new face. I smiled at it warmly. I was proud of it, and it smiled back at me with joy, with the smugness of a pregnant belly. I took with me the mirror face and went into the bedroom without turning on the light. Mary was on her bed, her blanket partly trailing on the floor and partly covering her long thighs. I undressed in the weak light that came in through the blind, slipped into my bed and quietly pulled up the covers. Sleep was far away. Indeed, I didn't want it. I was afraid it would deprive me of the new face I'd seen in the mirror. I crossed my arms under my head and from the joyous heights of the evening surveyed the arid desert of the years I had passed. I had been a corpse pulled by an invisible rope across the wilderness, and had expected to go on being pulled in this way until my breasts dried up and my belly shriveled and the flesh dropped off my bones, which would be scattered along the dismal route of despair.

I passed my tongue over my lips that had felt a man's kiss. The laugh that rose in my breast remained there, as I meant to relish it for a long time. Alex and I were on these lips. The taste of my sweat and his. The lips are the gate of the body. Life enters and exists through them. And Alex and I were embraced on the threshold.

"You'll drill holes in the ceiling with those looks," said Mary in a wide-awake voice.

"You're not asleep?"

"Are you in shock?"

"No, I feel good," I said. "I feel good," I repeated. Now I wanted her to share in my happiness.

But Mary was swimming in a different sea. "Huda," she said, "you remember I once worked for a couple of months as a pilgrims' guide in Nazareth? From tomb to tomb, from church to church, from moldy ruin to smelly excavation. Germans and Americans thrilled to bits, cameras clicking, ancient hymns. How I loathed them. I felt like a madam displaying her crooked girls as if they were beauty queens, but the customers are blind and can't see."

"Wahid again?"

"He's like those pilgrims. Instead of churches and tombs I offer him neck and tits and arse. My idiot is the weirdest tourist I've ever met. Wallah, he's an Orthodox Jew disguised as a Christian."

The laugh burst out of my breast, ringing merrily.

"Go on, laugh," she scolded me, amused and mournful. "They're also forbidden to go up on the Temple Mount because it's too holy. What can you do with an ahbal who sees a tit and thinks it's the dome of a church, touches an arse and thinks he's on the Mount of the Leap? Tonight we hit a new record. After two hours of hit-and-run foreplay, his eyes rolled up and a weird noise came from his throat, he couldn't control himself, begged my pardon and ran to the sea. The noise was louder than the waves, as if a herd of horses were pissing, not one single man. Niagara Falls." She collapsed laughing, jumped into my bed and butted my belly with her head. Her laughter was like a spray of petals. "Mary, Mary," I said with intense affection and kissed her forehead.

"Huda!" she was stunned. "You kissed me of your own accord. You're different." She sat cross-legged and held up a finger. "So, there has been some progress," she continued in the playful tone. "A man who dares to piss near a sacred shrine has already taken a step in the right direction. In the next two weeks he's got to do the rape, if I have to inject cement into his broomstick. The bastard in my belly is already screaming for a legal father." She laid her hands on my shoulders and leaned forward. "How about an aromatic, refreshing cup of coffee? Eh?"

"With pleasure."

"Why me?" she exclaimed. "Aren't you in the seventh heaven now? So stir yourself, don't be lazy."

When I came back with the coffee she was still sitting cross-legged, her back straight. "Now you tell me," she said, her eyes sparkling. "How did Abu-trumpet play for you?"

"He kissed me," I said proudly.

She choked on the coffee. "And you didn't faint?"

"No." Then my smile died. "Mary, your mother-in-law is an angel compared to Alex's mother. She threw his father out into the cold night and attacked Alex."

"Unbelievable—attacked Abu-trumpet? If he didn't tear her apart she must be the champion weight lifter of the USSR."

"She's aggressively mad."

"Allah preserve us."

"On top of which, she'll always regard me as an Arab whom she can step on. And I am not you."

"You can count on me—if war breaks out I'll be your chief of staff."

"It isn't funny."

"Why not? With laughter you can kill elephants." She raised her head and listened. "Abu-trumpet's coming up the stairs. Why don't we sneak up and visit him?"

I put her off. "I've had enough for one evening."

The following day, a Saturday, I lost my nerve. Without Mary's strong urging, I wouldn't have kept my promise to go up and mend his shirt. Mary saw me to the door and waved her hand to drive me up the stairs, whispering, "Yallah! Yallah!"

Once on the roof I froze. It must have rained in the night. Everything was gleaming, looking quite different in the sun's dazzling radiance. Even the feelings were not the same. The door of his room was closed and looked uninviting. Maybe he's still sleeping, naked on his bed? I was tempted to turn back, but knew that Mary was lurking downstairs. I went up to the door and listened. Not a sound. I thought I'd sit on the barrel for ten minutes, then go down and make up some story for Mary. But I'm a poor liar and Mary's a first-rate interrogator. I did what they do in films—I cleared my throat.

"Come in, the door is not locked."

I would have preferred him to come and open the door with a smile. When I went in he didn't even rise from the table, which was strewn with papers. "I did not believe you would come."

Having grown up in a family whose only breadwinner was Grandpa, who lacked special skills and earned a pittance, my senses were sharp enough to know that there was no food in the place. Other than a thick residue of coffee in a cup, there wasn't even a slice of bread in the room.

"When did you last eat?" I asked.

He pointed at a chair. "Sit, sit—what is that?" He pointed at the sewing basket I put on the table.

I blushed. Mother embroidered everything, obsessively, harking back to her grand youth—sheets, tablecloths, pillowcases, curtains and countless napkins with which to wrap things. Grandpa used to say that it wasn't safe to expose an area of skin in our house, or Mother would pounce on it and start embroidering. My sewing things were covered with an embroidered napkin in a little wicker basket, and Alex must have thought that I had brought him some breakfast.

"You're hungry," I stammered.

"I'm going down to buy something. On Saturday everything is open in wadi."

I got up. "Don't move. I'll get you something."

He took hold of my wrist and made me sit down again. "Wait," he said. My hand was still in his. I didn't know what to do with it. He held it loosely, as if leaving me to decide. It would have been over-bold to bring our hands to my hips, and silly to leave them hanging in midair. Our eyes met and we smiled. His thumb parted from his palm and stroked the back of my hand as if unintentionally. "She always does this to me. Forces me to shout at her and curse and look like I want to kill her. But from all her provocations, her beatings and my torn clothes, I only remember her tears. From when I was little child, I swim in her tears. But it is only her manipulation of me, of her son. She did not cry when they took Papa to prison in Russia. Nobody saw her cry when they took away the house also. Nobody saw her cry even when she went to prison. She was there years, but nobody saw one tear in her eyes. All the tears she left for me, and I swim in them. And I can tell you, even now her tears are right. She says I buried her when she is still living. She is old but still did not have life. Did not have time. Suddenly she is in old-age home with old people."

"How old is she?"

"Almost seventy. Sick, but she looks like sixty or even less. Yesterday she bit off red polish from fingernails with her teeth, all the time yelling, for who, for who. Around her they are pushing half-dead old people in wheelchairs, some people walking with difficulty on paths. Women with swelling belly and mustache, breathing like fishes. One man stood on grass in water from sprinkler and yelled Help me, like child in rain. One old woman opened her legs and pissed standing up. But Mother painted her hair and put polish on nails for Sabbath and for my visit."

"And your father," I said. "He's with her, isn't he? Doesn't he help her?"

"She is very angry with him. He was in prison many years. There you learn to live in all conditions. In Israel they gave him job, but now he cannot work, and he cannot take care of Mother or do shopping. He is happy in old-age home. He tells Mother that old-age home is like deluxe hotel, but she throws him out of room. He has friends there, so he runs to them all the time. All week she waits with dry eyes, and pours all the tears when I come. I think yesterday she did on purpose. She knows I will be sorry, and today I will have to go to her again. That is her tactic."

His cracked lips were almost white. The stubs in the ashtray before him were like a heap of twisted corpses. He took his glasses off with his right hand. Wanting to rub his eyes with his left he realized he was still holding my hand. He smiled and let go.

I stood up. "I'll get you something to eat."

"One minute. That is what I want to speak to you. I study and work and all the time I eat crap here and there. I can pay. I can pay good like for two people. The food of your mother is fantastic. Shame to spend money in restaurants, and I don't like restaurants. It is like orphanage. Your mother will agree?"

I tried to think for Mother. A bit more money won't hurt, but what of the distant past and her pride? "I don't know," I replied. I wanted to say that if she didn't agree, I'd cook his meals here on the roof, but I did not. "Why don't we go down and you ask her? Ever since you got rid of Zuhair she can't think what to do for you."

"And your grandfather, he will not say no?"

I smiled. "He likes you."

I need not have worried. Mother no sooner heard his suggestion than she made him sit at the table and stuffed him till he was full. Meanwhile Grandpa looked out of the window and hummed an ancient tune. He turned to Mother and said to her in Arabic, his voice filled with sweet sadness, "Soon we'll be left alone in this house."

Mother glanced at Alex, who this time was eating in a leisurely and moderate manner, and asked, as if addressing the air, "So what do you say?"

"You are speaking Arabic," said Alex. "I know you are speaking about me."

"True," said Grandpa. "Some things you have to say in your own language, otherwise it's like eating food without salt."

"That is true," Alex agreed wholeheartedly. "So what do you say?"

We burst out laughing. I hastened to explain to Alex that that was precisely what Mother had said, word for word, in Arabic.

"Son," said Grandpa, "you must learn Arabic."

"First I must get on in Hebrew," Alex replied.

He asked Mother to name the payment for his meals, but Mother was ashamed and stammered and then refused, so in the end he proposed the amount, which struck her as too high. Then Alex put the money on the table, to show there was to be no arguing. Mother said to Grandpa, "It's excessive—and from whom? From someone who may become Huda's husband."

Grandpa did not bother to demonstrate generosity. "You needn't feel ashamed. You'll feed him like a king and he'll lick his fingers and thank you."

"And if they do marry—then I am robbing Huda."

"Meantime you're just fattening him a little for her. Nothing has happened yet, it may all blow away like a balloon. At any moment he may pack his trumpet and scamper off without fanfare. You've seen his trousers and sandals. Everything he owns shows he's a man who travels light."

"Is that what you think?" she asked, alarmed.

"I have to think everything. Even the most devout person, who prays and fasts and obeys all the rules can't be sure that he's got God in his pocket. If he has any sense, he'll act like a sensible atheist and remember Satan, who turns Allah's sweet grapes into rotten vinegar."

I heard him and my spirits fell. His entire speech, uttered with such conviction, was meant for my ears. He wanted to cool my enthusiasm. A man like Grandpa, who walked barefoot for so many years of his life, does not float in the air. And here I was in my intangible kingdom, building castles in the air. I became depressed. Indeed, Alex hadn't yet said an unequivocal word. He's sniffing around me without committing himself. But is he? Surely it is I who've been sniffing around like an eager hunter. So he put his hand on my thigh. His lips touched mine. What man wouldn't do this to an available woman? If he told me about his mother who tore his shirt, it was because he is a candid man with the soul of a child, who has not yet learned to feel embarrassed.


Naturally it was I who took him his breakfasts and suppers. On the second day he said the food was sticking in his throat.

"It isn't good?"

"You are not waitress and I am not important man."

The next day he came to eat with us. He brought a small notebook in which he wrote the new words he heard in our conversations. At first I didn't like to interrupt and correct him, but he insisted. He also took better care of his appearance. He appeared shaved and scrubbed, his shirts neat and his trousers clean. I told him about the first visit of Wahid and his family, when they came to ask for Mary's hand.

"I remember," he said. "I came to you in middle . . ."

"Broke in."

"Broke in," he repeated and wrote it down in the notebook.

"That visit of Wahid's family ended dismally."

"In happiness?"

"No, in sadness."

"That is what will be with my mother. Very sad and dismal, yob-tvoi-mat!"

"Can't we invite her to visit?"

"Invite her is possible. She will run. The question is, how to take her back to old-age home. I keep this address secret. She does not know where it is. If she knew, she would fly to come here. I know it is very crappy for son to do this to his mother. I feel like lousy criminal."

"At least we can visit her."

He stopped eating and looked at me attentively. "You are beautiful girl, very beautiful."

"Like Assya?"

"Assya? Beside you she is like celery, long with funny hair on top. But she is very good and with intelligent head like you. She is also very soft. More than soft. Like a soldier who throws away gun and puts his hands up. How do you say it?"

"Surrendering, giving in, meek."

"Meek. You can see immediately that she is meek. That is why Mother was not afraid of her. In the end she did dirty trick on her. But she will look at you, and all her guns and rockets will be in front. She will see immediately that it is serious."

I was pleased, but wanted to make sure. "I'll try not to let her see."

"Then she will see it on my face."

He is making good progress, I said to myself. "Alex, does it bother you that I am Arab and you're a Jew?"

"Assya was not a Jew. And what sort of Jew I am? I do not even know holidays. I mix up Purim and Kippurim. I could not understand one word when Mother and Papa talked Yiddish in Russia. I also did not want to come to Israel, not at all. Mother fixed up everything."

## Chapter Fifteen

Alex did not come to Israel because he was a Zionist. His mother, who today loathes Israel and would flee from it as from a leper colony, is considered a Zionist and enjoys the privileges of a "Prisoner of Zion." She was the one who maneuvered everything and brought him and his father against their will.

Alex's parents were originally from Poland. His father, who had been an Orthodox yeshivah scholar, exchanged one faith for another and joined the Communist underground. While not exactly brilliant, his tireless commitment raised him to the middle rank of the party. His mother, a rabbi's daughter, a sickly but intensely energetic woman, had no choice but to follow him. Before the Second World War the persecution of Communists intensified and she subsisted on handouts and waited for him when he was periodically arrested. As a reward for his devotion and suffering, the Party sent them both to the USSR for a period of recuperation and further education. His mother's parents had disowned her because of her husband and his secular religion. She herself didn't believe in it and cursed the revolutionaries who'd hoodwinked him. Twice she went to work to support the family, and undermined her health. Lying ill, gasping stertorously, she wished on him and his comrades the asthma that was choking her. Her body could not retain her unborn babies, and she thought of the lost fetuses as children killed by the Revolution. But despite her illness she remained good-looking. The father loved her and deferred to her, as he deferred to his superiors in the Party hierarchy. He didn't understand why she couldn't cheerfully endure their suffering and poverty. He thought she was demented, especially when she let loose a stream of coarse profanity. It is rare for a rabbi's daughter to curse like a common whore.

Alex's father moved about the Soviet Union like a rustic pilgrim in the Pope's court. He was deeply shocked by a slightly anti-Communist joke told by the woman guide who had been assigned to them. That such people still existed in the USSR after so many years of socialist education! The conscientious and compassionate man could not tolerate the presence of pork in the Holy Ark. He could barely wait till morning. At the office they assured him she would be taken care of appropriately. He returned to the hotel room, beaming with satisfaction and self-importance. "They trust me absolutely."

His wife was outraged. "She's a Jew," she cried, "and still a child. You've killed a poor girl. You're capable of selling me too."

"You?"

She fell silent. With her sharp senses and clear-headed realism she quickly gauged the nature of the place. Informers and secret agents did not get sent to the front. Her husband had at long last, if inadvertently, joined the ranks of the privileged. She was right. They were sent to a provincial town and her husband was given an undefined but very important position in a plant that produced tanks. She was pleased and almost contented. The comforts they now enjoyed almost made her believe in communism; at any rate, she was willing to justify its manifestations. Now she cursed the enemies of the regime with the same stunning coarseness. They got a spacious apartment, received important visitors, she bought warm clothes, and for the first time in their married life enjoyed other people's envious looks.

As the Nazi forces swept across the USSR, she felt that Hitler was waging war against her personally out of sheer meanness. In those days she was a passionate Soviet patriot. She quickly learned the language and eagerly took her husband's place at the plant when he was sent to other provinces. Her picture appeared several times in the local newspaper. Her husband was sometimes absent from home for weeks or even months. But she continued to miscarry. With open mouth and gasping lungs she would trudge back to the empty flat, filled with a sense of achievement. She regarded every tank that left the plant as the fruit of her own labor. She personally sent it forth to repel the forces of darkness. After a brief rest in the flat she would go out again into the snow, to fire workers' meetings with the flame that burned in her. She inspired the exhausted men and women with her passion, her persuasive gifts and a captivating delivery which combined deep thought with tavern coarseness. Her spirits did not flag when entire Soviet armies were defeated and Hitler's armored divisions swept over the land like an irresistible plague. She felt full of mighty powers to block his advance. Had she not clipped his wings in front of Moscow, destroyed his cohorts at Stalingrad, repelled his attacks on Leningrad? Her arms embraced the vast expanses of her new homeland, and the new homeland did not fail to reward her. She was decorated on flag-draped platforms, given a better flat, and did not lack for firewood and food even in the worst days.

While her own faith was growing stronger, she became aware that her husband, for some reason, was trying to efface himself. Between his long journeys and her activities they did not see much of each other. A part of her had always looked down on him, but even without self-deprecation she realized that their comforts and status were due to him. The war crushed and ground down whole cities, armies, communities, while she herself bloomed and grew handsomer. In years to come she would tell Alex that many courted her, but she would evade them with a smile and remained loyal to "that idiot." But at that time his father had not yet become an idiot. Nevertheless, he was changing. His passion ebbed, his body shrank, he would sit before the stove without uttering a word and suddenly wave his hand before his face, as though driving away a fly. One day she asked him if he'd read the reports about the sniper Misha, who had killed two hundred German soldiers. Killing Germans was a righteous act. "You remember where you came from? You think the Germans left a living soul in your house or my father's? A secret agent is a hundred times more dangerous than a common soldier that Misha kills. And you feel sorry for spies."

He said to her, "You remember that girl in Moscow, the one I informed on because of a childish little joke? She has been in a closed prison, and now is being sent to exile in Siberia. She's grown old. I destroyed her."

"So go and destroy the USSR, which has given us too much and bled and saved millions of Jews from extermination. If you were at the front and talked like this they'd have had you shot."

"I've asked to be sent to the front."

"You told them that you're planning to desert your post but you never consulted me?"

"You've become a heroine. They won't hurt you."

"And how they will. To get at you."

"Anyway, they refused me."

"But it's on record. They'll bring it up against you when it suits them. And just now, when the Red Army has entered Poland, when it's time to get a bit of rest!"


Six years passed before they brought this up against him as she predicted. One day, some five years after the end of the war, he disappeared. She was used to his being called away for long periods and didn't worry, though for once he hadn't left a note on the table. In the meantime she found that she was pregnant again, and this time the fetus was holding on. Three months passed, she felt her belly and couldn't believe it. In the middle of the fourth month she went to the office. Two officers received her warmly, like the guest of honor on a platform.

"Where is he?" she asked. She knew the more senior of the two officers. Throughout the interview his gaze kept turning to the door. She imagined that it would open and her husband would come in, humbled and beaten but persisting in his stubborn opposition. In her mind she prepared a severe speech against him, and smiled at the senior officer, to indicate that she would support him if her husband needed to be taught a lesson. She would show him her belly, to demonstrate that there are truly important things in life. But the husband was not brought in. Instead a clerk came in and gave the officer a sheet of paper, which he handed to her solemnly, as if it were a commendation. It was a statement made in her name, denouncing her husband's subversive activities.

She asked them, "Is he dead or alive?"

"What are you thinking of?" the senior officer protested. "But he's stubborn, very stubborn."

If he'd said her husband was no longer alive she would have signed without a moment's hesitation. She was a Jewish woman who had reached a high position in a strange city, and made a good few enemies. The dead can't be helped, but there was a new life starting in her womb, for whose sake she would have been willing to publicly denounce her husband's name and memory, and satisfy the powers that be. The fact that he was still alive cheered her somewhat, but when she considered her situation and his, she thought it might have been more convenient if he were dead. She refused to sign.

"I'll convince him," she said to the senior officer. He arranged for them to meet in private. But her husband, who perhaps felt a compulsion to atone for something, remained immovable, and she reprimanded him harshly but left empty-handed. The senior officer was plainly sympathetic and invited her to return to his office. To his astonishment, she still refused to denounce her husband. She was certain that he had been condemned to stoning, but she could not cast a stone herself. Her access to the platform was barred, she was stripped of her privileges. She fell from her exalted position to the status of a cleaning woman. But her spirit did not break.

Her husband's trial was public and noisy, and people gloated. During that harsh winter her lips never stopped muttering. Above all she cursed her husband because in the end he broke down and confessed, so that her sacrifice was in vain. As he bent his back she straightened hers, as if to show the strange city that she was fiercer than the icy winds. One evening when she came home from work she found the front door of her flat locked with a new lock. The neighbors told her that her belongings were lying in a heap in the courtyard, that it was the senior officer who took over her flat and he had already moved in his own furniture. She borrowed an axe and they cheered when she used it to smash the lock. But they immediately realized the enormity of the act and fled to their own apartments. She threw the officer's furniture out of the window. That night she was arrested. Her trial was shorter than her husband's.

Alex was born in the prison. A week later he was taken away from her, because she was considered unfit to raise a Soviet child, and he remained in an orphanage even after she completed her sentence. The orphanage was his family, home, friends and school. Most of his memories of the place were warm and pleasant. He was not reminded that his parents were enemies of the state, nor was he taunted as a Jew. He grew up to be proud of his triumphant nation, of his country that became a superpower, and was devoted to the regime which treated him generously.

As soon as she was released from prison his mother hurried to visit him. She knew that they wouldn't let her take him away, but she directed at him all her bitterness and frustration at being deprived of her child. She had expected to find a wretched and neglected child who would eagerly stretch out his arms to her and kick at the nurses and teachers. She was furious to find a lively, smiling youngster. He sat beside her and gobbled the food she brought and answered her questions politely. He had learned from the real orphans how to live without a mother and father. She prodded him to complain and relate his bitter experiences, suspecting that he'd been threatened, but he was a frank child and only complained that he was short, much shorter than the other boys.

"And that's all?" she cried, thinking he was blaming her for it. "So everybody beats you here?"

"Sometimes," he said, "but they're afraid, 'cause I beat them back."

"I mean the big scoundrels."

He didn't know that she meant the staff and thought she was referring to bad people outside. "They don't let them come in here."

She burst into tears which brought on an asthma attack. A doctor had to be sent for. It was her first and last visit. The director forbade her to come again, for the sake of her health and the child's proper emotional development.

But Alex remembered how his mother was sent out of the orphanage, and although he didn't understand exactly what happened, he felt he had done her a terrible injustice. He, who was so important to her, had let her down. This feeling grew stronger after his father was released and rehabilitated, and Alex was returned to his parents' care. His mother talked about the injustice done to his father, but the father hardly opened his mouth. He shaved only once a week, went bowed and withdrawn, and let life flow over him. Alex thought of him as a man who was destined to become a victim in any country and under any regime. He had come across such pathetic, contemptible types in the orphanage. They were made to serve the strong ones and sometimes even provoked the urge to torment them. It never occurred to him to blame either the regime or the orphanage.

He had left the orphanage a devoted loyal son of his great homeland, and grew up amid bitter rows with his mother, who had come to detest his beloved homeland. His father kept quiet, and Alex interpreted his silence as another sign of weakness. He felt somehow responsible for his rebellious mother, who fought like a lioness, whose stock of profanities had been enriched in prison. He mediated between her and the neighbors she quarreled with, took her place in queues for meat and bread, where strong elbows were an asset, and dealt with the authorities. Inevitably, his education suffered. His father hardly contributed to the family budget and his mother earned a pittance. Alex did all kinds of odd jobs. His one hobby was the trumpet, and he used it too to earn money, playing at parties and funerals.

One afternoon he was lying on his back, improvising on the trumpet, and feeling that the melody was pulling him toward something hidden and mysterious. He was tired but couldn't stop playing, and thought he would go on till death closed his eyes. Finally he fell asleep and the trumpet sank on his chest. He was awakened by a knock on the door. His father was standing beside his bed and from his expression Alex guessed almost immediately the identity of the visitors. His father's jaw was trembling, making his false teeth chatter.

"Please, sit down, sit down," Alex said to the two officials and hurried to his father, who seemed to be perishing on his feet. Alex had never seen such terror. The blood had drained from his face and he looked as if he was about to throw up. Perhaps that was the moment when he first felt something for the prematurely aged man, and he realized that it was his father's shoulders he was gripping.

"You must come with us," one of the visitors said to Alex.

He was relieved to hear that they'd come for him and not his father. They placed him between them and when they left the house he was sure that he'd be back that evening to play his trumpet at a wedding party. In the doorway he turned back and was surprised to see his father smiling sadly and fearfully, as though pleading for forgiveness. He couldn't believe what he'd heard his father say, it seemed so irrelevant. On the way he said to the men, "His mind is affected. Why Israel of all things? He was a prisoner for many years."

He was full of confidence when he was taken before a gray-haired officer who gave him a fatherly smile. "What have we done to you?" he asked Alex in an injured tone. "The Soviet Union was still hungry and wounded from the war when she fed you well and pampered you. Why do you want to leave us?"

"Me?"

The officer pushed a filled form across the desk. "Come, you must know your own signature," he grinned. "Naughty, naughty. I know you've got an ugly girlfriend, but surely you need not flee halfway around the world to get rid of her."

Alex said nothing.

"Or maybe your father forged your signature. That's a very serious crime, son."

When his father was first arrested, in the late nineteen-forties, he was sent to Siberia and returned a broken man. If he were now arrested again he wouldn't last long in prison. Alex had to choose there and then between his father and the Soviet Union. He stated that the signature was his.

"Son, son," the officer sighed, "you're sacrificing the homeland, your friends, your language. And on the other hand what have you got? An old man whose mind is gone. You'll get to Israel and there you will strangle him with your bare hands for what he did to you. In your place I wouldn't hesitate at all."

At home he was not allowed to scold his father. His mother opened the door and stood between him and his father. "I made him do it," she declared.

He ran away. For a whole week he and Assya floated on vodka vapors at her place. She was not a Jew and she'd never be allowed to leave with him. They hardly got out of bed. Between drinks they made love with a desire that was like longing for death. They hardly ate anything. On the third or fourth day Assya awoke from her swoon and held his head as if it were a lifebuoy. "You remember— what was the name of that French writer . . . About a boy and girl trapped in a coal mine . . . They decided to die . . . not from the darkness and hunger but from love . . ." She tried to pull him closer with her babyish hands.

Alex slid off the bed and staggered to the tap and the dry bread.

A few months after their arrival in Israel his mother woke up from her dream. His father was broken. Their flat in Nazareth was burdened with debts. At first Alex and his father worked in the same plant, Alex on the production side and the father as night watchman. After a week the people in charge came to think that the father himself needed watching. Equipment was stolen and they suspected he had a hand in the theft. His mother was stricken by violent asthma attacks. She struggled to breathe the air of the Holy Land only to lash it with her filthy tongue. Alex fled to the port of Haifa. For a few months he lived in a tin shack on Shemen beach, where he met Abu-Nakhla's men. Abu-Nakhla regarded a Jewish docker as an asset, and a suitable tenant for the room on the roof.

"I am going down to buy cigarettes," Alex said but didn't budge. With my head resting on his shoulder, I was gazing dreamily at the sunlight on the roof. "I'll go and get you some," I said, but didn't make a move either. It was years since my head had rested on a man's shoulder. Alex turned and inhaled my hair. "I'll go," I repeated, remaining immobile. "I will," he said. He took my fingers and passed them over his tobacco-parched lips. Finally I tore myself away. Not finding a whole pack at home, I went out, bought five packs and returned to the roof.

There was an empty beer can on the table. He took it and crushed it with his fingers as if it were made of paper. "Sometimes I ask myself, what I am doing here. Sometimes it is like walking in cemetery at night. Sometimes I think nobody can understand me or hear me. There are days when I think that everything I can remember and is important to me will never be here. One day I felt so strange here, I almost wanted to finish. Because of you I want to live again."

Even in my youthful fervor I'd never taken the initiative with
Bahij. Now I touched Alex's hand and rescued the crumpled can. His
fingers gave like softened bars. Then they awoke and spread out and
thrust like a pitchfork into my hair. He didn't notice that I was trembling with fear. The hand in my hair pulled my head down to his
bare knees, while the free hand caressed my shoulder. My cheek
touched the hairy flesh bulging below his short trousers, and my
body waited anxiously for his invading hands. I was tired of fear.
And he went on stroking my hair and shoulder, as if absentmindedly,
until I stopped trembling and began to relax. I opened my eyes. Very
slowly, as if rising from a deep sleep, I felt myself growing aroused.
My cheek was on his muscles and his smell was in my nostrils. My
body responded to the sun-warmed odor. Or perhaps my response
was nothing but sweet torpor. Discovering that my lower belly was
waiting for his invading hand I blushed. His hands did not invade.

He'd had no choice, he went on, but to put his parents in an old-age
home. The mother rebelled. In the Soviet Union the talk had been
of orange blossoms and the warm sea, white houses and brave Jews,
and she thought about her lost years and about renewal, forgetting
that her husband was old and worn out and that her son would
escape her. She demanded from Alex, who wanted to work and
study, to make good the dreams she had been deprived of. "An old-
age home?" she shrieked. "Prison in Russia was better. At least there
were some young women there. What should I be doing with sick
old people? It's worse than prison."

The father secretly yearned for prison, any kind of prison. He
wanted to be punished for the young woman in Moscow who lost
her youth because of him, and for the loss of many other lives. He
was very frail, but didn't dare complain in his sickly wife's presence
and say that he himself was very ill. Her illness was her weapon,
and she had no intention of letting anyone take it away from her.

Alex took a taxi and brought his parents to the old-age home. His mother kicked and cursed him, despite the injection the doctor had given her. The taxi driver was disgusted and sympathized with the mother, till Alex indicated to him that she was out of her mind. She saw the gesture and went berserk. The driver asked Alex to hold her down. It was a spring day but a light rain was falling and the car was going down the narrowing, winding road from Nazareth to Tel Adashim. The vehicle seemed to be propelled by the shrieks of the mother trapped in Alex's arms. Near Afula he thought that she had weakened and he let go. She leaped up and struck her husband, who was sitting in front, on his head. From that moment until they reached the old-age home in Pardes Hannah, Alex's arms held her in restraint.

"I am shit," he said, blowing into my hair. "I ruined Assya. What kind of rat puts his mother by force into old people prison? She is right that she wants to leave Papa and come live with me."

My head was resting on his knee, a man's knee. I was so happy, so pleased with myself for being normal, I felt so good because I was wanted, that I said with great generosity, "Maybe you should bring her here. I'll help you take care of her."

"You?" He withdrew his fingers from my hair, raised my head and put his face close to mine. "She will swallow you. She is sick, but can destroy tank. She will not let you come up on roof and will not let me go down to you. She will tell you that in face. Even beat you."

"Your mother is a frightening person."

"I know. She did everything so I did not marry Assya."

My heart sank. "And now?"

"Now I am here and she is there. This time I will not let her. You I am ready to marry. Problem only with your family."

"They will agree. Maybe I'll convert, become a Jew. It's important for the children."

On the stairs I took my hand from his and went on ahead.

## Chapter Sixteen

When we entered our flat I was struck by the difficulty and absurdity of my situation. It appeared that we'd interrupted a rare monologue of Wahid's, who was sitting at the table, a glass of lemonade in his hand and a self-important expression on his face. He received Alex with smiles and ceremonious greetings, from which I understood that Alex's presence at that moment was not welcomed by Mary's fiancé. Alex, unable to read the Oriental masks, did not understand. He responded to Wahid's calculated smiles with his own childish ones.

Mother's looks also annoyed me. She looked at Alex as though she too suspected him of something, though she did not begrudge him coffee and lemonade. Even Mary was looking worried. Grandpa seemed amused, as if he'd just heard a salty joke. The only person in the living room to be at ease was Alex. But seeing that I did not make an announcement, he grew alert, examined the faces in the room and turned to me. I shrugged, sat at the table and joined the chitchat that was covering up something. Finally I excused myself and drew Mary to our room.

"What's happened to your man?" I asked.

"At last he had an important subject for conversation and you two spoiled it for him. He's found out that our cousin Hissam, who's also his cousin, is now in Beirut. Wahid was trembling when he told us that Hissam is the commander of a big unit. This is not a suitable subject for your Jew."

I sank on the bed. "And we came to announce that we're getting married."

"You and Alex?" she exclaimed, her eyes widening with joy. She forgot the complications and fell on me with hugs and kisses. "You sly thing!" she declared. "You brought it off in no time!"

"And what do you think your Wahid, for instance, will say about it? His cousin runs away from home and goes out to destroy Israel, and I'm marrying a Jew. Maybe I'll even convert, become a Jew and an enemy of his cousin and ours? Maybe he won't want to be the brother-in-law of a Jew?"

Mary's eyes flashed. "He has no right. He makes his living from Jews and they make a living from him. He's Israeli, with Israeli money and Israeli clothes. Israel isn't a shop, it doesn't belong to Alex or to Wahid, and they don't have the right to demand that it should sell only one kind of merchandise. If Alex agrees to have Arab relatives, how can Wahid presume . . ."

And before I could stop her she rushed to the living room. I ran after her but it was too late. She struck a dramatic pose at the table, with a regal hand on Wahid's shoulder and the other hand waving at me and Alex, and solemnly announced, "Grandpa, Mother, listen." Then, recalling her fiancé, beaming under her clutching hand, she added with a smile picked in a world free of wars and hates, "You listen too, Wahid. We yakked and yakked and never let Alex and Huda say a word. They came down to tell us that they're getting married."

Alex didn't understand why Mother and I turned to look at Wahid. Behind his back Mary mocked him, and I myself did not exactly admire him. I still think Mary deserved something better. But at that moment Wahid mattered, because he was more thoroughly Arab than Mary and I. He lived in the village and doesn't know Amichai's poems by heart. Though dressed in modern Israeli clothes, his soul, his thinking and habits had longer roots. He will decide, I thought, if I am to be an enemy of my people for the rest of my life. "I and my children and grandchildren will be the mortal enemy, and every armed Arab will be sworn to destroy us, and excoriate our memory for all eternity"—to quote Boaz's occasional harangues to us at the office. Mother's face revealed that she thought as I did. Wahid did not react at once. He was deeply absorbed in the feel of Mary's hand on his shoulder. I got ready to translate Mary's announcement into Arabic for him.

He stood up and looked at Alex, who also rose from his seat. And since one was an Arab and the other a Russian, they embraced each other warmly and gave each other loud smacking kisses on the cheeks. "Li kul al-sharaf, mabruk, mabruk!" Wahid exclaimed, and realizing that he was speaking Arabic added in Hebrew, "It's a great honor for me. Congratulations, congratulations!"

Mother breathed with relief.

"When will you have the engagement?" Wahid asked.

"That is what we are doing now, no?" Alex said.

Grandpa got up and went to the bathroom. Wahid smiled at Alex as at a silly child. "I mean, when will the parents come and the families? You have parents, right? Our custom is that the two families meet and agree between them. It's also a great celebration. People get together and see if the couple suit each other."

Alex looked at me. "We suit each other," he told Wahid. "We do not need somebody to tell us that."

"I also knew that I suit Mary and Mary suits me. All the same, we had a fine engagement. The two families were happy. Right, Umm-Huda?"

Mother nodded and glanced at the passage leading to the bathroom. Suspecting Alex of being evasive, she grew wary. She needed Grandpa, but he went to ground in the bathroom. She tried to catch my eye but I avoided her. She said uncomfortably, "Let's wait," and fell silent. It was awkward to admit that the question of betrothal must wait till Grandpa emerged from his present location.

Wahid was not a perceptive person. "What's there to wait for?" he growled. "I wouldn't betroth even an orphaned girl without a proper engagement party." Recalling that Mary and I had no father, he fell silent and looked at Mary contritely. Without saying a word, she let him feel that he'd put his foot in it. I'd already told her that compared with Alex's mother, Wahid's mother was an angel, so she said to her man, "You were willing to get engaged, even to get married, without your mother."

"But in the end there was a big party!" Suddenly he burst out in Arabic, "Maybe this man's a common crook. You have to beware of a man who keeps his parents out of sight."

Alex caught the unfriendly tone. "What did he say?" he asked.

It was an awkward moment. Mother looked at me reproachfully but I remained silent. The bathroom door was like the armored door of a vault.

Mary decided that complete frankness was in order and answered Alex. "Wahid says that you're hiding your parents, and that a man who disowns his parents is not to be trusted."

Alex did not know the word "disown" but got its meaning. He looked at Wahid for a long moment. Mother held her breath. If Grandpa had emerged from the bathroom at that moment she'd have told him to go back as everything was lost anyway.

"You are right," Alex said to Wahid.

Wahid couldn't believe his ears and said somewhat contritely, "Mary shouldn't have told you."

"I am glad she told," Alex said glumly. "It shows she wants Huda and me to marry and it is not good to have secrets in family. You are right. I also would think like you. But I simply cannot bring my mother."

Thoroughly trounced, Wahid said nothing more.

The sound of the liberating flush in the toilet broke the uncomfortable silence in the living room. Grandpa walked in delicately, as if tripping through a flowering garden, and addressed the table. "From so much joy, you forgot to put something on the table."

"Alex refuses to bring his parents," Mother told him.

Grandpa smiled. "In 1948 my daughter-in-law's brothers fled from this country and couldn't come to her wedding. Whether they would have wanted to come to a wedding with someone like him is another question. But is the border between Haifa and the old-age home so dangerous?"

"Mother wants very much to come to Haifa. She dreams to come and live with me alone, nobody else. She will not share with another woman the house she wants so much."

"She and my daughter-in-law's brothers must have gone to the same school. She hates Arabs that much?"

"She hates whole world. She had shitty life and now in old-age home she feels like in cemetery. So she hates more and more. She hates Papa most of all."

"If you only knew, son, how many Palestinians were killed by Palestinians just to kill one Jew. . . . So your poor mother is sick?"

"How you know?"

"Hate is a most serious illness."

"Yes, yes," Alex exclaimed. "That is very true."

"You see?" Grandpa said to Mother. "Everything is all right, only the table keeps screaming and nobody answers."

Mother went to the kitchen and called me and Mary to help her. She muttered angrily for a long while because of the hard things Grandpa said about her brothers.

Jamilla knocked on the door before we set the table, as though she sensed what was going on. Faced with three men who were sitting and waiting in silence, she cried, "Umm-Huda, where are you?"

"Here," Mother called back, still angry. "Sit, sit, we're coming."

We heard a chair scraping on the floor. Neither Wahid nor Alex volunteered to chat with her. Grandpa watched her with his green eyes, as if eager to hear the exciting news which had brought her to our door, but at her age most of the news she gleaned was meant for women's ears. She turned to Alex in an aggrieved tone, "Soon my cat will sleep at your place too and I'll never see him at all."

"He is nice," Alex said.

"What shall we do with her?" Mother whispered in my ear. I was also uneasy. Unlike Wahid, Jamilla was wadi born and bred, and though an old spinster, she had extensive connections with people and many doors were open to her. Even Abu-Nakhla was careful with the amiable old lady who could count on her lawyer nephew and on relatives in politics. Wahid might consider that it wouldn't hurt an Arab businessman in Israel to have a Jewish brother-in-law; not so Jamilla. Her finger was always on the pulse of the wadi, and she viewed events in the light of a balanced historical memory. When the owner of the bookshop near us was charged with espionage she did not hesitate to criticize him in the wadi, because people hadn't forgotten that during the dark fifties she was twice arrested for demonstrating against the Military Administration, and was even beaten by a policeman.

I said to Mother, "You may as well tell her."

I thought, she'll find out anyway, and I didn't care to start my life with Alex by running away from reality. I'd known from the start that I'd chosen the most difficult course for a couple in Israel, a land full of hatreds.

Mother emerged from the kitchen carrying a loaded tray, followed by Mary and me. Jamilla became aware of the solemnity of the occasion and her wrinkled face beamed. "Good news, inshallah," she said with sincere delight.

"Huda is getting engaged," Mother told her.

I had barely time to put the platters down. Jamilla's arms, her face, her flat chest and scrawny thighs clung to my body. Hearing her sobs Mother also started to cry. Grandpa slapped his knees, like an old bird trying to take off for one last flight.

"I knew it," cried Jamilla. "I knew that Allah wouldn't let a flower wither in His garden. All the time I kept asking myself, why are the men so blind." For some reason she looked reproachfully at Grandpa.

My chest was wet from her tears. I led her carefully to a chair, sat her down and clasped her shoulder till she calmed down. She pulled a tiny handkerchief from the front of her dress and wiped her eyes and nose. "And where is the man?" she asked.

A mischievous glint appeared in Grandpa's eyes. "Here he is," he said, pointing with his chin at Alex.

"Stop it!" she scolded him in Arabic. "I'm asking, who is the man?"

"That's who it is," Grandpa replied.

She stared at Alex for a long moment until it penetrated. Suddenly she yelled at him, as if driving some animal out of her yard. "You!" She turned to him. "His trumpet! I swear to you, he bewitched her. You ever heard of a cat being drawn to a trumpet? Now he's bewitched our Huda."

"What is she saying?" Alex wanted to know.

"She says you bewitched Huda with your trumpet," Mary told him.

"What is bewitched?"

"Hocus-pocus," she said.

Alex burst out laughing. He jumped out of his chair, went over to Grandpa's bench and whispered something in his ear, and the two of them went mad. They roared with laughter, rolling with it together, until they looked like one body having the laugh of its life.

Jamilla rose and pointing with her thin arm, in the gesture of an offended admiral, asked, "What did that Jew say about me?"

The two-headed body howled some more.

"Birds of feather," said Mother.

But Jamilla wouldn't give up. "I want you to tell me what he said about me."

Grandpa wiped his tears with his fists and began, "He said . . ." But he groaned with laughter, took Alex's head between his hands and kissed him resoundingly on his forehead. "He says he's willing to lend you his bewitching trumpet for a whole year."

Jamilla looked at Alex from the corner of her eyes. Her cheeks twitched until she couldn't control her laughter. "He should have brought his trumpet here forty years ago," she said and sank into her chair. "So that's the man! I should have known. The joker's granddaughter waited until she found a peculiar joke." She leaned toward me and asked, "Where will you live?"

"I don't know. We just decided today and haven't thought about that yet."

My head was in a whirl. Today we decided. What did we decide? That the blood-soaked gulf between the two peoples does not exist? I know Israel better than he does. I live in its backyard. Yet neither Mother nor Grandpa nor Wahid nor even Jamilla, who grew up in the wadi and absorbed the Palestinian history, found fault with the difficult choice. Jamilla was dubious not because Alex was a Jew, but because she still hadn't figured him out. But presumably she relied on Grandpa's judgment. She whispered to me in Arabic, "He's short as if somebody forbade him to grow upward, so he grew sideways—look at his muscles! And he's got the eyes of a shrewd man."

"I know you are talking about me," Alex said, "but it is all right."

She turned to him. "If you and Huda should need a lawyer, my nephew will help you for free."

"Thank you, thank you very much."

Mother was alarmed. "God forbid! Why should they need a lawyer?"

Jamilla said, "He's a Jew and she's an Arab. The rabbis won't even look at her, and no priest will dare to give his blessing. You heard of civil marriage? No? Where are you living?" Jamilla enjoyed our surprise at her familiarity with such an apparently remote subject. "When there is nothing doing with either rabbis or priests, you go to a lawyer. You'll be surprised to hear how many Jews go to lawyers. For instance, a war widow who doesn't want to lose her pension but still wants a man."

"Enough!" Mother admonished her. "What else? Widows! On a day like today, what's the matter with you? Not at all, they'll get married like human beings."

Jamilla turned to Mary. "What does she imagine, that the Jews will accept her? Their religion is closed tight, like a pea pod."

Mary pulled me out of my chair and led me to our room, ostensibly to talk in private about this matter. She closed the door and spoke in whispers. "Listen, the time bomb is ticking away in my belly. My ahbal is absolutely incapable of rape. Something must be done. I've looked into it. We need a change of air and scenery. Sometimes men need a special setting."

"How can I help?"

"Wahid says the two of us can't go alone to Eilat or the Dead Sea. So let's go in a foursome. In the village he'll be able to say that you and I shared one room in the hotel and he shared a room with Alex."

"It'll cost a fortune. I don't know if Alex can—"

"Never mind," she broke in. "Wahid will pay. Maybe the desert air will stiffen his miserable tool."

"Maybe you're frightening him?"

"Of course I frighten him. I'm in a tearing hurry, and in the car in the darkness he probably thinks I'm going to devour his little bird. Is that what you think? You see what stuff all that reading has put into your head? At the hotel I'll have time, plenty of leisure to take care of him. I beg you."

"I'll talk to Alex."

"You can tell him everything. That will be my wedding present to you."

When we returned to the living room we found Jamilla going on about Alex's parents. There can be no family celebration without parents, she said. Finally a kind of compromise was reached. The next day Alex wouldn't go to work and the two of us would visit his parents at the old-age home. Alex was not looking forward to it at all.

*Chapter Seventeen*

In the evening I asked Alex what I should bring his parents, and he said, "Jams. Mother loves jams, all kinds of jams. Papa? I do not know what he likes." He didn't pretend that the visit wasn't forced on him and even tried to dissuade me from going, knowing that I was not especially keen. But I said, "I promised Grandpa and Mother, and I must keep my promise."

"So what if you promised? We will go in pickup to some nice place and come back. Nobody will know where we went."

"I always tell the truth at home."

"That is very cruel," he said, "always telling truth to people."

The following day at the office I convinced myself that I didn't love him and it was doubtful if I would ever even learn to like him. Those parents of his—they were probably a tissue of lies. The whole story about the prison, the orphanage and the old-age home sounded unbelievable. Later I understood why I was clutching at doubts. Truth is scarier.

That morning there were hardly any customers. At ten-thirty I made up my mind, with a sense of relief, that this was it, I was through with Alex. Backaches, Valium, insomnia, insane delusions, they were all better than this mess. Warning myself that I was running away from life, I shrugged it off as a worn cliché. Who can say that an ascetic nun in her cell is running away from life, while Mary who wants to be raped by a man who disgusts her is the life-loving one?

It was a fine winter's day. The white masts of the ships in the harbor reached up to the limpid azure of the sky. Rain had fallen in the morning and its scent clung to the foliage of the trees along Independence Street. Now the sun shone on the women's dresses and gleamed in the eyes of men. And I sat at the window looking out and thinking that none of it was for me. Unfortunately there were no customers to keep me occupied. The trees and the light outside seemed to concentrate on Shirley. Shirley has a new lover now, a lecturer in Kobi's department. The sun is on her forehead and she's chewing the end of her pencil. "He's the man of my life," she tells us. "Married with two children. His wife's really terrific. Such a beauty, and so brilliant!" As if these facts were to his credit, and so indirectly to hers.

Boaz and Adina have always adored her. How can they fail to do so now that they no longer hide their own love, and have even involved Shirley and me in the secret, to help shield Boaz from his wife? They caress each other with their eyes, light flowing in and love pouring out. And the three of them make an effort not to look at me with pity.

"I'm going to leave early today," I said. "And next week I'll be away for a few days."

"Medical tests?" Adina asked.

"No. I've got a boyfriend."

I might have said I was about to undergo plastic surgery to enlarge my bust. They stared, wondering if it was a good thing for someone like me. To reassure myself as much as to impress them, I added, "We're thinking of getting married."

They remained silent, waiting to hear about the fly in the ointment. Perhaps the groom is old. Or maybe he's crippled. Or it might be an arranged match and I haven't met him yet.

"There's a certain complication," I said.

"Aaahhh," the three of them breathed.

"He's a Jew."

Boaz sank onto the armrest of Adina's chair and mechanically stroked the back of her neck as if it were his own neck. Adina, fearful that the chair would collapse under his mass, automatically supported his broad backside with her delicate hand.

"Don't tell me it's that funny new immigrant you brought to the beach!" Shirley shrieked.

"Yes. He's coming at two to pick me up. We're going to visit his parents."

Boaz rose from the armrest and went to the door of his office. He looked in, as if consulting the photograph of his son in the elite corps. "I don't know," he said. "I really don't know. Have you considered it carefully, Huda?"

At that moment, if I didn't know how kind he was, I'd have hated him.

Adina scolded him, "Boaz, what's the matter with you?"

"Why does she need such trouble in this fucked-up country?" he exclaimed almost angrily. "I wouldn't have wished it on her."

Suddenly I began to fear for myself. The past few weeks must have worn my nerves thin. Tears welled in my eyes against my will.

"I'll help you," Adina said in a challenging tone which was aimed at Boaz. "I'll be with you any time you want."

Boaz shut himself in his room. After a while Adina said to me with a warm smile, "Forgive him. Men are like that."

"There's nothing to forgive him for." But in my heart I thought, Grandpa is also a man, and he doesn't make such pronouncements about other people's lives. Adina had to go to Boaz's room and pacify him and take him out of his self-imposed solitude, as though it was she who had been out of order.

But what if Alex didn't show up at two? I wasn't worried about him but about my own pride. He arrived at exactly two o'clock. Adina made him a cup of coffee and served him herself. When we left he stopped on the pavement and looked back at the office. "Terrific woman, so beautiful. She is . . . she is . . ."

His Hebrew died on him and I wasn't about to help him out. For the first time in our relationship I felt a twinge of jealousy. It was too sharp, and yet in a way thrilling. We drove out of the harbor car park toward the old road. Near Tirat Hacarmel I told him about the problem of Mary and Wahid. It took him a while to understand why they could not go away on their own. When he heard that the four of us would go to a good hotel in Eilat his face brightened—and at once became gloomy. "Damn, I finished all my money this month. Arranged teeth for Papa. Russian teeth were moving in his mouth like a too-big shoe. Maybe we go next month?"

"Wahid will pay."

Nearing the Ata-Turk Woods he began to whistle a cheerful tune. On our left the Carmel was already clothed in the green foliage of early winter. But when the orange groves joined together into a solid dark-green mass his good mood evaporated. I also recalled where we were going. Joining a line of cars waiting at the level-crossing barrier to the sound of the bell, I wished that the train would be endlessly long. But then the barrier lifted. My knees shook in terror. I slid closer to Alex until my breast touched his elbow, but I could not calm down.

"Alex, is she really so scary, or are you exaggerating a little?"

"She is my mother. I love her. She is very brave and everybody forgets it is hard in this world for brave people. She is brave like crazy. And I love her," he repeated, as if issuing a warning.

At that moment I'd have changed places with Mary, with her village mother-in-law and the bastard in the belly. My jaw began to tremble. "I'm not brave," I said. "I'm a big coward." His hand came and covered my face. I closed my eyes in the shelter of his rough docker's palm.

No, when it came to the men I wouldn't trade places with Mary. Some cowards are fated to stumble into the path of the brave ones.

In Binyamina we crossed a narrow stream and entered a magnificent avenue of palm trees and eucalyptuses. I did not dare to ask whom he would choose if he had to choose between us.

"Is it far?"

"Five minutes more."

I slid down in the seat, like a child trying to become invisible. He wrapped his arm around my shoulders, dug his fingers under my armpit and pulled me up like a sack. "Listen," he said, "anybody can forge documents of lawyer or rabbi. They can forge anything. That is why I don't believe in documents. I had document of orphan and I was not orphan."

"What are you trying to say?"

He stopped the pickup by the side of the road, near the fence of an orange grove. "I want to say that you are already my wife. You don't want to come to my bed because you want to wait for document, all right, so it is difficult for me. But you are already my wife. I am glad we came. You must think of yourself as my wife, and Mama must live with that. If you don't want . . . I don't have document to force you."

"You don't have to force me. I want to be your wife." I took his hand and covered my cheek with his palm as if it were a warm compress against pain. He pulled my head close and kissed me on the forehead. His lips were soft and it felt like a kiss from a distant childhood pact.

The parents' room was full of old furniture and objects, evidently useless, as though the old people could not bear to part from them. The fridge stood on the balcony. Alex insisted that I give them the presents we had bought that morning. I laid on the table jars of jam, a basket of dried fruits, a scarf for his mother and a pen for his father, who was not in the room. Alex introduced me to his mother by my first name only. The hand she gave me was limp and noncommittal. She looked in silence at the things I put on the table, as though making up her mind if they were lethal weapons or innocent gifts. She clearly had little faith in innocent intentions. She whispered to Alex some questions in Russian, repeated them three or four times, but he pretended not to hear. His face bore a ceremonious smile which put her on the alert.

We sat at the small table, facing each other, and her face was close to mine. Her breath came like a whistling bellows, the whistles growing shriller the longer she observed me, until I feared that they were leading up to an explosion. She was shorter than I and fatter. She fell silent and stopped pestering Alex, who was sitting on one of the beds, legs outstretched, back leaning against the wall. There was a wary smile on her lips the exact meaning of which was still obscure, but it hinted at a devastating power, suggesting that she could be grateful or she could wage war. My knees began to itch, but I was afraid to move. Her right hand lay curled on the table and I knew, from what I'd heard about her, that she was capable of hitting with it. I almost wanted her to wipe the smile off her swollen face and raise her voice to drive me out of the place. But then, she might be thinking that I was a possible means of leaving the old-age home. So far Alex had not told her anything about me.

I asked, "Where is Alex's father?"

She turned to Alex and fired a question in Russian, to which he responded with a smile and a wave of the hand. She turned back to me and her curled fingers opened on the table, like the hand of a gambler impatient for the rest of the cards. "He is outside," she grunted. "Must be coming. Shall I call him?"

"No, no," I replied hastily.

"Why?" she asked. "You not in a hurry?"

I sent Alex a distress signal. How could he abandon me like this facing a lump of meat that could at any moment turn into a raging bull? My head felt empty and feverish. Alex jumped up. "Here is Papa."

His father looked like a child's drawing, a stick man with stick arms and legs and a little ball of a head on top. His smile looked too bright in the gloomy room. "A guest?" he called out in relief.

"Still don't know," the mother said, throwing cold water on his delight. "Maybe official from Jewish Agency or government." Her Hebrew was fairly good. Perhaps a remnant from her rabbinical father's home.

Alex's father greeted me with a slight bow. His smile was genuine and his look warm and direct. While looking at me he said to his wife and son, "You have not given our guest any refreshment?" His Hebrew was good too. He was a rabbinical scholar in his youth; all he had to do was remember.

"Tea with lemon," the mother stated, as if it was the last remaining refreshment in her world.

I nodded and Alex put a kettle on the gas ring in the corridor. He said aloud to his father from there, "Papa, this is Huda."

A warm smile lit his father's face. "Pretty girl."

Alex's mother's voice extinguished the smiles. She addressed a long speech in Russian at the corridor and a few words in Yiddish at her husband. I moved my chair back, as if to smooth down my dress. I was ready to leap for the exit.

"Just a moment, Mama, patience," Alex said in Hebrew.

"It is sad here," his father said to me. "Everybody is old."

"Old?" his mother exclaimed. "Why old? They laugh like in kindergarten, dirty pants like one-year-olds, eat porridge like babies. Soon they will go back to their mothers' bellies."

Alex's father breathed deeply, probably relieved that she did not go on to describe their return by the same route through which they had come into the world.

Her eyes flashed red. "Suddenly you remembered that you live with stinking cadavers?"

"Because of this pretty girl who came with Alex. Beautiful and so young," he said with a bold smile.

"I still don't know what she wants. You see this basket and the jams and flowers? All this she brought—for what? Because I am sick and my son is having good time in Haifa, forgetting his mother? You think she comes to give us little house with window to sea? I know them. She probably thinks this old-age home too good for us. I hear in Kfar Saba there is home for people who cannot wipe their nose alone." She pushed aside the jam jars as if to clear space for her immense bosom while she leaned toward me. "Here we eat too much food for free. You had enough, huh? You want to take us to Kfar Saba, because there it is nearer to ground?"

"Mother," said Alex from the corridor, "she does not want those things at all."

His mother pursed her lips and wiped them with a savage gesture, as though to tear them off. "So who is she?"

Alex came in, seized the chair on which his father was sitting and moved it playfully nearer me. Then he pushed a chair between his parents, sat down and said, "Huda is my wife."

His father immediately took my hand and pressed it between his hands. "It is true? True?"

"Moment!" his mother shouted and banged her fist on the table. Tea spattered on the red cellophane wrapping of the dried fruit basket. "Moment!" she shouted again. "Since when?" she demanded an answer from me.

Alex should have sat between her and me, but I realized that he saw fit to protect his father rather than me.

"We are not really married yet," he said. "Just engaged."

"Ah," she said to me, showing her teeth in a predatory smile. "Presumingly it was nice there. Alex can sing and play music. There was not enough food for everybody, so you forgot to invite Mother and Father? At the wedding also presumingly you will forget somebody gave birth to him."

"It will not be very soon," Alex said. "She is not Jewish and we do not know how it will be."

A spark of either worry or hope appeared in her eyes. "You are tourist?" she questioned me. "You want to take Alex far from here?"

Alex laughed. "She is not tourist. You did not hear how she speaks Hebrew?"

His mother picked up a jar of strawberry jam and said, "She is like a foreigner. From moment she came in I did not hear her. So who are you?"

"She's an Arab."

"Arab," his mother repeated, but I heard none of the revulsion, hatred or contempt I'd expected to hear. The tension in my spine relaxed somewhat and I leaned back in my seat. I saw that she was evaluating the new situation, and evidently decided not to be too hasty. She stared at me while calculating the pros and cons. Perhaps, she said to herself, an Arab woman is no great danger, her status is weak, she can be dominated. If Alex must marry, perhaps it's better this way. On the other hand, what if I converted to Judaism—having had the courage to cross boundaries, I might also have the courage to stand up to a powerful mother-in-law. But for once her piercing glare was of no avail, it encountered my sole strength—my inner armor. At last she gave up and said to Alex, "I don't know. She does not talk, she only looks. What did you see in her?"

"She's a pretty girl," his father said.

"Wipe your mouth!" she scolded him. "You know what he did yesterday?" She was speaking to Alex, but it was plain to see that she enjoyed humiliating her husband before me. "Suddenly he went all elegant with stick. Walking on pavement, throwing leg here and leg here, knocking with stick on pavement like blind man. He is jealous of stinking old people. Maybe he is afraid they will take him into army?"

She laughed. I couldn't believe my ears. Her laughter was light and youthful and almost contagious. I would gladly have joined such a cheerful laugh but for the intention to hurt Alex's father. The old man hung his head.

"I was feeling dizzy," he apologized with a sheepish smile.

"And why not dizzy? Since your son spent so much money on your teeth I don't see you anymore. You still remember you have sick wife, she needs a glass of tea sometimes? Never! He runs from club to rooms of his friends, from workshop he goes on trips."

"Papa," Alex said anxiously, "what's this about dizziness? You asked doctor to look at you?"

"Ask your mother how she feels," his mother exclaimed.

"Not necessary to ask. You always tell."

"You see?" she said to me, almost as a friend. "That is a son? And where will you live?"

She caught me unprepared. I realized that the intimate tone was calculated. "I . . . I . . . don't know. We haven't thought about it."

"No, darling. When you catch a man like this presumingly you know everything and think of everything. You will not live in street."

"We'll find a place. Alex . . ."

Her fist shook the table. "You must not do this! When I speak to you you must not run to Alex . . ."

"Leave the girl alone!" his father begged.

"You shut up!"

He shrank. Alex kept quiet. I saw his face go rigid, but he preferred not to open his mouth. I was furious. My knees shook. I didn't want to burst into tears in her presence. They could all go to hell—including the pathetic father and the son who sat on the sidelines as in a circus, watching a dangerous beast baring its jaws. What was he waiting for? For her to strike me with her fist? This was the man who said I was his wife? Who gave me a pact-sealing kiss that tasted of childhood?

She kept glaring at me. I clenched my teeth. I wanted to respond to her with the bold, challenging, crushing smile she was asking for. To my dismay what came out of my mouth was a feeble twitter, and the words themselves were weak and submissive. "We'll live in a house, we'll find a house," I told her. "If Alex wishes it, you could both come and live with us."

I glanced at Alex. His frozen face had turned into gray steel. "Mama, she is talking nonsense."

"She is talking like human being," she said.

The cooling tea tasted like a horrible medicine. I didn't know whom I'd betrayed—myself, Alex, his father or mother. Or perhaps I was being faithful—to myself, to the culture of my forebears, their tribe and family.

## Chapter Eighteen

The house was full of excitement, as if everyone was getting ready for a school outing. In the evening Mother and Jamilla baked biscuits and prepared food for a long journey. "But we'll get to Eilat in the afternoon," I said to Mother. "What shall we do with all this food?"

"Throw away what's left," Jamilla replied instead of Mother, who kept quiet. Grandpa dozed off about ten, woke up at midnight and stood by the window smoking. Mother was still busy wrapping, tying and putting things in the fridge, and grumbling about Alex. "Why did he have to go to work tonight? Tomorrow he'll be tired. How will he take turns driving? How will he watch out?"

"Take a leaf from Mary's book," Jamilla lectured me. "She knows how to control a man."

Grandpa's voice came from the cloud of smoke near the window, "Dear neighbor, it's very late. You should have gone to sleep long ago."

Jamilla shrugged, as though to say, "I know Umm-Huda wants me here, so don't you meddle."

This was the first time that Mary and I were going away together. Mother and Grandpa would be left on their own. When we were children Mary and I went to bed early, so after Father's death they were on their own every evening. I don't know what used to happen in those days, but I couldn't help noticing things now. Mother was avoiding Grandpa's eyes, and my imagination put all kinds of inter-pretations on the quick glances. The tension sharpened Jamilla's senses, and perhaps that was why Grandpa wanted her out of the way. He was flustered by Mother's excitement, because he was also excited.

"Let's make coffee," Jamilla proposed.

"Now?" Grandpa squawked. "Even the stars are tired."

Jamilla's shoulders twitched. "Who needs to sleep?"

Grandpa's voice rose from his belly, "I waaaant to sleeeep."

Mother laughed despite herself, and Jamilla interpreted this as permission to raid the coffee and sugar jars.

I went into our bedroom and found Mary sitting cross-legged on her bed, surrounded by books, her eyes shut.

"There are already three people going mad in the living room," I said. "What's this supposed to be?"

"Meditation," she replied in her clear voice but didn't open her eyes. "Tomorrow I must be fresh and attractive and dynamic. Wahid is totally unnerved. Huda, you're distracting me."

I wanted to distract her, but more than that, I wanted her to distract me. I was the most jittery person in the house. Tomorrow at this time she would be busy getting raped, and Alex and I would be alone in a strange room. I had never been to bed with a man. This idea was rushing about in my head like a runaway train. "How is it in a hotel?"

"We booked rooms in a good hotel. With bathrooms and probably fine curtains and fruit on the table."

"I'm not interested in the bathrooms and fruit."

"Ah, you mean the beds. Well, it's not very logical. In some hotels there's only one bed, a huge one, and in others there are twin beds which can be pushed together."

"How is it in this hotel?"

"I've no idea. Of course I prefer one bed, or my ahbal will fall on the floor between them. Enough, Huda!" she exclaimed, and closed her eyes again.

"Mary! Don't play games with me. I'm already thinking about IVF, pregnancy without sex. I'm scared to death. Suppose there's only one bed . . ."

Mary looked at me with sympathy and pity. "Huda, I'm not lying to you. Believe me, love is like war—you plan and plan, but once on the battlefield things are always different."

"You call that love?"

"You'd rather I called it a first fuck with a man?"

"No!"

"Then listen. Even with a man who really loves you, and you're so crazy about him that you think life was created just to bring you together, even with such a dream lover you can never tell in advance. It could be just 'poof' and that's it, like a sneeze, and you lie there dazed and wondering what it was all about. Or it can be like a hammock made of flowers, and you swing between fire and water, swooning, and you want more and more fire and water."

"I prefer 'poof' and that's it," I whispered.

"That isn't up to you either."

"You're a great help," I burst out.

Her eyes were still open but her voice was already veiled in meditation. "Huda, that's the truth. It's chiefly up to the man. At least the first time. There are men who know how to make music and others who don't know the difference between a violin and a chamber pot, and you can't tell in advance. A man who looks self-effacing can turn out to be a great artist, a little weakling can attack you as if you murdered his mother, and a powerful man can turn into slime all over you. The decorations are given after the battle, not before."

"Now I understand why the fighters are afraid of war."

"But you don't die of it. If only all the wars were like this. Now go to sleep and let me finish the meditation."

Mary's imagery must have affected me. In the morning we were not two couples out for a pleasant vacation in distant Eilat, but something like a tank crew rushing to the front, both comrades-in-arms and enemies. Mary arranged things so that Alex sat in front next to Wahid while she and I sat in the back. Alex had returned at dawn after an exhausting night in the port. Wahid's face showed that he too hadn't slept a wink.

Wahid and I were like fresh recruits on their way to their first trial by fire, and we both looked it. I developed a psychosomatic cold and wished Alex were a hypochondriac who would refuse to get into bed with me. I visualized the room with two beds and what I would do then. I would get into the shower and drain all of Eilat's freshwater sources. Finally I'd get into bed and encase myself in blankets, even if the room was boiling hot. But what would I do if there was a double bed? How would I walk on my feet out of the shower, and in my netlike nightgown—which unfortunately I'd allowed Mary to buy me—get into a man's bed?

Wahid chain-smoked and twice slid off the road and swung back onto the tarmac in a spattering of gravel. At times he overtook other vehicles at great speed and at other times crept along like a loaded lorry going uphill. He wanted to stop at every roadside inn, proposing that we have something to drink and stretch our limbs. After Herzliya he began to swing from lane to lane like a sniffer dog. His fingers searched for knobs and switches, like a shepherd trapped in a spaceship. He'd had air conditioning installed two days before the trip, and now he tested it by alternately roasting and freezing us. Now and then we heard the squealing of the brakes of the cars behind us.

Mary screamed, "You'll kill us all today!"

Wahid gave in. He stopped the car under a tree and said, "That's it. I'm not driving any more."

Alex got out without a word, walked around the car and waited for Wahid to take his feet off the pedals and his hands off the wheel and move into the passenger seat. I hushed Mary before she could scold him again. His nonsense had saved me from making a fool of myself, for which I was grateful. He leaned against the window to calm down, not daring to turn around and look back at Mary. Now I began to worry about Alex. I noticed that his shoulders were slumped and from time to time his head bobbed up.

"Alex, I'm afraid you're falling asleep at the wheel."

"Him?" cried Wahid. "He keeps laughing all the time."

"Serves you right," Mary told her man.

"I am not laughing about him," Alex said. "I am laughing about my mother and your sister."

"She came home looking like someone pissed in her face," Mary said in her inimitable style.

"My mother kissed her. Papa also wanted."

"I was terrified, so I lied. I said we might get a big flat and she and Alex's father could come and live with us. It's what she's dreaming of."

"Give me a cigarette, Wahid," Mary said.

"You smoke too much for a beginner," he replied.

Mary lit the cigarette like a practiced smoker and waved it in the manner of a Tel Aviv cafe lounger. "Huda telling fibs! Who'd believe it? My sister Huda."

In Beersheba Wahid was himself again. The packed food was left in the trunk, while he generously took us to an expensive restaurant.

"Ask them," he said to Alex, "how to get out of town onto the Eilat road?"

"Everybody speaks Hebrew better than I—and I must ask?"

I told him frankly, "It's better for the Jew to go forward and the Arabs to follow."

"You are Arab like I am Mongolian."

"But I am an Arab, Alex, and so are Mary and Wahid. Has it ever happened to you that a policeman asked for your identity card just because he thought you were an Arab?"

"It happened to you?"

"No. I look like a Jew and speak like a Jew. Mary and I don't talk Arabic in public. Like many Arabs, we disguise ourselves as Jews."

We were traveling south on the Dimona road. Bedouin encampments dotted the bare landscape.

"I do not want to know," Alex said. "In Russia they told me Israelis are screwing Arabs. I was sorry for them and I gave blood for Palestinians to annoy my mother. Here I hear all the time Arabs are making plots to kill all Jews."

"And you believe it?" Wahid asked.

"I don't want to believe nothing. Papa believed too much and screwed up his life. I spit on all that. They can all kill each other. I don't care. I just want to live in peace. What all that nonsense about identity card?" he said to Wahid. "You were asked?"

"Yes," Wahid replied. "One day I was arrested because of my identity card." He took the card from his wallet and put it on the steering wheel for Alex to see.

"And because you are Arab they catched you?"

His ironic tone annoyed me, but Wahid remained calm. "There was an explosion at the central bus station in Tel Aviv. They stopped all the Arabs in the neighborhood, me too, even though I was injured. This wouldn't happen to you in Israel. Huda is right. It's best that you're driving. If anything happens on the way you could say that we are with you and we're good Arabs. It's not easy to be a good Arab, especially when you don't know exactly what a good Arab is. Many Jews think that a good Arab is a dead Arab. How can you manage to be dead the whole time?"

This was the longest speech I'd ever heard Wahid make. I repressed an impulse to put out my hand and wipe the sweat off his forehead—me, the girl who was plotting to capture a Jew, who was selling daydreams to his mother, who was willing to convert to Judaism for his sake, while in my mind a bed alternately formed and fell apart.

Wahid turned on the radio and we traveled like silent landscape lovers until we reached the prairie.

There we stopped by the side of the road and watched animals we couldn't name. I walked away from the others to climb a hillock for a better view. Mary came and rested a hand on my shoulder. "What's this new interest in beasts? You can hardly tell the difference between an elephant and a donkey. Soon you'll join those groups

who are ready to kill people for the sake of rare foxes and rab-
bits. . . . Why did you suddenly bring up the business of Jews and
downtrodden Arabs?"

"And didn't you jump violently on Wahid? Mary, if we've come
here to quarrel we might just as well go home."

"Easy for you to talk. This isn't a pleasure trip for me. I need to
make a future for the bastard in my belly. I'm not selfish like you."

"I'm selfish?"

"And how! If you'd had such an accident, you'd have rushed to
the nearest doctor to get rid of the embryo. You see how much I'm
willing to pay to keep him. I'm selling myself. Don't you see?"

Suddenly I did. We cowards abjectly assume that rebels are driven by selfishness. Since they dare to realize our own secret desires,
it suits us to argue that they're acting without consideration for others. But have I, Huda, shown consideration for Mary? What did I
know about the horrors of her affair with Zuhair? How much older
sister's support have I given her? I viewed her submission to her
mother-in-law as an amusing game and laughed.

Alex was saying, "Wahid, you must be careful of me. Look at
them. Huda and Mary are like one parcel."

"A parcel?" Wahid queried.

"Not parcel. It is like . . . like bunch of grapes. You cannot eat half
then say enough. Look at them."

Wahid's conservative soul could not tolerate such jokes. "Mary is
my wife!" he announced.

"We'll fight for the two sisters," Alex proposed. He threw an imaginary foil to Wahid and began to cavort about on the dry ground like
a fencer.

Wahid refused to take part in such an immoral game. He turned
his back on Alex, unconsciously throwing away the imaginary foil.
"Wallah, he's crazy."

Alex ran after him and touched his back with the tip of his foil.
"The two of them together or nothing."

"Aren't you ashamed?" Wahid rebuked him. "And I don't want you to look at Mary, you hear?"

"Mary," Alex cried, "your boyfriend does not have any fantasia."

"You're telling me."

"What nonsense is he saying about me?" Wahid asked us.

"No imagination," Mary explained.

"Al jnoun fonoun," Wahid quoted an Arab saying.

"Is he cursing?" Alex asked me.

"He is saying that madness is art."

His eyes lit up. "Then I am artist!" he cried, threw his sword at the beasts and ran over to me. Before I could make a move he swept me off the ground and swung around with me like a spinning top. I saw the revolving horizon, the jagged ridges of the colorful hills, Mary's sad smile and Wahid cautiously withdrawing from the site of madness. I wanted to remain in midair, like a fruit that would never ripen or fall.

## Chapter Nineteen

Mary and I sat in grand armchairs in the hotel lobby while Alex and Wahid went to the reception desk to fill the forms. "Alex," Mary called out, "take adjoining rooms."

The two men nodded. When they came back to us Alex had the key ring dangling from his finger and a boyish smile on his face. Wahid was clutching his key in his fist, like a child who has caught a frog and doesn't know how to get rid of it. I had sunk into the armchair, and like an old woman held onto the armrest and the nearby table to get up. A group of children rushed out of the lift, their mouths open, but I heard nothing. I dragged my boneless legs behind Alex, Wahid and Mary down the endless corridor. Mary took the key from Wahid's hand and opened a door. Alex opened the door next to it. I went inside and sat on the edge of the bed because I could hardly remain on my feet, the smile trickling from my lips like a body fluid out of control.

"Beautiful bathroom!" Alex announced happily after a quick survey of the place. "We're going to bathe."

I jumped up. The bed was a double. Mary said you don't die of it.

"Why are you sitting?"

I hadn't noticed that I was sitting down again. I wished I was in Haifa.

"We must bathe and quickly eat something. I am starving."

I wondered where he'd got all his energy and cheerfulness after working all night and traveling all day.

Mary and Wahid's voices could be heard from the next room.

"I'm tired," I admitted.

Suddenly I was in the air. In his arms. His laughter rolled like stones over my face. "I'll wash you." And he pushed the bathroom door open with his knee.

Only when I saw the grimace of pain and surprise on his face did my fingers let go of his hair. "I'll wash myself," I whispered. He put me down and his eyes sought mine, which evaded him. Without a word he left and closed the bathroom door. I turned the taps on full to overcome the heavy silence. I lay in the bathtub and forced myself to think. Think of it as an operation, I said to myself. At that moment I didn't love him. I only wanted to believe in him as a patient believes in his doctor.

After wallowing in the water for a long time I began to wonder why he wasn't urging me to come out. Maybe he'd left the room. I'd behaved like an animal. And he didn't even try to kiss me when he carried me in his arms. Only brought his face closer to mine and his nostrils flared as he playfully sniffed my skin. And I pulled his hair out, to the point of pain, of tears. He must have fled from the room. Maybe he took his bag and left the hotel. What shall I tell Mary after she gets raped?

Without drying myself I threw my nightgown on and rushed into the room. He was sitting in an armchair, reading a Russian book. He closed it at once and said, "Crazy. You are crazy," and went to the bathroom and slammed the door.

I felt ashamed. I was also angry with my treacherous body. In the past it always came to my rescue with backaches, with pains in the shoulders and legs. And now when I desperately needed a good excuse it remained passive like a bystander. But it was feeling cold—at least that. I threw it on the bed and rolled it up in a blanket, and it promptly thawed and would not let my bones shiver with cold. I licked the sweat from my upper lip. Alex came out of the bathroom and I pulled the blanket up to my eyes. At first he didn't look at me. A low cry came from the next room, but I couldn't tell if it was Mary or Wahid. Alex sat down again in the armchair and opened his book, his face expressionless. I thought, let him read and I'll pretend to sleep. But despite myself I felt vaguely offended. His hair above the book was damp and shiny. I saw how long his lashes were. If he moved I wouldn't be able to escape, being trapped in the blanket. Then I realized that he was not reading but waiting, like my body, for me to decide. And neither of them understood that I was incapable of decision.

The book dropped on his feet. Suddenly the blank expression dissolved and he burst into a great laugh that shook the air, the bed and the walls. "Like mouse!" he bent over, laughing. "You are peeping like mouse from blanket!" I turned away so he wouldn't see me being swept by the wave of his laughter. Smiling at the window, I saw the top of a palm tree thrashing wildly in the wind, as if invisible fingers were tickling its roots. The mattress sank and sighed beside me, and still I looked at the fronds flapping heedlessly in the air. His rough fingers were on my forehead and interlaced with the palm fronds to soothe them. My body stiffened and clung to the trunk of the palm that refused to submit to the wind. His fingers were on my eyes and my head shook free. The fronds returned to the wind and his fingers moved down to my mouth and slid down to my neck. For a moment the fronds stopped, as though panting after a wild dance, and the stars twinkled among them. Then they re-awoke as if hearing a distant, irresistible melody. Even the trunk moved when his hand skimmed over my breast. The wind and Alex were whispering and blowing and I couldn't hear because of the roar of the fronds and the turmoil in my belly. I knew that my head wanted to thrust against the headboard as the palm tree thrust its fronds into the starry sky. The palm and I were stretching out in agony, because there was no other way of expressing what was happening to us. I spread out my arms to the air, to the dancing fronds. The trunk split when struck by something stronger than the wind, it pleaded for its life, to go on raising its fronds to heaven, and I longed to hold it up, to keep it from falling or letting me fall. We were both hurting in the wind. My arms clasped the tossing treetop and Alex's breath blew on my face. His hands cupped my face and turned my head. The tree vanished and instead of the stars I saw the triumph in his eyes. His chest was panting on me, as if it captured the storm, and he whispered, "I love you, Huda, Huda." Suddenly he was as light as a little cloud on faraway peaks. In his eyes there was no more triumph but loving tenderness. I wanted to yell something that I had never had in me. The shout struggled but found no words; then I understood that it needed no words. The triumph I saw in his eyes was now in me. I was a normal woman, a real woman. I turned to the window again and the palm tree was in its place. Its roots were in me, and it grew and became stronger.

Alex was lying beside me, holding my hand and sucking my fingers as if extracting the juice from the rind.

"So now I'm pregnant?" I said, but I didn't care.

"You did not even enjoy," he said sadly.

When I saw the palm tree fighting for its life in the wind I did not think of enjoyment. Triumph overrode it.

"You are not pregnant. I was careful. But now you are not virgin."

Still thrilled with a sense of triumph, I looked at him and he no longer appeared menacing. On the contrary, he seemed so vulnerable lying on his back with his head on his folded arms. His silence suggested remorse, which I could not account for. I touched his shoulder with my head and showed in my eyes what I was too shy to say. His arm came and embraced my head. "Huda, you are not angry?"

"Why should I be angry?" I loved the sound of my voice. "I just don't know how to do this."

"It is not important. Love is important. You never said that."

"You wouldn't have believed me," I replied, smiling. "I love you."

He pulled out his arm and leaped out of the bed. I saw him bending over his suitcase, rummaging inside, and when he straightened the trumpet was in his mouth. His cheeks bulged and I managed to yell, "No, Alex, no! Not in the hotel! They'll think we're mad!"

I meant Mary and Wahid. Mary would interpret the trumpet blast in her own way. I wanted her to see before she heard. I wanted her to see my limbs, my movements and face, and realize that I'd become a woman.

"I beg you, Alex, don't touch the trumpet."

He sat down on the edge of the bed and I moved closer and curled around him. "I want to tell you with trumpet how I love you. Let me play to your breasts. They are so beautiful."

I grabbed the mouthpiece of the trumpet with one hand and with the other covered his hand that cupped my breast. "No!" I yelled.

"Only one note, one note. You will see how your breasts will dance." Throwing the trumpet on the bed, he spun around and landed beside me, ready to pluck me off the bed, when we heard someone pounding on the door. At that moment I saw nothing but his naked maleness.

"Who is it?" Alex asked.

"Open up!" Mary whispered. "Open the door, damn you!"

When at last we opened the door, having dressed hurriedly, she burst in like a storm. Her hair was disheveled and she stood before the mirror and yelled at it, as if examining her distorted features, "He's a beast! Did you see? A criminal!"

"Why is she yelling at the mirror in Arabic?" Alex asked.

"She wants Wahid to hear," I whispered.

She pointed at Alex and turned to me furiously. "What's he standing and grinning for? He should look shocked."

"Alex," I said coolly, "pretend that you saw Mary almost murdered."

"She is all right. Just a little crazy—who screams at mirror?"

"He's an ahbal just like my man!" Mary declared. Her eyes fell on the shiny brass trumpet lying on the bed before I could hide it, and immediately the grin I'd been so afraid of appeared on her face. "With a trumpet?" she whispered, still in Arabic. "I never heard of it being done with a trumpet." She repressed her laughter. "Huda, what happens if he gives a blast on the trumpet and the trumpet starts to choke and cough? You probably suffocated it completely."

"What is she chattering?" Alex inquired.

I looked into her eyes and said to Alex, "She thinks you did it with the trumpet."

He could appreciate a joke. He looked at Mary and lied in his teeth, "Huda plays better than thousand trumpets."

Naturally she didn't believe him, but at that moment she noticed the glow on my face. "Huda," she crooned and hugged me. "Oh Huda!" Then she remembered, flung herself on the bed and wrapped herself in the blanket, as though shivering with cold.

"What should we do when he comes in?" we asked.

"Nothing. Just stand there and look at him as if he ran over a child and drove away. Don't say a word."

Alex was now quite amenable to taking part in what seemed to him an amusing comedy. To be on the safe side—never knowing what Mary was capable of—he took the trumpet and tucked it out of sight in the suitcase. Mary lay in bed, trying to make her teeth chatter. She checked the lighting and turned off the wall lamp. Her face looked almost gray.

"I am hungry," said Alex. "Maybe I can go and call him?"

"What's your Abu-trumpet thinking of now?" Mary grumbled.

I defended him. "We really can't go on like this till morning."

"Suddenly you're in a hurry. All your life you let the years drain away, and now you worry about a single night?" The fresh coloring returned to her cheeks and her eyes shone. "Is he that good, your Abu-trumpet?" she asked in Arabic.

"Alex," she went on in a coaxing voice, "Huda told you that this is very important to me. Later we'll go to the best seafood restaurant."

A few minutes later Wahid knocked feebly on the door. Alex opened it to him. Wahid glanced at the shivering Mary and collapsed in an armchair, prepared to submit to any verdict. He felt shy before me and Alex and didn't know what to say. But Mary did not treat him harshly. There was a conciliatory note in her voice when she asked, "What will your mother say about this?"

He took courage from her tone. He had come in looking as if his life was shattered, but now he raised his head defiantly. "What has she got to do with it?"

"Don't be naive, Wahid," Mary said. "Your mother and all her generation value virginity above all. They sniff, examine, they're capable of canceling everything. My life is ruined."

"Mary, listen to me. I won't let any woman come near you. I won't let them, you hear? I'll tear out any tongue that dares to say one word. You're my wife, Mary."

"Only your fiancée. They'll throw me out before the wedding. I trusted you, Wahid, and you . . ."

"We'll go home and get married right away."

I didn't know whom to pity. He was being made to bow down by a bogus trick, but at that moment I could not condemn Mary. She didn't do it for pleasure or out of wickedness. I was well aware that she knew she was degrading herself. If she were Jewish, like Shirley, or if she came from a different class, she would have aspired higher. With her sharp wit, her vitality, temperament and beauty, she should have had a better start in life. Women who were inferior to her sat at groaning boards, while she had to snatch furtively at forbidden fruits. Meditation, Yehuda Amichai, good Hebrew and English, the brilliant matriculation—they availed her nothing. She would be digging holes in the village earth in which to bury her crushed dreams.

# Chapter Twenty

On the way back from Eilat we were different couples. Mary was at ease, despite her look of being resigned to her disability. Wahid was the husband—a loving, generous and understanding husband. He drove the car with confidence and made Mary sit beside him.

"On Monday, two weeks from now, we'll get married," he said, "and the next day we'll fly to Greece."

Mary was silent.

The effervescent lightness that filled my body made me self-conscious. Giving me a thrilling sleepy look, Alex took off his glasses and laid his head on my lap. His hand crept possessively under my skirt and dozed on my flesh. His long lashes came down and his mouth opened slightly, and my body sang like a forest full of birds. I leaned forward as if to adjust my shoes, so as to touch his forehead with my breasts and enfold his fingers. The night before his eyes were bright with the light of discovery: "You are a warm woman."

Bahij had said that my body was more frozen than the sides of beef imported from Argentina. He didn't say it to hurt me, but because he felt sorry for himself. I love you, he almost sobbed, but I'm a man, you see. And I felt as if I'd deceived him, as if I was hiding under my clothes a body that had absorbed the wrong hormones. Such a misfortune, I thought, must be a congenital defect. I suppressed my own pain and wept for his grief. He said it was my body that had driven him to give up the love of his life and follow the German girl. Her body was like a warm nest, he said. It was enough to touch any spot on her body with a fingertip. Her body was lined with sensors that set bells ringing. Whereas I, the more he fondled me the more I became a cross between a tortoise and a hedgehog.

He married the girl of the ringing bells. I understood him. I saved up and bought them an expensive wedding present and sent it with Mary. Three months later he came to pour out his heart. It was because of me that he'd married a woman who didn't understand him, a woman he didn't love, who couldn't adjust to village life, who felt homesick for the frozen rains, whose body quivered at the sight of every black mustache, a woman who loathed sheep and went mad because the village houses were unheated, a woman who wore shorts and got drunk—really drunk—in male company, and who wouldn't hear of children.

He came to me again after she ran away from him to the rain-soaked forests of Germany. He said he would learn to live with my disability. I was the only person with whom he could talk. There was no one else in the world with whom he could hold such conversations. He had abandoned the Palestinian revolution and become a lawyer specializing in real estate. He had Jewish friends and partners. He would have my body treated medically. Perhaps the doctors could install some kind of bell in it, or awaken a dormant one. He wanted an educated woman, and children too, because he couldn't live with a stupid peasant woman. What was the point of making so much money if not to have a wife he wouldn't feel ashamed of before his Jewish partners and friends. He was willing to forgo sexual relations for the present. That German woman had destroyed him. He couldn't even bear to think of her.

"And after we're married?"

"Who needs bells then? You'll be mine."

In other words, a piece of conquered property, whose wishes and desires only a fool would consider. And the odd thing about it is that I loved him even then. It seems to me that I still do. He was my first love, after all. And he didn't give up easily. He even sent his father to our house. His father's astonished expression said plainly,

All this for a skinny little thing like you? My son is fasting and going crazy for such a dried-up creature? But he carried out his commission faithfully and talked to Mother and Grandpa. They thought I was missing the chance of my life. Mother wept, recalling the villa from the old days and the relatives whom she saw only at funerals. She felt it was blasphemous and a betrayal of the past to reject such a match. I asked myself why I was being so stubborn, and blamed Amichai, all of Hebrew poetry, and the delusion of equality which suffuses every page of modern literature.

Now Alex said I was a warm woman. For that alone I could love him. He doesn't lie. My flesh thrills to the touch of his sleeping hand.


Even before we reached the house I sensed that something was wrong. In the midst of the teeming bustling wadi our house usually stands quietly aloof. Since Abu-Nakhla's boys quit the roof strangers rarely entered it. Yet here were three men coming out and two going in. Formally dressed, their faces expressionless, they exchanged subdued greetings and walked on staidly. They were not visiting Jamilla—her front door is visible from the street, and the newcomers walked past it. I reached over and dug my fingers into Mary's shoulder. "Mary, Grandpa's gone."

I looked up the street as far as the cafe, searching for confirmation for my premonition, but everything appeared normal. Cars crawled down the streets, children ran around, in the cafe the men bent over the backgammon boards, a boy walked past bearing a tall stack of pitas on a tray on his head. The sky above the roofs was winter blue. But the people who entered and left the house were youngish, not at all Grandpa's companions.

Mary blanched but didn't lose her head. She flung open the car door and rushed to the house. Wahid called after her, "I'll park the car and come right up." Alex and I ran after her up the stairs, which smelled of coffee and cigarettes. Our door was wide open and we could hear a low murmur of voices, as in a respectable cafe. The living room was packed with men sitting and standing, speaking in low voices. They'd even taken over Grandpa's bench, but there he was, tall and straight, backed against the window, his green eyes on the ceiling as he blew smoke upward. Jamilla emerged from the kitchen with a tray of coffee and disappeared among the men. So it's Mother! I shrieked inwardly, but before I could utter a sound I heard her voice from the kitchen, "Jamilla, there's more coffee for the guests."

Suddenly they all fell silent, as if on command. Grandpa made an odd movement with his hand. The tray shook in Jamilla's hands and she had to press it to her belly. "You're back," she murmured. "Umm-Huda, the girls are back."

Mother came out of the kitchen. Her eyes were red, her face swollen, and she was dressed in black. She too tried to signal to me but I didn't understand. It was hard to stand thus in the doorway with everyone looking at us without a trace of sympathy or commiseration for the tragedy of which I was still ignorant. Then I realized that they were looking at Alex and their eyes were growing increasingly hostile. I pushed through the crowd and reached Grandpa. "What happened?"

"Your cousin Hissam was killed in Beirut. The Jews assassinated him." He spoke drily, merely stating the facts. "Take your man away from here, find a way to get rid of him before anything happens."

"He's not to blame," I said, but I knew Grandpa was right. A young man in a red sweater grinned contemptuously over his coffee, and leaning forward to light his cigarette at his neighbor's lighter, said, "Her cousin is killed, and she's with her Jew."

Grandpa seized my shoulder and turned me around to face him. His eyes looked into mine. "Huda," he said softly and stopped.

Over by the door Alex asked, "What is happening here?"

His Hebrew sounded very alien in the atmosphere heavy with

Arabic murmuring. The people standing near him moved away, as though from a bad smell. He looked around the room and didn't know what he was accused of.

Wahid came in and asked Alex, "What's happening here?"

"Another one who's forgotten his Arabic," muttered the young man in the red sweater.

"I don't know," Alex said to Wahid, who shrank back. Alex threw out his chest and I grew anxious. He stepped and leaned against the door jamb, protecting his back.

The young man in the red sweater stood up and went to confront him. "How many more will you kill before you've had enough?" he demanded.

"I don't understand this nonsense, and don't talk to me like that," Alex warned him.

Someone called out, "Leave him alone, Adel."

But Adel didn't let up. "No. I want to know if they won't rest until they've killed the last Palestinian."

Wahid clung to Mary, alarmed by the threatening atmosphere.

"Will you tell me what happened?" Alex asked.

"I will tell you," Adel said through gritted teeth. "You murdered Huda's cousin."

Alex looked around, as if seeking the body. "Where?"

"In Beirut."

"Then he was enemy, no? He wanted to kill, he knew he could be killed—he himself would not call it murder. A terrorist should be killed."

I closed my eyes, expecting a major explosion. I stumbled when Grandpa pushed me aside and rushed over to Alex. Some men were already trying to separate the two, who were cursing aloud in Russian and Arabic. Grandpa interposed his tall figure between Alex and the others. "Shame on you," he roared. "You've come to express condolences and you're desecrating the house. Out! Out!"

"But you're leaving the Jew here," said Adel and spat on the floor.

"Shame, shame," one man murmured and left the apartment. To the sound of shuffling feet the living room emptied, and I sank into a chair and struggled to suppress my nausea.

"How did he get killed?" Wahid asked.

"In an Israeli paratroop raid. He was driving a jeep on the coast road near Beirut. All the passengers were burned to death." Grandpa reported the facts in Hebrew. He was speaking to Wahid, but kept glancing at Alex and at Mother, the opposite ends of a crumbling world.

Mary wept. "When did you hear?"

"Yesterday morning."

"We didn't want to spoil your holiday," said Jamilla, who was gathering the untouched cups of coffee in order to drain them one by one.

"You must be hungry and thirsty," Mother said in a neutral, everyday voice, which emphasized her grief.

Alex stopped beside a little table which was draped with a black kerchief. Mother had many of these. On it were displayed photos from the family album. A baby with a shock of black hair swaddled in a white blanket; an infant in a bath of clear water, crying in terror with his eyes and his mouth wide open; a little head peeping over the side of a white baby carriage; boyish legs running after a ball; carrying a schoolbag on a straight back.

"That is he?" Alex asked.

Jamilla wiped her mouth with the back of her hand. "Yes, that's Hissam."

"And what is this?" Alex asked again.

"The flag of Palestine," Jamilla replied as though casually, but with unmistakable pride.

"It is forbidden, no?"

Jamilla picked up the tray with the empty little cups and said, "His body was wrapped in this flag. They took him to Amman in this flag. Today his father will bury him in this flag."

Mother uttered a sob, but at once suppressed her tears, refusing to let Alex see them. Alex turned to Grandpa and said, "That is not true."

Grandpa invited him to sit beside him on the bench. I breathed with relief. Grandpa hadn't changed. But I saw the anxious look in Mother's eyes, as though she feared that he would do something to the pictures on the nearby table.

"What is not true, son?" Grandpa asked.

Mother jerked her head at the word "son," as if it disparaged her grief.

"When young man dies, no matter how, he did not die for flag."

"Hissam died for the Palestinian flag!" Wahid cried.

"Wahid," said Grandpa and offered him a cigarette. "I want to hear Huda's man."

Finally my tears overflowed and streamed on my face. Huda's man. Dear Grandpa.

"Next month I go on reserve duty in the Golan," Alex said. "I am in fighting unit. I don't have another country. I don't have strength to go to another place, speak another language like a baby. Here I found Huda. I love her, I want to marry her, even this evening. So now this country is my home with Huda. I want to live. If I get bullet in Golan it will be stupid accident, like a sack falling on the head from crane in port. I don't want to die for flag. It is not fair that the men who were here hate me, and Huda's mother does not want to talk to me."

Grandpa waited for Mother to object, but she remained wrapped in her sad silence. "You said," Grandpa returned to Alex, "that Hissam was a terrorist. As if it is allowed to kill him."

"Of course it is," Alex declared.

Pure hatred glinted in Mother's eyes. Her mouth shrank, as if holding back a bitter outcry. She looked at me and something of her hatred for Alex splashed like acid on my face.

Alex turned to her. "When they tell me to put on khaki and give

me gun and tell me to go up to Golan Heights, I know that every
Syrian soldier is allowed to kill me. I don't want Jews to hate Huda
for this."

Mother burst out, "And now they don't hate her?"

As if I'd become a stranger. I hung my head. That's how they
speak in respectable families about a daughter who's become a
whore.

"Mother," Mary cried, "you're talking nonsense."

"You too!" Mother choked. "At least wipe the red muck off your
lips. They murdered Hissam. Can nobody understand? I don't want
to cook for him any more," she went on in Arabic. "He won't receive
any more food from my hands."

I felt that she was disowning and rejecting me as well. I didn't
dare open my mouth. I understood her pain and it hit me too, but I
objected to her attempt to make Alex the target. I couldn't suppress
a wicked thought that Mother enjoyed the stream of condoling visitors. Perhaps she recalled the glorious times in her father's house.
Alex's appearance shattered the funereal stage set. Now she would
have to confront a gray, solitary bereavement. She believed that
many who had come to express sympathy now felt she had no right
to mourn. If she went out in black—and she liked to wear black—
people would see it as hypocrisy. Perhaps she already imagined herself going to Amman to take part in her nephew's funeral, and there,
at the side of her brother, her own flesh and blood, she would be
treated like a leper. Adel had spat on the floor as he was leaving her
house. There too she would be spat at and driven out.

I was completely at a loss. For weeks I had carefully ejected all
troublesome thoughts, but I'd known that sooner or later I would
walk barefoot into a field of thorns.

"Grandpa," I whispered.

Her reddened eyes widened. "Don't try to get around him. You eat
the filth you've cooked."

I didn't want to pronounce Alex's name. "He is filth?"

She squeezed her dry lips with her fingers and let go. "Do we know where he came from? Bahij waited for you, he crawled to you on his hands and knees, and you threw him out. What kind of dirt got into your soul that you seek out such types?"

I never imagined that grief could be so vicious. And this was my gentle mother, the warm soul who believed in me and valued me, and whose faith and regard had kept me from going mad in the past few years. I burst into tears. At that moment I thought I must be horribly ugly. A woman whose mother says such things to her makes herself ill.

Alex did not understand the words but perceived their import. "Huda," he said firmly, "let's go."

Grandpa wrapped his arm around my neck and said, "No, son. It was a bad shock and we are all tired. Go rest a little." He let go of my neck and touched Alex's chest. At such moments a physical touch is needed to underline the words. He led him to the door and said, "Take a shower, rest, forget everything, and I will come up to you later."

"Not necessary, not necessary," Alex insisted, and his hardened eyes rested on me. "I am not tired. I want Huda."

It was like plunging into a limpid pool. "I want Huda"—like a mutinous child refusing to part. A long moment passed before I noticed that Jamilla was speaking. The sentimental, romantic old woman must have imagined she was watching an Egyptian film, and as usual couldn't resist joining the action at its climax. "Go," she called out in her rasping voice, "go up to the roof. Nobody is going to take Huda away from you."

"I need my suitcase," Alex said to Wahid. "It is still in car."

When the two men went out Grandpa rebuked Jamilla, "Keep quiet, woman!"

She sat down as if he'd paid her a compliment. Grandpa returned to his bench. Mother stood leaning against the wall, as though it was her last support in the house. "So let's burn down the house and start walking to the border," Grandpa said to her. "If Huda's man is such an enemy, what are we doing among all the other Jews?"

"God damn them all to hell! He was still a baby and they murdered him. God damn them!"

"Huda's man didn't murder."

"Huda's man is glad he was murdered."

"Huda's man is like me."

"He's not like you. You're an Arab."

"You think that in my village I knew whether I was an Arab or an Indian? They told me I was an Arab and I said, so be it. If the beetles had told me I was a beetle, I'd have said, so be it. Huda's man is like me. They told him he's a Jew, and he had no choice in the matter. They'll tell him to go and kill children who are out to kill children and he'll go. The one certain fact you know about him is that he loves your daughter and wants her to be his wife. What a terrible crime!" He rolled his eyes, and I couldn't tell if he was speaking seriously or mocking us. "It was for something like this that they wanted to kill me in the village. That's why I'm here. So go on, woman, kill him. It's possible to kill with words, too. Think about it, woman."

"What will they think of me if I keep feeding a Jew after Hissam died a martyr's death?"

There was a knock on the door. It was Abu-Nakhla, impeccably attired from his red tarboosh to his burnished shoes. His mournful expression seemed sincere. For some reason, the sorrow of a well-dressed man is more impressive, perhaps because it does not act alone. Jamilla sat and stared at him shamelessly. Mother remained glued to her patch of wall, but Abu-Nakhla's dominant presence intensified the grief which seemed to be exclusively hers. And it was to her that he addressed himself after clearing his throat and wiping imaginary sweat from his brow.

"We have heard, Umm-Huda, we have heard," he opened in the plural, like a spokesman for many who did not wish to be seen ripping their clothes and tearing out their hair in public. His eyes lingered on Jamilla, as though considering how to remold her gray form to suit the sacred occasion. Jamilla blushed, pulled at her dress, straightened her back and immediately slumped again, despairing of the effort.

Abu-Nakhla took off his tarboosh and set it on his knee like a warrior's helmet. He went on in a sonorous voice, "He was a Christian, but I am here to tell you that the paradise of Allah's messengers is open to receive him. His name suited him—Hassim—a man of iron will and a clear destiny. Hassim!" The name rose from the depths of his lungs and was borne like a treasure on his lips.

"Hissam," Mother corrected him softly.

"Hissam!" Abu-Nakhla pounced on the name, almost kneeling down with awe. "Umm-Huda, your brother was prescient. Many whispered that he was too subservient to the monarchy in Jordan, yet he gave his son such a bold and noble name: a sword! Here we've been wallowing in muck, while he was sharpening such a sword. Why are you mourning, Umm-Huda?"

"He was still a boy, and they killed him."

Abu-Nakhla put on his tarboosh and stood up. "He was Hissam. A sword may not be killed. In the ancient poetry it says, A broken sword is a source of pride, a testimony to a tireless warrior. Be sorry for your poor brother, not for Allah's sword."

"I'm sorry for him too," Mother whimpered.

Having finished his eulogy, Abu-Nakhla decorously resumed his seat. He looked meaningfully at Jamilla, who did not understand at once, but then she jumped up and hurried to the kitchen to prepare the princely coffee.

Abu-Nakhla turned to Grandpa, "You are important people now."

Grandpa shrugged off the mantle. "We are what we've always been, poor souls in poor bodies."

"Not anymore," said Abu-Nakhla to Mother, "not with such an asset."

"Asset?" asked Mother, confused.

"A fighter who's been granted such a death is an asset, Umm-Huda. The Palestinian revolution has spread its wings. Yasser Arafat appears in the United Nations and heads of state stand up in his honor. Honor and power, Umm-Huda, honor and power. . . . Jamilla has spilt the coffee on the gas."

Mother detached herself from the wall and peeped into the kitchen. "She's making you some more."

"Honor and power," Abu-Nakhla repeated. "Honor and respect for the families of the fallen. And money," he added significantly.

"Money?" Mother repeated in amazement.

"Don't be naive," he chided her gently. "Thousands are rotting in the Jews' jails. Thousands more are wounded, many remain crippled. Hundreds, many hundreds of martyrs sacrificed their lives. Have you heard of any hungry families? Has the light gone out in any house because there was no money to pay the electricity company? The Palestinian revolution rewards generously, it does not abandon the orphans, the widows and the bereaved parents."

"Can you think about money at such a time?"

"Not about money, Umm-Huda, but about honor and a loaf of bread. When the men languish in prison, someone must feed the children. Otherwise the daughters would have had to sell their bodies to save their families from starvation. The revolution guards the honor of Palestine. And that means money." He took the little coffee cup from Jamilla's hand like a priest receiving an offering.

"My poor brother," Mother said in a low voice. "He is not thinking about money. He's lost a son."

"He doesn't have to—he's got plenty. But you should think about it. You shouldn't have to go on living in this ruin. It would be a shame if the aunt of a martyr had to live in such a dump."

"We don't need the money," Mary burst out.

He seemed to notice her for the first time. "You certainly don't. Having finished off my son you found yourself a golden cage. And what's that lipstick doing on your lips? Is this a party or a house of mourning? Have a little shame, girl. You've got yourself a fool who's willing to patch up what's been torn. Why drive other men crazy?"

"Abu-Nakhla!" growled Grandpa. I looked at the front door in fright. I wondered where Wahid went when he left with Alex. Maybe Alex invited him up to the roof.

"Egyptian," said Abu-Nakhla with a good-natured smile, "I haven't come to offend or to quarrel. But it still hurts me. Despite everything, I was willing to indulge your granddaughter in every way. Now Zuhair is on the road to damnation. What granddaughters you've raised, Egyptian!"

"What do you want?" Grandpa asked.

Abu-Nakhla bowed his head. "I came to offer my condolences. Also to tell you that the Jew who almost buried my son has sucked my blood because of you."

"Your son also shed his blood."

Abu-Nakhla tapped the tarboosh on his head and stood up. "Not bad, not bad at all. You're covered on all sides. On the one hand a martyr who died for Palestine, on the other hand a Jewish son-in-law. What more can a man ask for in this crazy country? Goodbye, Umm-Huda . . ." He stopped in the doorway. "Or has your daughter already got a Jewish name?"

## Chapter Twenty-one

Mother fasted and Jamilla took over the kitchen. Grandpa gritted his teeth and said nothing. The following day when I came home from work I loaded a tray with Jamilla's cooking and went up on the roof. Alex was sitting stiffly on a chair.

"I'm hungry," I said. "Let's eat."

Alex raised the corner of the napkin covering the food and said, "The pitas are white. I don't touch bread without Christian blood in it."

"Don't be crazy, Alex. Maybe I'll be a Jew as much as you are."

"Because you're an idiot."

He went to work without any supper. Mother was sitting at the window with her back to us. Jamilla was offended. "My food is not good enough for his lordship?"

"After what happened last night," Grandpa said, his eyes caressing Mother's stubborn back.

She slapped her thigh sharply. "Maybe you would like me to crawl and beg his forgiveness? Leave me alone."

"All Jews bear a grudge," said Jamilla. "For the least thing they won't forgive you till you die."

Mary came out of our room, her legs smeared with wax and swathed in strips from an old sheet. In her blue dressing-gown she looked like a hobbling patient in an orthopedic ward. "Mother," she trilled, forgetting that the house was in mourning, "I can't find the scissors."

"Leave me alone," said Mother. She turned around and shrieked, "What's this?"

"Defuzzing my legs."

"You heathen! Your cousin was buried yesterday. Burnt all over he was."

Mary had dreamed about this cousin, yearned for him, taken pride in him. At the same time, he was only a series of fading snapshots in an album. "That's no reason for me to grow fur all over," she replied.

Mother stood up. "We're in mourning and you're thinking about your legs, damn you!"

"Mary," said Grandpa, "you must show consideration for your mother's sorrow."

"Your mother's sorrow!" Mother cried. "None of you has a tear to spare for the murdered boy!"

"A tear," Mary raised her voice. "Yes, if you like, I'll give you a bowlful to send to Amman. Consideration? For whom? You were a widow and Grandpa broke his back to feed us. In winter we walked in torn sandals, and were glad when it rained. In the evening we washed the one dress, and it wasn't always dry by morning. So we were glad we could say it got wet in the rain. Did any of them ask how we were?" She ran to the side table, grabbed the photographs and shuffled them like a pack of cards.

"Don't defile the martyr's pictures!" Mother screamed.

Mary's low voice shook. "He died a martyr's death and we lived martyrs' lives of misery and privation. You want to go on like this, Mother? You've driven Alex out. Shall we drive out Wahid too?"

"You're vicious." Mother turned to Grandpa. "Can't you say something to this wanton?"

Mary lost her self-possession. She grabbed Jamilla's shoulders from behind and shook her hard. "Look at her, Mother. Look at her!"

Jamilla was startled and flung off Mary's hands. "Are you mad, girl?"

"Mother," Mary went on, "in thirty years' time Huda will look like this."

Jamilla was hurt. Grandpa was embarrassed and gave her a paci-fying smile.

"I won't speak to you, Mary," Mother ended the squabble.

She didn't speak to me, either. Day after day, I was a pariah in my own eyes. When she resumed her position in the kitchen I refused to eat her food. I'd buy something on my way home from work and set a table for Alex and myself. In the morning I rose early and bought pitas and cheese. After a fortnight Alex said to me, "We get married immediately."

I went down and sat beside Grandpa. "If you say no," I told him, "I'll give up. Alex wants us to get married at once."

"I suppose he's fed up with the rubbish you buy outside," he joked.

"I haven't the strength to fight the Jews and the Arabs and his mother and mine. I haven't the strength, Grandpa. I'm not Mary."

Mother remained silent but stuck out her chin. Grandpa's eyes did not leave her. "So I'll have Jewish great-grandchildren and Arab great-grandchildren," he said slowly, delving into his thoughts. "I hoped to have a great-grandchild from you before Mary."

"I'll try, Grandpa." But I knew Mary's condition. There was no chance that I could fulfill his wish.

The next day I asked Adina how one converts to Judaism.

"So it's still serious?" she asked.

"We want to get married right away."

She laughed at my naiveté. "Boaz," she called. "Huda wants to know how one converts to Judaism."

"So tell her," said Boaz, laughing.

In the evening I told Alex to forget about a wedding in the near future. Conversion takes a long time, sometimes even years—there will be interviews, then a lot of lessons in Judaism, investiga-tions . . .

"Why investigations?" Of all the obstacles, his Russian ears picked out that word.

"To find out, for instance, why I want to become a Jew. They'll say I want to convert so as to grab myself a Jew."

"It is true, no?"

"I'm afraid it's not allowed. I mustn't say that I want to become a Jew just for that."

He grew suspicious. "It is because of your cousin. You are here to say goodbye."

"I'm just telling you that it's a long process."

"So we will make it short. We will marry in civil marriage in Cyprus. You arrange in your office a trip to Cyprus and we will marry there." His eyes examined my face. "If you are not trying to run away from me . . ."

"Because of you I quarreled with Mother at a difficult time for her. And I come to you on the roof . . ."

His lips sought mine. He asked, "So what now?"

I knew what he was getting at and it pleased me, but I pretended to misunderstand. "We'll go on like this. . . . You'll have to eat the food . . . the food I bring . . . Grandpa says . . . he says I'm feeding you rubbish . . ." I couldn't speak because his tongue moved into my mouth and his hands were on my body.

He spoke directly into my throat. "We talk and talk about it, and I think of nothing else."

He'd learned to explore my body and make it respond, and my body learned to surrender and long for him. I felt like a cluster of bursting, ripe grapes. My skin tingled as though assailed by a swarm of ants, and I was filled with an inward hum that grew into a soundless roar. Later I loved to gaze at his face above mine. His eyes would close while mine opened and examined his features.


Downstairs Grandpa motioned me to sit down. Mother was still in mourning, but she had changed into a navy blue dress. I realized that it signaled a reconciliation, which cheered me up. Grandpa was waiting for one of us to make the opening move, but I didn't know what to say and she was too proud. I did not need an apology from her, a smile would have been enough, or an outstretched hand.

Mary looked at my face and grinned. "Shame on you."

"What for?"

"Look at your eyes, your skin, your lips. You're radiant and shining—shame, shame."

"She's more beautiful than ever," said Grandpa.

"She's skin and bones," Mother uttered her first whole sentence since the row.

"That's love," Mary beamed.

"Shame on you," Mother rebuked her.

"What for? Because she is loved, because she's in love?"

"You're jealous," Grandpa taunted her.

"Just a little bit," Mary admitted.

"You should be happy," Mother said severely and turned to me. "So, you'll become a Jew."

She said it as if I was moving to a world with which her world did not even communicate by post. It gave me a twinge of pain. "You'll always be my mother," I said with unconcealed emotion. "Alex's mother is not like Mary's mother-in-law. She's like a shark. I'm afraid of her, but I love you."

"You hear! You hear!" Grandpa sang.

"And if they ask you to cast off your family? Tell me the truth, Huda."

"I would never agree to such a price. Ever since I can remember I've been without a father. My greatest fear was that one day I'd wake up and find you and Grandpa gone. That fear is still in there. And I'm not sure I'll convert. Maybe we'll have a civil marriage."

"Next week is Mary's wedding. Will he come?"

"Why shouldn't he come? He's even talked about the wedding present. He likes Mary and Wahid."

"It's only me he hates."

"Mother, he wouldn't touch Jamilla's food either, though it made his mouth water. He was very hurt by what you said, but he never uttered a word against you. He's used to people going mad and hitting out. He reacts immediately, but he is incapable of hate. And I think he's missing Grandpa."

"Tell him to come, tell him now," Grandpa said.

I didn't move. Mother herself had to tell me to bring him. Suddenly I remembered. "He's going on reserve duty on Sunday. I'm not sure they'll let him come to Mary's wedding."

"He must," Mother declared. "What would people say?"

I chuckled. This was the real reconciliation. "Earlier you were afraid what people would say if I married him."

"Many of them will be glad to think he's thrown you over. I don't want them to have the satisfaction. He will have to tell them in the army that he's got to come to the wedding."

"We go on talking about him and meanwhile he's alone on the roof," Grandpa protested. "Go and call him."

## Chapter Twenty-two

I was ironing Alex's uniform in his room when the significance of what I was doing came home to me. Many Israeli men dressed in these uniforms had killed Arabs. I went on working mechanically, smoothing the cloth in front of the iron, smelling the rising steam. And once in this uniform, Alex would be a target for any Arab soldier or Palestinian fighter.

The night before leaving Alex didn't go to work. He lay on his back, holding the trumpet. Jamilla's cat fled from the roof at the first roll of thunder. Rain and hail rattled on the roof-tiles and the wind shook the loose window and the creaking door. The warmth inside was pleasant, but it did not reassure. Somehow it felt fragile, as though the rising storm would soon break in. The room seemed as frail as a gazebo. I imagined books flying, table and chair taking off and soaring over the roofs, and Alex, still lying on his back, being carried away to the raging sea.

"What can you do on the Golan Heights in such a storm?" I asked, raising my voice to overcome the hail and the trumpet.

"Not much, but the army has to be there."

"I want to know what exactly you do there."

Alex put the trumpet on the floor and gazed at me in wonder. Deep in his heart he was an Israeli soldier and required to keep his service secret, and suddenly he saw me as an Arab. At least, that was how I interpreted the dry answer he gave me as though against his will. "I can't even see where my gun is shooting. Everything is in numbers and angles and range, and there is smell and noise. You are satisfied now?"

"I was just asking," I protested.

His eyes were hard. "You ask what I do there, and I don't know what is worse for you—that I am dangerous to Arabs, or that Arabs are dangerous to me."

"Both. I don't want you to get hurt, and I don't want you to hurt anyone."

"Come, come here."

I went over to him and rested my head on his chest, and he stroked my shoulder which used to know nothing but pains. For a long time his hand rested dreamily on my neck and then touched my breast. I raised myself to help him take off my jumper, but he drew my head down on his chest and his hand went back to sleep. His body was warm and dimmed the roaring wind and the barrage of hail.

"Suddenly I am thinking about children," he said. "And I still don't have profession and don't have home. I threw away years."

"We'll have a home and we'll have children."

Many times before I'd heard his trumpet filling the soul with sadness, but this was the first time that I heard the sorrow in his voice. I even raised my head to see if there were tears in his eyes. They were dreamy, but not wet.

"You'll phone?" I asked, and at once realized how strange it was. An Arab from the wadi behaving like her co-workers in the office, waiting for a phone call from a soldier. But then, everything's been strange from the first day I met him.

"Of course I will phone. I will also get leave. Ask Wahid to take you and Mary and come to visit me."

"Three Arabs driving around on the Golan Heights, looking for a gun battery?"

"Yes," he said. "I forgot, I am stupid. For one minute I was glad I also have family to visit me, like other soldiers."

"It's the situation which is stupid, not you."

He put my jumper back on. I rose and he pressed his head into my stomach and said, "There is break in rain, run down."

He was mistaken. I ran through pouring rain from his door to the stairs. Mary was awake in our room. "Why did you come back?" she wondered. "I thought you would stay with him till he goes."

"I can't before Mother and Grandpa." I was ashamed to tell her that he didn't ask me to stay till morning. "He'll freeze on the Heights," I said. "It's snowing up there and the men are outside the whole time."

"I'm glad my children will not serve in the army and won't take part in any wars."

I asked myself what made her so sure. Who could have imagined, when she and I were born, that Palestinians would bear arms and hold military parades and die near Beirut? When Hissam was a schoolboy his future also looked very secure.

"I'll only be here a few more days," she said.

The idea hit me like a physical blow. A whole part of life was coming to an end. The bed opposite would be empty, and I would remain alone with Mother and Grandpa in the aging house. My heart throbbed for Alex who saved me from awful loneliness. "I'm sorry you're getting married before Alex comes back. I'll go mad here on my own."

She patted her belly. "The fetus in there won't wait for reserve duty or the turn of the seasons. He's growing in the dark and has a very accurate watch of his own. You could come with us to Greece. It'll be fun! The roof will be empty anyway."

That's just why I'll stay, I thought. I'll take my book and read upstairs. The quiet of the roof is a good setting for Amichai's poems.

We heard some low murmurs and soft footsteps, and the tinkling of cups in the kitchen. "I'll go and see," I said.

"Don't disturb them," Mary said, laughing.

Grandpa was lying on his bench with Mother bending over him. Mary's words echoed in my mind and I almost turned back. Then in the light from the kitchen I saw that Mother was placing a wet cloth on Grandpa's forehead.

"Is he ill?" I asked.

Mother was startled. "You're not asleep?"

"Go to sleep, all of you," said Grandpa and sat up. The compress fell on his lap. Mother picked it up and pressed it to his forehead. "Lie down," she said and pushed him back. He obeyed.

"What's wrong with him?" I asked. Mary was already beside me. I was worried. All my life Grandpa was tall and strong and healthy, always smiling and joking. I approached his bench. "He must have a high fever," I said to Mother. "He seems delirious."

"Yes, yes," she agreed.

Only then did I notice the anguish on his face, as though a cruel hand had passed over it and remodeled its features.

"Go to your room," Mother ordered us. "You're disturbing his sleep."

Mary pulled me away. I thought she didn't understand the situation, that she was suppressing a giggle and implying that we should leave them to themselves.

"Go, go," Mother said again.

But once in our room Mary's face was grim. "What's the matter with him?" I asked.

"He's old, Huda, very old. He's got a strong handsome exterior, so we think . . ."

I seized her shoulders. "Mary, what is it?"

She turned toward her bed and I followed her without letting go of her shoulder. I sank down beside her. "Huda, Grandpa has never believed in eternity. He's always laughed at people who cultivate their hates and loves and their morals as those that would last after all the mountains have fallen."

I lost my patience. "How come you know things and I walk around the house like an idiot?"

"I found out by accident and they made me swear not to tell you."

"So here's another one who keeps her word!"

She put her hand on my knee. "Let's say that they persuaded me."

"Of what? That I'm retarded? That I shouldn't know?"

"You seemed ill much of the time. Your illness was not like Grandpa's. We didn't understand it, or maybe we did and were more worried about it."

"So you thought I was crazy."

She nodded and her eyes twinkled like Grandpa's. "Long live Doctor Alex and blessed be his clinic on the roof. Oh the miracle-working saint!"

Suddenly she knocked me down on her bed. Her kisses were like flowers on my face, her hair fell on my eyes, and her laughter rang like a bell. "Huda, I love you, really love you. Pity we're sisters and not man and woman." She bared her shining teeth. "I'd eat you up!" she growled and flung herself on her back. "Sometimes I'm jealous of Alex and sometimes I love him because of you." Her body froze. Then she said in a low voice, "We'll be two estranged and hostile families. A Jewish family and an Arab family . . ."

I was alarmed. "Why should we?"

Mary sat up, wiped the corners of her mouth with her fingertips and in a deep, slightly raw voice imitated the late President Sadat, "No more war! Peace!"

That night I lay on her bed, my ears pricked to the living room as well as the roof, but nevertheless slipped into a blissful doze. At dawn I rose quietly, and stood in the living room for a moment watching Grandpa sleeping, bundled in his blanket, a focus of myriad memories. Then I went up on the roof, made tea for Alex and me, and woke him up.

"Why did you leave?" he asked.

I squashed his nose with my finger. He must have forgotten that he'd thrown me out into the rain. His room was cold but his chest was warm under the blanket. He pulled me to him and we mingled together for a long time, till I felt he was being plucked and torn away from me and a huge cavern called The Army was swallowing him up. When we went downstairs Mother was waiting for him with a bundle. Her eyelids looked heavy and her shoulders slumped.

"What is it?" Alex asked.

"I baked a little for you. You must come to the wedding." They shook hands almost formally and he went down without looking back.

"What did Mary tell you?" she asked inside.

"What you've kept from me," I replied.

"At his age it's not so dangerous. Sometimes he's unwell, but he'll live for years."

He was not on his bench. I took my handbag and fled to the office. I didn't want to see anyone this morning.

Adina looked into my face, searching for some hidden alteration.

"It's Alex," said Shirley. "It's just his influence."

Adina smiled and said, "Boaz said to invite you to my place next Thursday. He will be there and some friends."

I didn't know then how much I would need that evening at her place.


On the day of their wedding Wahid and Mary flew off to Greece for five days. Mother and Grandpa said it was young people's madness, and Wahid's parents agreed. Nevertheless, I had the impression that Mother suspected something and preferred not to delve too deeply.

Two days before the wedding I had bought Alex a shirt, though it was uncertain that he would be given time off. I asked Boaz, who assured me that you don't get leave for a sister-in-law's wedding. Alex telephoned the office. I thought it was a customer and was puzzled about the sizzling and creaking on the line, but when I realized it was Alex I strained my ears to find out through the noise if he was cold and if he wasn't being fired on. He told me that he'd given up a weekend leave, that he would come to the wedding and that it was indeed bitter cold on the Heights.

He liked the shirt a lot and said it was a shame to wear anything over it, so he was cold at the wedding. By evening they were gone, both he and Mary.

The house felt as if the lightbulbs had become dim. The shadows lay in the corners like mute beasts. Grandpa tried to crack jokes and failed pathetically. Zuhair walked under our window, humming a sad song. I sat on the edge of my bed looking at Mary's empty one, and said it was unthinkable that the roof should be empty at this time. I took the Amichai but didn't open it. After a while I tucked it under my arm and went out.

"Where are you going?" Mother asked.

"To Alex's room."

I left the door open and a damp wind blew in from the sea. I swept the floor, cleaned the gas rings, folded trousers, dusted books and polished the ashtray. Then I locked the door from inside and lay down on his bed. I felt lost in a snowy wilderness. Yet not long ago I used to sip the passing time on my own, drop by drop.

There was a knock on the door. My heart leaped—Alex! I jumped up and opened the door. Grandpa was standing there, his head wrapped in a towel against the cold. "Better not to be here alone," he said. "Zuhair is still hanging around down below. Lock the door and come home with me." But he himself was in no hurry to leave, and came inside, sat down on a chair, bent over the little electric heater and took off the towel. His white mustache was like snowy blossoms on his dark face. Suddenly I knew that one day he would die. He saw something in my eyes and smiled sheepishly. His voice sounded strange. "You're a beautiful woman, Huda. Very beautiful."

I couldn't help smiling as a woman does at a compliment. He was probably teasing me. Why did he come up?

"It's pleasant here," he said with a sigh. "Very nice in front of this wicked heater. It heats the face and feet and doesn't let you forget the cold sitting on your back."

Again he was playing games with me. Did he come up to talk

about the cold? "Grandpa, you shouldn't have come up in this weather."

"Come, let's go down, my dear. He's away and it doesn't matter where you wait for him. Your mother is worried."


The following evening I fled to Adina's place. The two couples who were invited did not show up, but Adina seemed unconcerned. She sat on the sofa and folded her legs under her, a cat-like expression on her face which I'd never seen at the office, making her look youthful. Boaz played host and overflowed with warmth and eagerness to please. It was plain to see that they'd made love before my arrival. With the generosity of the well-fed they wanted the fireflies that hovered in the fine apartment to land on my face too. Yet their eyes were childishly innocent. I was grateful to them for letting me share their stolen moments. Boaz put various delicatessen on the table, played background music and made jokes as he poured our drinks.

"That's too much," I protested. "I won't find my way to the bus."

"Boaz will take you," Adina promised.

Boaz sat beside her and stroked her toes which peeped from under her skirt. I wondered how I'd feel if I saw Alex stroking another woman's foot. He'd seen Adina at the office and was dazzled. I stifled the thought.

"Where will you live?" he asked. "Adina says he lives in a storage shed on a roof, and it isn't even his."

"It all seems so out of reach that we've stopped thinking about it."

They felt uncomfortable. He has a thriving travel agency, as well as a propertied family to back him. Adina's parents compete with her dead husband's parents in lavishing gifts on her and their grandson, and she has her salary and her army widow's pension.

"In the beginning, at least, it may be better if you live among Jews," said Boaz. "It may not be easy to live among Arabs."

"Any flat or room with a bathroom, whether among Arabs or Jews, will do for us. Alex is very adaptable."

"When is the wedding?"

"In the summer, when he finishes his studies."

"We'll gamble with your money," he said.

I glanced anxiously at my handbag, as though it contained all my savings. "I've got very little, and I don't like taking risks."

"I didn't mean to gamble just with your money. I'll give you a big loan and invest it all on the stock exchange."

"I'm afraid of the stock exchange."

"The profits will be yours, the losses will be mine. The market is hot, I won't be taking a chance."

"I'll contribute the same amount," said Adina.

My mind was in a whirl. I realized that the guests who failed to show up were imaginary.

"What do you say, Huda?" Boaz asked.

Like asking a thirsty person if he wanted to drink. "Are you serious?" I couldn't even smile. "We'll repay every penny."

The telephone rang. Adina jumped, like any soldier's mother. She listened and then covered the receiver. "Huda, it's for you. How did they know you're here?"

"It can only be Alex," I said. "I gave Mother this number in case he called." I shouted gaily into the receiver, "Alex! How are you?"

His voice sounded mournful. "What happened?" I could hardly hear him through the whistling and rustling on the line. I didn't want to ask him to speak up and repeat what he'd said. He was sobbing. Adina's hand rested on my shoulder and she led me back to my seat. I sat down and got up again. The whistling and humming continued in my ears, and Alex was standing there alone and crying.

"What happened?" she asked.

"I think his father died."

"You think?"

"Yes, he died," I snapped. "The line was bad. I understood that he's going straight to the old-age home. The funeral is tomorrow."

"I'll take you there if you like," said Boaz.

I hung my head. And what if Alex didn't get there till morning? What would I do there with the corpse and the predatory mother without him to defend me? "How will he get there tonight?" I wondered aloud.

"Catch rides," said Adina.

"In this weather? Who will pick him up? He'll spend the whole night on the road."

"You should have told him to get to some particular place," said Boaz. "I'd have picked him up."

"I'm a fool," I said.

## Chapter Twenty-three

The storm passed, but a thin drizzle continued to fall from a darkened sky. Some thirty people clustered on the porch of the funeral departures door at Rambam Hospital. People don't mind late arrivals and hold-ups on happy occasions, but when it comes to funerals everybody is pressed for time. It was already a quarter past two. The first to grumble aloud were some Russian friends of Alex's from the Technion. His mother wiped raindrops from her forehead and wheezed, as if she was climbing a steep staircase. The dock workers smoked and talked in whispers.

Grandpa arrived in a black coat which I did not remember. He took out a handkerchief, made knots in its corners and put it on his head. Clearly this was not his first Jewish funeral, and it was strange to see him thus when most of the Jewish men present remained bareheaded. Mary suppressed a smile at the sight of Wahid standing at attention. She touched him with a red fingernail, and he relaxed with a sigh of relief.

Two-thirty.

Alex stood at the gate and watched the road through his steamed up and streaming glasses. His windbreaker dripped water on his trousers and shoes. His mother came out of the shelter, pushed aside some umbrellas and demanded, "Where is your father?"

Alex put his hand on her shoulder and led her back to the porch. "He will get here," he said grimly. "He can't escape now." He motioned to us to keep an eye on her and went back to the gate. Mother took his mother's hand between hers, to give her some warmth. I was afraid to approach her.

Grandpa asked me in a whisper why they had to bring him to

Haifa—couldn't he have been buried nearer the old-age home? I hadn't considered it, but I heard myself saying, "His mother insisted that he be buried in Haifa." Then I understood what she was getting at.

Three o'clock.

By three-thirty most of the mourners had slipped away. Suddenly Alex's head jerked with relief. An ambulance drove into the court and an unshaved young man in sandals got out. He and Alex went around to the back of the vehicle and opened the door. I heard Alex roaring at the driver in a fury, "What is this?"

I hurried to the ambulance and saw Alex holding two of the stretcher handles, as though to fling it with the body into the puddles. "What is this?!" he shouted again.

"What do you want?" asked the driver, who didn't understand Alex's rage.

"That is not my father," Alex snapped and pulled the stretcher further out. "Papa is little man, and you brought an elephant!" He pulled off the black plastic covering and long hair fell out into the rain.

Behind me his mother groaned, "Genya! It is Genya. What is she doing here?"

"You brought a woman instead of my father!" Alex yelled at the driver.

The man fled to the porch. His eyes swept the remaining mourners, pleading for understanding and support. "How am I to blame? I'm an ambulance driver, not the burial society. They gave me a body and said take it, so I did."

Alex pushed Genya back into the ambulance and shouted to the driver who was hiding behind people's backs. "You go back right now and bring my father!"

Alex's boss went up to him and pressed his shoulder. "Alex, take the pickup and go and bring your father."

"No," said his mother. They turned to look at her in surprise.

"While he goes and comes back it will be dark. Presumingly they close the cemetery. We will not wait outside until they open." She looked angrily at Alex. "He was always like this." She went back onto the porch and sat down on the bench in regal silence.

"Who did she mean?" Grandpa whispered to me in Arabic.

"Her husband," I replied, and implored him with my eyes not to forget himself.

But he could never resist a joke at death's expense. "Wallah, no wonder he sent someone else in his place. He's afraid to meet her."

Alex went up to her. "All right," he said. "Come, I will take you back."

"I do not have strength to go. I am sick. You have room in Haifa, no? Don't ask her with your eyes!" she said, indicating me. "You don't need to ask permission to take your sick mother to your room." She gave me a warning look that said, Don't you dare meddle. "I am very sick, I tell you."

"But he is one who died," Alex said and turned away.

That night she slept in his room, on his bed.

Alex asked me to take his mother up to his room and he drove to the Pardes Hannah to sort out the confusion about the bodies. Mother urged her to come to us until her son returned, but she waved her hand dismissively. "Where is Alex's room?" she asked me, and put out her hand for the key.

Mother signaled to me to give in. I wanted to accompany her to the door and climbed ahead of her. But she didn't budge and even pressed against the wall to let me go down without touching her. Her eyes were on me until I entered our apartment. Inside everyone looked at me, as though I was responsible for the day's bizarre events. Grandpa kept quiet, and his silence disturbed me.

I spoke to him. "What if she can't open the door? Sometimes the lock sticks. She'll stand on the roof in the rain? She'll die there."

"No great loss," Mary said softly.

"You mustn't say such things about a living person," Mother scolded.

Grandpa remained silent. His gray face expressed pity. I recalled that he himself was sick, his time was running out and the non-funeral must have been a galling reminder. Alex's mother feigning illness, or exploiting a real condition, no doubt upset him. I avoided his eyes and felt ashamed of my own petty worries.

Mother proposed that we leave our door open.

"This evening I'd prefer not to see Jamilla," said Grandpa, as though a closed door ever stopped her.

"I'll make some coffee," said Mother.

"Tea for me," said Mary. "I mustn't drink too much coffee." Wahid looked at her still flat belly with proprietory pride. He and Mary were to spend the night with us.

Alex returned close to nine. He looked tired, with a two-day beard on his exhausted face. He collapsed into a chair like a blind man and motioned with his head at my room. "Where is my mother?" We told him.

"This thing is like a present for her. Now a bulldozer will not get her out of here."

A green spark appeared in Grandpa's eyes and relieved my mind. I thought he was feeling sorry for me.

"Suddenly she decided she is religious," said Alex. "She said she will sit shiva here on roof."

"You must honor the dead," Mother interjected tactfully.

"First you must honor the living," Alex replied almost savagely. "She made him crazy. I believed her that he was pretending sickness. You know what it is, to be dying and nobody believes you? Shit, shit. I was also shit."

Grandpa put a bottle of arak before him, but I grabbed it. "He hasn't eaten since yesterday," I said to Grandpa. "He shouldn't drink."

"Let me," Alex whispered.

"Let him," Grandpa urged me. "He is a strong man, Huda."

Alex tossed back a shot which visibly restored him. "I must go up to mother. She is also hungry, and maybe she needs help. After all, she is really sick."

"Go up," said Mother. "Huda will soon bring you some supper."

At the door he turned and thanked Grandpa. After a while I went upstairs with supper for three. The rain had stopped. I didn't have a free hand and it seemed inappropriate to knock with my foot, so I called to Alex to open the door. His mother was already huddled on the bed under a blanket. Where would he sleep tonight? There was no additional bedding in the room. I saw she had on a nightgown and understood that she had come well prepared. I set the tray on the table which Alex placed near the bed. He put two chairs on the other side of the table, facing his mother. She rose on her elbow and stretched her hand to the tray, but when I sat at the table she withdrew her hand and growled something in Russian.

Alex said emphatically in Hebrew, "She eats with us. In the summer we will be married."

She rolled back and lay flat. Clearly she wouldn't touch the food while I sat there.

"You must get it into your head, Mama," Alex said.

I got up. "I've eaten already," I lied.

Alex begged me to stay but I wouldn't. I left the room. Outside he shouted to me in the sea wind, "You must not give in to her! You are not helping me like this."


Wahid squirmed on Mary's bed, lying between her and the wall. "You are used to reading late?" he asked me politely. He was a working man, an industrious artisan who went to bed early and rose early. It was strange to see him in the room which had been exclusively Mary's and mine.

"I'm turning off the light," I said.

"Thank you very much," he replied in a tight voice.

Suddenly I felt hungry—I hadn't had any supper. I slipped quietly out of the room. Grandpa was awake, listening to the trumpet's mournful song which informed the sea and the wind and a faraway land that Alex's father, who had missed his life, was also humiliated in death. There was an arak bottle on the floor beside the bench.

"Huda," he called me softly when I was in the kitchen. "Come and eat here."

"Can I get you anything?"

"No. Just come."

I sat on a chair near his bench and ate in the dark, blinking away my tears.

"You've got a good man to rely on," he said.

"He wants me to be as aggressive as she is. He refuses to see that I'm not like that."

"Don't be aggressive, my dear. He wants you to, but not really. Anyway, he wouldn't let you hurt her."

"But she's allowed to hurt me."

"He thinks it's best that you know what she's like, and that she is part of him."

"So I'll have to put up with it all my life?"

"Your man wants a wife and children and a home. For that, he will even stand up to his mother."

Alex's mother remained in his room for nineteen days and nights. I know now that at the time I neither hated her nor was I even angry with her, but only afraid. She viewed the whole world with suspicion—people were conspiring against her, plotting to harm her, even Mother, who cooked every day and sent heaped trays up to the roof. Mother invited her to tea three or four times. Sitting on the edge of her seat, she devoured Jamilla's biscuits and sipped the tea, while her head turned around like a periscope, her eyes as watchful as store cameras and her ears alert to sounds on the stairs, in case it was a cunning plot to entice her away from the roof and bar her way back. Mother almost groveled to her. Jamilla shamelessly fawned on her. But what Alex's mother feared above all was the sly twinkle in Grandpa's green eyes. Perhaps in her paranoid mind he was the sorcerer he'd been in his youth.

"Why are you hurrying to marry?" she asked me on one of her visits.

"Alex decided on the summer," I replied. "He'll finish his studies then and get a good job, so he won't have to work nights in the port."

"Alex, Alex! Say what you think. A man never thinks for himself. You don't think it is too soon? What about a house?"

"It's not easy. We have to wait a while."

"And in the meantime?"

"We'll live in the room until we find something."

"The room is too small, not enough for three people."

Silence fell. In a sudden gesture of intimacy she put her hand on mine. "Why not you two live here and I will be on roof? I don't want to go back to old-age home. No."

"Is it not good in the old-age home?" Jamilla inquired.

"It is cemetery for living people." She let go of my hand and caught Mother's eye. "You will soon be same age as I—how will you like it if they take you out of your house, throw you in a place with strangers who dirty their pants and talk to themselves?"

Mother, who dreamed about the grand villas of the past, was alarmed. "What? Oh no," she stated proudly. "We don't do such things. We don't throw our parents away like this."

"You see?!" she turned on me. "But you and Alex think only how to throw me away like sick dog. That is nice?" She wept.

Jamilla and Mother shed tears in sympathy. Even Grandpa gave me a quizzical look, patted his knee and said in Arabic, "I don't know. Wallah, I don't know."

She turned to him, blushed, wiped her tears with the back of her hand and asked, "What did you say?"

"I see you are not happy."

"What I am asking, after all? To be near to my son. I don't have brother or sister or daughter. Even husband gone. There is nobody. All alone. Like a bird that cannot go back to its nest."

That night I said to Alex that there was some sense in what his mother said. We could live with my family and she could stay on the roof till we find a flat of our own. He was firm. "Nothing doing! She is jealous of you. She will ruin your life. Patience, Huda, just a little patience. I am waiting for opportunity."

And the opportunity came. It came on a warm night that presaged spring. There are no trees in the wadi, so the warmth and scents of spring come not from the ground but are wafted there by the breeze. Alex stayed in my room in the few hours spared from his studies, his work in the port and his mother.

"Another few months, all nights will be ours." The promise in his voice inflamed my body, which had abstained from his since his mother's arrival. I no longer felt ashamed of my physical longing for him. I'd come to know the intensity of a woman's desire. At first he loved me in Russian, aroused me with strange murmurs, enfolded me in soft incomprehensible sounds. The words of love and desire were intense, but I met them as a guest. He led and he initiated, and I was swept along. When he learned to love me in Hebrew I discarded the last veils. I stopped turning off the light and was thrilled by his powerful muscles in their shameless nakedness. He said he was drowning in my green eyes, and his laughter blossomed in me, rose and returned.

The tremendous banging on the roof reminded me that the world did not only contain joy. It sounded hysterical, and because I knew its source it sounded vicious, too.

"Your mother is calling you," I whispered, but my arms did not release him. The magic moment was over. "What is she banging on?" I wondered.

"On a pail," he laughed.

"Has she gone mad? Why isn't she calling you, instead of banging?"

His mother was not the sort to go out of her mind, he said, but nevertheless he got up and went calmly upstairs. A moment later I heard him calling me, "Huda! Huda!"

I found him on the roof supporting his mother under her arms and dragging her to his room. "She is choking!" he shouted.

"Give her mouth to mouth resuscitation," I cried.

"She does not let me. She bites. Call an ambulance, now!"

In the ambulance I clasped her hand in both of mine. Her hand was limp and cold. There was a deep terror in her eyes which frightened me and I looked away. The screaming of the ambulance siren made me feel that she was dying. Traffic was congested on UN Avenue and the siren shrieked with superior authority. Her fingers twitched in my hands. I was still too frightened to speak and tried to catch Alex's eye, but he was peering impatiently through the front window. Then I saw her looking at me, her eyes wide open.

"You are happy now."

At first I didn't catch the words, only the hatred in her voice.

"You are very happy now," she reiterated. "Arab whore, kills mother and takes son."

I whimpered in terror. My voice vanished and I was unable to call Alex to my rescue. I felt she was trying to drag me down to the abyss with her. Her fingers closed like a vise on my hand.

"Now they will put me in ground and you will come to laugh on my grave."

After an eternity Alex turned his head. "She is awake!" he cried happily. I tried to signal to him with my eyes that she was dying and there was nothing to rejoice about. He didn't notice. "How nice!" he sang. "Hand in hand, at last."

"Alex, Alex . . ."

"What is happening to you?"

"She . . . she . . ." Then he saw the horror in my eyes and quickly released my hand from her clutching fingers. They immediately closed on his thigh, and she dug her fingernails into his flesh as she tried to rise from the stretcher. But before she could spit in my face—as I believe she meant to do—she fell back in a faint. I was petrified. A stench like rotten earth invaded my nostrils. It clung on for hours and days afterward.

After a week in the hospital Alex took his mother back to the old-age home.

*Chapter Twenty-four*

There is no street like Independence Street. It has a split personality. During the day it's a main artery connecting the north and south sides of the city, lined with government departments, lawyers' and accountants' offices, as well as restaurants, clothes shops and banks. It's a bustling, noisy and congested street, but a respectable one. Even the policemen maintain a subdued presence, although this is also the site of their headquarters, a sombre gray building. Tens of thousands of men and women make their living on this street, and hardly anyone ever strolls there. It is a workaday, down-to-earth street, and idle people avoid it.

When evening comes it loses its proper, serious aspect and turns into a port street. The office buildings sink into the gloom to be dominated from above by the ships' masts and the wharf cranes. Colorfully attired prostitutes parade along the pavements, pimps scurry from den to den, groups of drunken or drugged seamen hang out in the doorways of bars and pubs that are unnoticed during the day. The street ceases to be a place where men and women mingle in assured equality, and turns into a macho arena where women enter only as merchandise, peddled after dark like the falafel and burekas in the daytime—to be devoured quickly in the sharp-smelling damp air.

There is also a distinctive wartime Independence Street, different from the peacetime one. Israel's wars pass through it, grave boys and men in jeeps, trucks and pickups, tanks and armored vehicles, their faces expressing a grim resignation, like people about to undergo a risky operation. They hardly look around, they don't laugh or wave or whistle at the girls. Even the comedians among them keep silent. Already they see in the thronged pavements the shadows of another world. The blue sky above them resembles those insipid posters in travel agencies' windows, promising far-away Edens.

That morning I saw them on Independence Street on my way to work. Alex had taken a day off from work in the port in order to prepare for exams. Over the weekend he'd had a bad headache and a high temperature. The imminent exam made him very tense and the usual Russian expletives fluttered between the walls like trapped birds.

Then I saw the war rolling through Independence Street.

I had linked my fate to a Jew, but my fears were still those of an Arab. I didn't dare to stop and ask the worried-looking passersby what was happening. I was sure that they would know me for what I am. I felt I was walking like an Arab, looking around like an Arab, thinking like an Arab. The men and women on the pavement were gazing with Jewish eyes at sons and brothers, husbands and fathers, being led to fight a Jewish war. My alienness intensified with every step. My legs turned boneless. I reminded myself that Alex was a Jew, but what came to mind were some Arabic lullabies from my early childhood. Then suddenly they disappeared, leaving me blank, neither Jew nor Arab, in a street that was a solid mass of anxiety and fear, hatred and anger. In this war-minded street the Jews might let me share their laughter but not their sorrow, whereas the Arabs would eject me from their laughter but expect me to participate in their sorrow.

And all the while I said to myself, surely they won't take him, he was on reserve duty not long ago. I didn't know much about the usual procedures of war and the general call-up. And anyway, I thought, he has a high fever and in a couple of hours he has to sit his first exam for the engineering diploma.

Armed with this reassurance I entered the office, not knowing how to disguise it from the others. There were no customers that morning, and Boaz and Adina were submerged in the anxieties of soldiers' parents. Adina had obviously neither slept nor eaten for many hours. Her face looked gray and there were blue circles around her eyes. She got up and plugged in the electric kettle, leaving a gray cloud in the air behind her.

Boaz emerged from the inner office. Adina's eyes flashed gray beams at his clouded face, which saw nothing. "Coffee?" she asked.

"All right," he replied.

A friend of Shirley's rang her to say goodbye. It seemed to me that the other two looked at her indulgently, as though her solemn sadness was a luxury, seeing that she was in no danger of being orphaned, widowed or a bereaved parent.

"Was he called up?"

Shirley's question hung in the air like a vile insect, but no one moved to dispose of it. Boaz tugged at his trousers and his belly shook under his shirt. Strangely, he did not reply. Then I saw that the three of them were looking at me and realized that the question was addressed to me. But surely I was not likely to become an orphan, widow or bereaved parent.

"No, he wasn't," I said in a low voice, which despite myself sounded defensive.

"He hasn't been called up?" Boaz said, perhaps a trifle louder than he meant to sound.

"He will be," said Adina softly and put a cup of coffee on my desk.

Boaz calmed down, even gave me a weak smile of sympathy.

"She still doesn't realize . . ." Adina said, back at her desk.

"Wanted to be a Jew," he said with sincere affection. "It costs, you know. It costs a lot all the time." He stood behind Adina and stroked her hair sadly. She leaned her head back on his paunch and said, "I'm crazy. He phoned and I could sense his fear. He was laughing like a child. He really is a child still." She seemed astonished, as though it was something new.

Another phone call for Shirley. Another boyfriend going to war. Adina and Boaz detached themselves. "There's work to do," Boaz said, as though recommending a miracle cure, and went into his office. A little later Adina went to him with a heap of files. I pulled a chair over to Shirley's desk. "I didn't hear the news," I said.

"How come?"

"Just didn't. Alex was studying for an exam and we didn't turn on the radio or the television."

"It's war in Lebanon. The army has gone in." She pointed at the silent transistor radio on her desk. "Adina doesn't allow me to listen to the news. Flipped her lid completely."

When lunchtime came I didn't take out my sandwich. Adina was still dazed with Valium and still hadn't eaten, and for some reason I felt embarrassed about eating in her presence. I was also beginning to fret. Alex was supposed to phone as soon as the exam was over, but hadn't done so. Shirley's extension was also silent. Apparently all her men had gone to war. The only phone call in the afternoon was from Boaz's wife. Adina eagerly picked up the phone, but her face fell immediately. The woman on the other end was also a soldier's mother. On this day Adina had no moral advantage over her. Perhaps that was why she didn't respond with the warmth of uneasy conscience, but quickly switched the call to Boaz.

And still no word from Alex.

Maybe he failed in the exam, I thought, and is wandering about the Technion in despair. Yet he had studied so hard for it that love and marriage and his mother were all pushed to one side. Or maybe his temperature rose and he went straight home. He had said he would take a taxi to the Technion if need be, even crawl all the way there.

I could not bring myself to phone home and ask Mother about my man, who was indulging himself in exams at such a time. Even to speak Arabic on the phone so that Adina wouldn't understand was out of the question. Today Arabic was the enemy's language.

At three Boaz emerged from the inner office. "Yallah, everybody home," he said. "There's nothing to be done here."

Adina looked at him and froze. She was afraid to go to her empty flat, but knew that Boaz could not stay away from the telephone at his house.

I ran. I flew up the steep street, my breath whistling like a bellows. I didn't go into our flat but hurried up to the roof. Alex's room was locked. I groped blindly for the key in my handbag. Inside there was a smell of burnt coffee, bedding and a sense of disaster.

I went down to our flat. Mother looked at me as if I was sick. "He went to the war," she said fearfully. "They came and took him, a quarter of an hour after you left. He asked us to phone you and let you know, but we thought it best to wait and tell you in person."

I almost screamed at her for not letting me know before, but there was no point. Everyone was confused, and she meant well.

I sat down in the living room.

Grandpa came out of the bathroom, holding his stomach, his face agonized. He didn't say anything. Mother waited until he settled on his bench and said, "He's a good man."

"Yes," I said.

"I was not blessed with a son," she mused. "He hugged me and kissed me and then I cried a lot. What a world. He is sent to kill our children, and I cried for him. What a world."

"Enough, Mother."

I rose and went into my room. Mary had taken away her books, and the exposed stretch of wall looked like an ugly scar. Later that evening I went up to the roof, washed the floor, folded his clothes and polished the ashtray. The trumpet was hanging in its case on the wall.

# Chapter Twenty-five

"You still haven't heard?" Shirley asked.

It's the stomach-churning question; as if there's something wrong with me that disrupts communication, or as if Alex is guilty of something. Grandpa was silent and Mother didn't know who to pray for. Mary, who'd given birth to a boy, wanted to come and spend a few days with me. I said she shouldn't travel with the newborn. She rang every day and always asked, "Haven't you heard yet?"

Adina was an embodied scream, alternately uttered and suppressed. She stopped making up her face and looked ten years older. I noticed Boaz glancing at Shirley from time to time. He didn't make a pass, but evidently Adina's worn looks made him want to look at something fresh. It turned out that his son was not at the front, but guarding a quiet border far from the line of fire. Perhaps that was why he went out of his way to comfort Adina. To her, the war was a dreadful monster but a sacred one. Her son Eyal was in its maw, but still untouched, and she was afraid to attack the monster, for fear that her son would be harmed.

Boaz, by contrast, was free to attack the monster openly. "It's madness," he growled, and Adina looked at him reproachfully. It was unthinkable that her son might be a victim of madness. But he ignored her. "What do they think they'll achieve by it? Do they think they can finish the Palestinians for good? Nowadays you can't crush a people's will by force. This is a game conducted by idiots without any vision."

Adina pressed her fingers to her temples. "Boaz, how can you say such things? Children are getting killed over there. Enough." She didn't scream, because earlier that day she'd received a message from her son. A soldier from his unit had come home on leave and phoned her.

I didn't open my mouth. I agreed with Boaz, of course, but I also feared the monster that had Alex in its maw.

"It's almost two weeks," Boaz said to me.

I was abashed.

"It's irresponsible," he criticized Alex.

"Maybe he has no time to write," I protested.

"What about his mother? Has she heard?"

"I don't think so. Maybe she doesn't even know he's there."

"That's good," Adina said softly. "That's very good."

I didn't hurry home. The wadi is Arab. Almost every family has relatives in Lebanon.

The Israeli war machine had swept over Lebanon like a tidal wave. Some were already mourning cousins and nephews who had been killed over there. Every morning I sneaked out of the house and returned to it furtively in the evening. Grandpa stayed away from the cafe. Mother asked Jamilla to do some of her shopping, and I carried the rest of the purchases up the steep street.

At home I found Mary with her baby and her husband.

"We've come to fetch you," she announced. As if the village air was a cure for fear and anxiety. As if the clouds of hatred hadn't reached there.

I smiled and declined. Mother begged them to stay the night and Mary gladly agreed. It was almost impossible to get the baby out of Jamilla's arms. She danced and cavorted with him all over the living room, and Grandpa kept jumping up from his bench, fearful for the baby.

Then Mary put him to the breast and we were all entranced by the wonder of it. She turned into a flowing spring before our eyes. It seemed that the very roots of her hair were nourishing the little creature. She talked and moved while nursing him, but to me she looked like a great gushing breast.

"You've lost weight again," she said to me. "There will be nothing for Alex to take hold of when he comes back."

"She fasts the whole time," Mother informed on me.

"What's the point of it?" Wahid said reproachfully.

"You'll be an ugly bride," Mary laughed.

A motorcycle roared in the street below, startling the baby. With the instinctive knowledge of mothers since time immemorial, Mary squeezed her breast and squirted a few drops of milk on his face to soothe him. I felt a spasm in my lower belly. It was a feminine spurt, an intense, abundant and vital spurt. Moved by shameless yearning, I touched the thick warm milk on the child's face.

"You'll also have such a beautiful baby," Mother sang.

A lump formed in my throat and I couldn't speak. I was not upset by the pity in Mother's voice, nor by Wahid's fear of the evil eye. Inwardly I shouted, Me too! No one in the living room noticed, except perhaps Mary. Somehow it seemed to me that she guessed. The monster had swallowed Alex, but already I was carrying his son.

Later I said the guests could have my bedroom and I would sleep in Alex's room.

Mother objected to my staying there alone, but I insisted. His books and his clothes were mute, and the ashtray on the table, which I polished needlessly every day, seemed to wait with me for a miracle we knew wouldn't happen. Tomorrow I'll be terribly tired, I thought, but perhaps it's for the best. Tiredness sometimes overcomes longings and fears. It was two weeks since I'd heard from him.

Just before midday the phone rang on Shirley's desk. I heard her saying in her pleasant professional manner, "One moment, please. . . . It's for you, Huda."

Lights and shadows seemed to spin around me. I asked hoarsely, "Alex?"

"I don't think so," she said in a cool, restraining tone.

Nevertheless, my heart was thumping when I picked up the receiver. "Hello?"

A man's deep voice asked, "Is that Huda?"

"Yes, yes . . ."

"You have greetings from Alex."

Wanting to laugh and sob, I asked, "You've seen him?"

"Of course. We're in the same unit. He's all right."

His laconic manner annoyed me, but all the questions slipped from my mind. "How is he feeling?"

"I said, he's perfectly all right."

Luckily a rational question came to my mind. "When did you last see him?"

"Yesterday morning, before I came out on leave. Excuse me. I still have a long list of numbers to phone."

"Is it dangerous where you are?"

He condescended to chuckle. "Safer than the central bus station in Tel Aviv."

"Tell him . . . tell him . . ."

"What should I tell him?"

The words simply evaporated. "Goodbye," I said, and hung up.

I looked up and saw I had no right to feel miserable. Adina was looking at me enviously. She had not heard from her son for four days, and my Alex was alive and well up to yesterday morning.

The week before I'd asked Boaz, when Adina was out of the office, "How will I know?"

"He must have put your name in his personal details card, as his nearest relative."

"But we're not yet . . ."

"He can give any name he wants. But perhaps they'd contact his mother if anything happened, God forbid. Would you like me to inquire at the old-age home?"

"No! No!" I said in alarm.

Mary went back to the village. The weather was hot and humid, and I was no sooner out of the shower than the sweat broke out again. I was too jumpy to sit at the table.

"Eat properly," Mother scolded. "You know he's all right, so give thanks to God and calm down."

"I am thankful," I said sincerely, "but I must go up to his room."

"Wait a minute, first try on this dress."

Ever since we set a date for the wedding she hadn't stopped sewing—dresses and kitchen cloths, shirts and bedsheets.

"Not now, Mother."

"That's how you thank me."

"Leave her alone," said Grandpa.

I sat on Alex's bed and my eyes caressed his books and shoes and the clean ashtray. I took the trumpet out of its case and polished its golden curves with an old towel. I put it to my lips, but couldn't bring myself to blow. For years it was animated by Alex's breath and spoke for him.

I lay on the bed and stroked my stomach, wondering when exactly I'd become pregnant. I was glad that Alex already knew about it. A man who has an unborn baby waiting at home will be more careful of his life.

I took down the volume of Amichai's poems and switched on the reading lamp.

> *A soldier filling bags with soft sand*
> *in which he had once played.*

As a child Alex did not play in the sand of Israel, and I didn't know if there had been a sandbox at the orphanage. He was filling bags with sand that other people had played in, was scorched by a hatred others had kindled, was harvesting a war others had sown. Once they played in the sand; now they were playing with his life. Only don't let them get carried away and stuff him into a sack as well. I thought about his sturdy shoulders, his powerful legs, and trusted him—he won't let them. He's got something inside me and he's strong, he defeated Zuhair. No, he won't let either the Jews or the Arabs put him in a bag.

I hear footsteps on the stairs.

"It's all right, Mother, I'll come down in a little while."

But there is no answer. The silence outside tells me it isn't Mother, and before my eyes, I see the woman in the doorway, short, bulky, her bosom rising and falling like a bellows from the climb, her eyes so protuberant that at any moment they'll fall out and roll on the floor. She enters and says, "What are you doing here?"

I tuck my shirt into my jeans. She can tell that I lay with Alex before he was called up and I haven't yet dressed.

"Shame that the room is a mess, I should have tidied up immediately."

"You hear," she says contemptuously to the policeman standing behind her, "She's tidying Alex's room. An Arab whore who enticed my son, now she comes to his room to steal. Search her."

But he is gone, and it's her strong fingers that grope over my body, invade my blouse and bra, slide into my trousers, feel my buttocks. My body doesn't belong to me—it's permissible to body-search Arabs, and I know it's best to cooperate with the searchers so as to end the horror quickly and run away and cry in private. I mustn't be cheeky to her, she is Alex's mother after all, and she is crazy and a monster and very unhappy. The tactic pays off, and she whispers, "Go away," but without hate or contempt. I slink out so as not to annoy her, but I'm afraid of what she might do to me when I turn my back.

Here is Alex coming up the stairs, only let me reach him before she plunges her claws into my nape.

I wake up drenched in sweat. Morning light fills the window.

## Chapter Twenty-six

I was in the thriving white town at the foot of the Carmel. Neat rows of little homes banked with flowers. It's a model town, with a splendid view of the blue sea, limpid sky and green mountainside. There are no bad smells, no slums or noisy crowds. Yet no one wants to settle here. People have to be killed before they can be brought here and settled in these fine marble residences that gleam in the sunlight.

Adina had checked and found out for me and showed me which way to go through the symmetrical rows, then with her kindness and tact left me alone. She is at home in this town. She goes in the glaring sunlight to visit her husband, perhaps to plead for their son Eyal, who is still in the monster's belly. She was right—you can't miss it, the names are engraved in black on the shiny marble.

There are living people here as well. Here a woman is kneeling and hugging the marble slab in her arms, as though trying to uproot it. Further down the row an attractive well-dressed man of no more than forty is standing immobile while the scorching sun roasts him in his clothes. He might have caught fire but for the sweat that pours out of him, drenching his clothes down to the edge of his trousers. He doesn't turn his head when I approach, he neither hears nor sees anything, he only blinks because the salty sweat stings his eyes. He's totally absorbed in listening to the stubborn marble which refuses to say a word to Daddy.

There is another silent tomb on my left, with a girl visitor who keeps saying, "Why? Why? Why?" In her white blouse and full skirt and the delicate sandals on her feet, with her fine spiritual face, she is as exquisite as a bouquet of flowers. But her sound system is jammed and keeps repeating again and again, "Why? Why?" until her madness turns on mine and I have to stop myself from rushing over to locate the switch under her blouse and turn it off.

We are all mad here, except the inhabitants of the little homes.

An old woman in black is sitting on the edge of a grave, nibbling a rusk, a thermos flask of coffee at her feet. She seems to be at ease, as if on a sitdown strike in front of a government office. Perhaps that's why her mad citizen's protest is so piercing, as she picnics on the grave, demanding to have her grandson restored to her. But can childhood and youth be given back to old age? No fear—God is as silent as the local residents.

I am mad too, I've come, in full awareness of my insanity, to explain to Alex and apologize to him. Adina said nothing, the gynecologist was shocked, being himself a bereaved father. Mother wept, Grandpa's green eyes flashed when he said, "I do hope for a grandson from you." He must be crazy too, since he understood at once.

I haven't brought Alex flowers. After all, I may yet throw the bouquet that I'm carrying inside me down the drain. Also it isn't easy to discuss it with him while he is lying down and I have to stand. I would have sat down if they'd offered folding chairs to the crazy visitors. So I couldn't tell him everything, I stood in mute protest in front of the grave, like a sullen delinquent.

Boaz said that the profits made on the money he and Adina had loaned me, which he'd invested on the stock exchange, came to a substantial sum, and together with my salary it would be enough to secure my future and that of the child.

"So you see, Alex," I said to the grave, "this will probably decide the issue. I mean the child's future. If I bring him up in the Arab society, will I have to tell him, before he hears it from others, that he was fathered out of wedlock by a Jew? Or should I raise him in Jewish society? In another eighteen years I will not be attractive and strong like Adina, sustained with warm care by parents and lover. Your mother even snatched away your trumpet before she returned the room to Abu-Nakhla. You can imagine what my position will be when the time comes to send your son to another war. He will want to join an elite unit. All his life he will try to prove himself, because his mother is Arab, and he will be a stranger among both Arabs and Jews."

The old woman with the thermos flask washed her grandson's tombstone with water from a little plastic bucket. Perhaps it was the bucket with which he used to play on the beach. Adina was waiting at the gate. Her voice was tense. "I must rush home. Eyal may phone . . ."

## About the Author

Sami Michael was born in 1926 in Baghdad. At the outbreak of WWII, Michael became involved in a leftist underground group acting against the oppressive regime in Iraq. In 1948, his activities were discovered and he fled to Iran. A year later he made his way to Israel.

Michael has been awarded several prizes, including the Ze'ev Prize, the ACUM Award, the IBBY Award in Berlin, and a special prize by SID, the Society for International Development, promoted by the United Nations, and AISI, the Italian Association for the Promotion of Peace in the Middle East.

In July 2001, Sami Michael was appointed President of the Israeli Association for Human Rights. He is the author of eight novels, including the international bestseller *Victoria* and lives in Haifa.

## About the Translator

Yael Lotan was born in Palestine under the British Mandate and has lived in Jamaica, England, and the United States. She is the author of *The Other I, Mangrove Town, Phaedra,* and a documentary book, *The Life and Death of Amos Orion.* In addition to being a translator from Hebrew to English, Lotan is a magazine editor, literary critic, and a journalist. She lives in Tel Aviv.